I0533498

Blood Kiss

A Vampire Love Story

M Kenyon Charboneaux

MacDonald, Barclay & Co.   Little Elm, Texas

A MacDonald, Barclay & Co. book

MacDonald, Barclay & Co. (www.macdonaldbarclay.com) is a very new, very small press located in the also very small town of Little Elm, Texas. MacDonald, Barclay specializes in whatever demands our attention. We have a small but talented group of authors covering a broad genre range.

For more information, or permission to use material from this text, contact us by:
Email: info@macdonaldbarclay.com
Mail: MacDonald, Barclay & Co.
                Suite 100-436
                2701 Little Elm Parkway
                Little Elm, TX 75068

PROLOGUE - SPRING, 1991

Black ocean, tipped and streaked by moon-white here and there. Wheels and time and the smell of old blood on the wind, and I thought I saw Mae standing there, at the sea's edge, as she used to do ... small and slender in white lace, her blond hair washed to silver by the moon, her skin to alabaster.

I had seen her die, yet here stood one so like her, that I must move to her, walk the yards that separated us, with legs like a dead man's and a heart singing like that of one who has finally found his lover after searching for her years along the freezing corridors of hell.

I must reach through the thickened air to touch her shoulder, stand trembling as she turned to me, and breathe out heavily and sharply with shock, in spite of myself, when she presented the perfect face of a Botticelli angel to me.

Perfect eyes, lips, cheekbones, but not Mae's eyes, nor her lips, nor her cheekbones.

Not Mae, and not one of her children, for she had made none during the period of her undeath, yet so very like her, in the porcelain perfection of skin and hair and shape, in her voluptuous, scintillating vampirism.

"Pardon me," I said gently, "you resembled

someone, standing here alone in the moonlight."

"Mortal or immortal?" she teased. Her eyes were violet, the color of dreams induced by the poppy. Unlike Mae's, they were open and clear, as innocent as it is possible for any vampire's to be and I stepped closer to her.

"I am Michel de Brissault," I said, with a small bow.

"And I am Celine Robards," she answered, holding her hand out to me.

I took it carefully in mine where it lay lightly, faintly warm with the lingering traces of a recent feeding, and perfectly, heartbreakingly formed.

"Of whom did I remind you?" she asked, her eyes still teasing.

"A woman I once loved," I said, and released her hand. The hurt of Mae was suddenly new and vicious.

I turned to go and she stood uncertainly in the sand, the incoming tide brushing her toes with sea-foam.

"It sounds like a long and romantic story with a sad ending," she said, a small falter in her voice. Like a child, she put her hands behind her back, bowed her head, and kicked at the sand.

"It is," I answered. "Although the ending was less sad, than tragic. I am sorry to have interrupted you." I bowed again, and began to walk away from her.

Instantly she was at my side. She reached out to touch me, then hesitated. I stopped and faced her. "What is it you want?" I asked, not gently.

"You are one of the Old Ones, aren't you?" she said wistfully. "I've never met an Old One. Won't you stay with me awhile? Talk to me? I haven't been changed for very long and I am alone."

"What of the one who changed you?" I asked sternly, for it is a foolish thing to transform a human being into a vampire, and then leave him or her to make their

4

own way in a literal darkness.

"I did not know him," she said without emotion. "He was a rock star, one of those splatter-gore punkers who pretend to be undead for the benefit of their fans, but this one was not pretending. My company assigned me to him as his chauffeur. He took me from behind, there in the limo, then left and I have not seen him since that night."

I nodded at this story whose general outlines was dismayingly familiar, if not its details. She might yet survive; he certainly would not if he continued to make others in such a shockingly careless fashion.

"You are lonely," I said at last. "You must learn to cope with that. You will be lonely for centuries. If you live so long."

"Like you?" she asked, and now her eyes were not teasing. They were solemn and full of purple shadows like clouds before a storm.

"Yes," I said shortly.

"Then can't we spend this night together? Be lonely in company? I will tell you my story and you will tell me yours. You can learn nothing from me, but I could learn everything from you. One night only, I swear to you. I will not cling to you after tonight," she pleaded, yet with dignity and grace, and, I saw, hopelessness. I slid my arm through hers.

"Shall we walk here along the beach," I asked, "or do you prefer to sit somewhere, have drinks, listen to music?"

She studied my face for a moment, finally saying, "Let's go to a quiet park and sit on wooden benches and watch the moon set through Royal Palm leaves. We will pretend we are lovers, once parted, now together again for just these few hours."

5

I had never done such a thing with Mae. Perhaps she sensed it and that was why she suggested this quiet interlude, rather than some other, more frenetic, frantic place, and I nodded, tucking her arm securely beneath mine.

"You must not say I can learn nothing from you," I said as we walked to my car. "I may, in fact, learn very much from you before this night is over."

"I would like that," she smiled.

I opened the passenger door of the Lotus and she slid onto its fine leather seat as if she had never ridden in a car before ... much like Tony the first time I persuaded him to ride in my, then hot from the factory, Model A Ford.

We drove through the night, not speaking, to a small park in Matheson Hammock. I choose a bench, well shielded by Royal Palms, through which the moon silvered her hair as it had on the beach, and she sat still and silent beside me while I remembered Mae for her.

My too beautiful, flaming, and, finally, monstrous Mae.

CHAPTER 1

I was not looking for Mae. I was not looking for someone like Mae. I was not, in fact, looking for anyone or anything.

I believe that it is always better, if one has enough to sustain existence, to be content with that, for anything more has its inescapable cost. Seven centuries have taught me that there is a curse in life attached to the good things as well as to the evil or the unnatural.

Love, of course, and in point of fact, always exacts its price. Immortality, also, but being nosferatu is, on the whole, a satisfactory thing, and so it is that in every major city of the world you may find them, those mortals who, for whatever reason, have seized upon becoming not-dead as a panacea for their ills, be these of the spirit or of the body.

Walking in their silences, amid the secret pulsing of their human hearts, spurred on by movies and books and late night television, they cry out for a vampire to come to them, to give them this aloes gift of immortality, and in return, they promise eternal love.

They throw aside the very lessons their movies and books attempt to teach them ... that earnest belief that vampires are evil, loveless, and incapable of love ... choosing instead to believe that it is love which bestows the gift, love the lure which attracts it.

Nothing could be further from the truth.

It is solely loneliness that drives us to create another of our kind, and better to transform a friend, even an enemy, than a lover, for the passing of the centuries dulls even the fiercest love to friendship, the most hallowed hate to mere indifference.

More importantly, it is easier to keep an eye on a friend during that crucial first year of transformed existence and an enemy will always have his eyes fixed firmly on you, few being willing to die to satisfy their desire for your death.

Nevertheless, we still ... I still ... believe that somewhere, a great love is waiting for us; a soul whose fire will catch our own and set it to blazing with the very stars overhead.

Tony and I used to play a game together. Standing in a crowd, we would look into each face and say, "Is she the one?" "Is she?" In my nearly seven centuries of existence, I had found love like that twice and both times, her heart cried to mine in an audible voice. It is this heart's cry I have come to associate with both love and death, the curse and the Kiss, and I avoid such cries; I flee from them.

I first heard Mae call as I strolled the wet streets of Florence. The rains that had fallen since dusk were not completely past but the theater district was alive with wet, reflected light in the puddled walkways, the squeals of ladies holding their gowns up and off the moist sidewalks and the

8

essence of blood and living flesh drifting to me on the damp breezes.

I, too, drifted among these tourists, feeling a pleasurable affinity with the people, a kind of peace that only so many centuries among humans can bring to us. In that peaceful state, I was more inclined to listen to her call, to muse upon it, to play the game Tony and I had used to play at country fairs and on market days, back in 14th century England.

The world, I thought, hearing her heart's wail, is not as simple as it was in 1323, when I was first changed. How much easier then to believe in all things, even in love that could last throughout all time.

In 1323 I would have heard her even had she been a prisoner of wealth in Tangier and, I, dancing at Whitehall. I would have run to her despite the risks. Now, I would only safely amuse myself by trying to guess which she might be of all these people pressing their succulent flesh against mine.

The fat lady with her graying hair and fatter husband just entering the dinner club, or that wealthy woman, there, with her diamonds and fold-draped neck, wrists and hands alight with emeralds, topaz and ruby, lipsticked mouth laughing, eyes blank as she gazed upon her hired companion with his model's face and weightlifter's body; was that weeping heart within either of these women?

Or perhaps it was the schoolgirl, hanging with sullen tightness to her father's hand, glaring about her with eyes full of angry tears, wishing fervently to be anywhere else, anyone else? Or it might even be, and I smiled at the thought, that American woman, bespectacled and bunned, her sensible shoes belying the madly flowered print dress with plunging neckline that she wore with careful

9

nonchalance.

Whichever she was, among this pre-midnight crowd, she was one of them: one with their laughter, their wide gestures of pleasure, yet she was alone. Alone in her weeping, rapt in the silence of her heart's begging for one such as I to set her free from death, from mortality with all its fears and failings, with no true understanding of what it was she wished for and no belief that there was anyone to hear her anguished plea being sent out into the newly washed night.

I felt compassion for her, pity for myself. Had I not also once been mortal, dreaded King Death in his myriad disguises ... the plague infected sailor, the pock-nosed highwayman, yes, even the innocent child with her long teeth and beguiling song? Feared age and hunger and war and prayed most mightily that the God in whose existence I hoped, would prove Himself real to me by protecting my life and saving my soul?

Once I had been as she was, believing in love, believing its possession worth its price, afraid of death, wanting, wanting ... but not now. Now I dared not open myself to her, dared not want her, could not bring myself to risk her, so I closed her pain and desire out of my mind, and walked on into the brilliant Florentine night.

In Venice, some weeks later, I again heard her.

Leaning on a balustrade, of the Scalzi Bridge after midnight, watching the black waters of the canal spread lazily before a gondola lit with red and blue Chinese lanterns, I felt her whisper through me like wind among wheat, golden and clean.

Seductress, I thought, with wry and rare humor. Is your tourist bus now here in Venice? Do you follow me, woman? I immediately regretted allowing myself to reach out to her, even for an instant, for her wail intensified,

10

becoming very nearly a taste in my throat, very nearly true contact from which I could not easily have drawn away.

I fled to Cairo then. Tours of the European continent rarely include a stop in Egypt and I freely admit thus running from her, to putting even more distance between her desire and my own growing one to answer. Too, I knew Tony would be in Abu Simbal at that time of year and I yearned to see him, to take advantage of his always prudent mind and great love for me, to seek refuge in his practicality.

We always sense when our own kind are near, especially those to whom we are bound by the passing of blood through the Kiss. Within three hours of my arrival, Anthony Tinsley IV, only scion of the Earl of Wiltmanshire, my fostered brother and childhood friend, came striding into my Cairo hotel suite, mouth stretched in laugher, his two Afghan wolfhounds tittering at his heels.

"Michel, you gadfly," he cried, swinging his arms around me with more good fellowship than good sense, for though it requires much strength, whether applied by mortal or vampire, to hurt those as old as we, Tony had always been, even in life, stronger than most. With the heightened strength of the undead, he is dangerous without meaning to be so. He has broken my ribs before with his playful hugs, and once my nose, in anger.

"God's Nightgown," he whooped, "but it is good to lay my eyes upon your sweet face, brother. It's been nearly half a century since last we hunted together. You'll tell me, of course, everything you've done, everywhere you've been, what new sights you have seen, and I shall bore you with the same, although after so many centuries, there are not many new sights to see, eh?" He bellowed laughter and love over me like a wave breaking on a near and hungry shore. "Where have you been, my Michel?"

11

"Not where you've been, it seems," I said, hugging him in return.

"I've been right here," he assured me solemnly, holding me away from him by the forearms so he could examine my face with his bold eyes. "You could have stopped in to chat me up anytime. You know I do love Egypt despite her hellish sun. I never leave her, for she never changes."

"And you are still a liar," I smiled. "I was in Akhenaton's old city last year and you were not anywhere along the Nile then. Tell me, now, what lady were you pursuing in what land, for you were nowhere in Egypt a summer ago."

"Oh, well, perhaps I had gone to ground," he grinned, for he never did any such thing. He released me and waved the air about with his hands. "Or yes, I think I was in Nairobi, which is still Africa and so very nearly Egypt. As for the ladies, they are a prey too dangerous for me." He roared out his laughter as once the lion of Egypt had roared among the marshes, but his eyes had caught mine now and they were uncomfortably speculative.

"I am hungry," I said to kill, with distraction, that speculation.

He grasped both my hands and squeezed until I felt the bones crack. "Have you not fed then? Why, the streets here are a feast! No one cares a rap for these poor fellahin. They belong to no one now feudal times are gone, and there is no one to miss them when they, too, are gone. I tell you truly, Michel," he said, shaking his head in disgust and squeezing my hands again, "this is a cold age in which a man can be so easily lost among the crowds."

I would have answered him, reminded him all ages have ever been cold, made some jibe at his perpetual philosophizing, but she called for me, and her cry passed

12

from my mind to his, running down my arms and onto his hands, like the passing of human sweat during lovemaking.

"God's Blood, Michel!" Tony swore with the same exuberance with which he did all else, but there was now horror beneath his apparent gaiety. "Another one? How do you still manage to attract them, and at your age?" he asked with consternation.

What he meant was, how could I still manage to allow myself to be open enough to receive these summons when I was old enough to know better? How could I tell him there was no defense against one as strong and determined as she?

"Your choice of expletive dates you as well, my friend," I said absently, really listening to her for the first time.

She was quite as audible here as she had been in Italy and Venice. An impossibility in these times of unbelief, I would have thought, for she was so very distant, in terms of miles, from me.

She was not in Europe, nor in Africa. I could feel that distinctly now as I reached for her. She was in America. The amount of psychic energy she must be expending, I marveled and reached again down the echo of her cry.

She _was_ an American. Their taste is different from that of Europeans. Younger, cruder, more alive, less resigned, and I was intrigued at her strength and her passion, indicating as these did a faith deeper than I had seen in two centuries, a faith more desperate to be proved substantial ... but I will not answer her, I told myself firmly, and shut her out.

Still I had blundered in allowing myself to taste her, for in doing so I had, in turn, brought her close enough to sense my reality. She would weep for me all the harder now, and I must be more cautious, less accessible. Antarctica, perhaps, I mused. Yes, that would likely be far enough away.

Tony threw himself into an armchair and lit a slim, only marginally foul smelling, cheroot. "If I recall, you were born in 1290 and I in 1291. You were transformed in 1323, yet you forgot all about me until 1325. Me, your truest friend. Your only friend, if truth be told, Michel, my brother," he said, grinning around the cheroot.

"I did not forget you, Anthony," I smiled in return, and poured us both a glass of wine.

He took his and swirled its deep redness for a long minute, watching the slow play of light within the ruby folds, his eyes distant and speculative again. Then, as if her plaintive
promises had sobered even his unquenchable and careless spirit, he said quietly, "No, I do not believe you did forget me. I think there was not a minute of those two years when you did not struggle with whether or not to give me your Kiss. It must have been horrible for you to be so alone, and after all, we had shared all else between us, even women, eh? Before you took the collar."

He drank off the wine in a single swallow, though it was Egyptian wine and raw on the throat, licked his lips and stood abruptly, grasping my head between his hands. "I'll share this with you now, my boyhood friend and fostered brother," he said, shaking me lightly. "Let her be. Nothing but pain has ever come of answering these calls. Do not endanger yourself again. Leave this one alone, Michel."

There spoke the prudent mind I had come to avail myself of, and, "I am far too old to put myself through that again," I assured him. Myself.

"Then you do not know your heart as I do, Michel,"

14

he said, shaking me again until my ears rang. "You were always to compassionate. Too much the romantic. You read too many books. You need a keeper, my brother. But, come," he bellowed, throwing his arm about my shoulders again and snapping his fingers for the dogs, "let us go to the prostitute district and feed. There is nothing like the misery of street women to destroy these illusions of love in a man. Such a night we'll have, blood and stories, eh, Michel?", and I nodded, smiling for him and his great energies, his great appetites, his great capacity for love and loyalty.

In the last days of December, 1325, this bear of a man had lain dying in a frozen field in Yorkshire, driven through the gut by a husband jealous, not of his wife's virtue, but for her dowry lands, and I had taken the last of Tony's mortal life from him with my blood Kiss, giving to him this immortal existence he lived with such elan.

We had grown up together, been best friends all our lives, and, in death, we were yet. Friendship stands the movement of years with a grace that love cannot. Friendship lasts forever,
if its beginnings are properly laid and nourished, like a fire smoldering in the home hearth, while love flares and burns out, in imitation of a lamp whose wick has been turned too high.

It would be well for me to remember that, even out of his presence, I knew, but memory is such a tricky affair. How odd now, for instance, to remember that I had once been a priest. I had not thought of that time in years, but as we walked through Tony's hunting grounds, I remembered the black soutane, the devout man who had worn it, as if he were a relative of mine, dead for years, whose name had been mentioned in passing.

Devout he had been, yes, but too much concerned

15

with theological argument and the reading of many books, too little solicitous of the people he was sworn to shepherd.

As I fed on a prostitute barely out of childhood herself, I remembered the child who had fed on me, and those first days of darkness and ignorance.

The feeding is a reflex, the stilling of blood-hunger, but despite the legend, our victims need not become undead. We have only to snap the neck at the moment before death to still the body and when, in the 1500's, the Inquisition found that they could also destroy a vampire by breaking its neck, we learned that we, too, were vulnerable from this same method by which we protect ourselves, for there can be death for us, though, perhaps, no release.

"Is the soul then in some type of central nervous system?" Tony asked me when the news was first brought to us by a fellow vampire who later died himself at the hands of the Dominican Inquisitors. 1526, I think it was. Tony wanted to know how our bodies differed from those of mortals, and he had been studying anatomy with some quack who later hung in gaol for graverobbing. He has always had this insatiable desire to know everything. I never have been afflicted with such rampart curiosity, and for its lack, I made an excellent priest. I believe this same lack of curiosity has helped me to survive the centuries since the child-fiend transformed me.

Walking back to the hotel, Tony cheerfully telling me of his last half-century, the women he had loved and lost (for we lose them all eventually, to time or death or indifference), I found that somewhere between the hotel suite and the spilled blood of the hunt, I had made a decision.

I would find this seductress who called so persistently and over such incredible distance, but not from curiosity and still less in any vain pursuit of love. I had never been a curious man, after all, and I had too often fallen for love's fraudulent promises and substantial dangers to do so again. I would seek her from compassion, a vice of mine, as Tony had said, to flame her inherent disbelief in the very thing she cried for, to turn her to a normal lifetime, lived normally. I was very firm with myself on this last point.

So easily do we delude ourselves.

I would see her, I promised myself, but I would not change her. I would not love her, bring her with me into eternity, risk my existence for her unquestionably temporary love.

Had I told Tony of my foolish decision, walking with his arm through mine, his laughter in my ears beneath Egypt's sliver of a new moon, he would have bound me with wild rose vines for clean half-century, maybe in Antarctica beneath a blue and icy white glacier, until the danger was past and the woman dead or entombed in a living death of old age and senility.

But I said nothing, for the holocaust had already begun between Mae and myself, and being a romantic man and thus, as Tony would say later, a fool, I wanted no one to stop me in this rush to my burning. Not even the friend I had come seeking so that he might indeed stop me with his wit, his good sense, his proven love.

I was eager to burn, while persuading myself I was too wise
to be so much as scorched when I came, like any blind pilgrim, to lay my heart among the sacrificial flames.

17

CHAPTER 2

I flew the Concorde from Orly to Kennedy three nights after my reunion with Tony Tinsley in Cairo, having spent the intervening days at my villa in Cannes preparing for the trip to the States.

Tony has been a passionate fan of vampire literature since <u>Varney The Vampire</u> first appeared on the newsstands, although even he admits <u>Varney</u> can hardly be classified as literature.

He is enthralled with mortal ideas about us, always curious to discover how they perceive our not-life. Having been mortal, we do not wonder at their lives; having never been endless they dream of us, desire us, and recreate those desires and dreams with words spilled out on white paper.

I think, though Tony would disagree, that there is a measure of soured grapes in their idea of what it is to be undead, for we have been stripped of nothing but our mortality and yet they persist in depicting us as incapable of love, of sex, of everything bodies were made to do, with or without the connivance of a soul. Humans write of our existence as a dreary, sometimes terrifying dreamscape of bloodlust and night, when in truth, we eat and drink and smoke, we make love, we fight, we weep.

And we have gained from our conversion, gained strength, heightened emotions and physical senses, deepened insight and the ability to change our appearance at will, if not our essential selves. We retain our human need for love and friendship and sustenance, and in their theology, not to mention their fiction, mortals grant even to the demons of hell these same needs they would deny to us. It is true we have lost much, but what is lost, we learn not to mourn too deeply.

Tony read Dracula almost immediately it was published. He became enamored with the idea of traveling as the Count did, sequestered in the lower hold of a ship, ensconced in a box of earth; he thought it so-so romantic. He scowled for days after finally admitting that he could not summon storms while at sea as the Count had done in the novel, but he has always persisted in his love of traveling in luggage compartments.

Tony's infatuation with literary vampirism was just another of my rationalizations for not telling him of my trip to America. Had I told him, he would have insisted on accompanying me (always assuming he did not prevent my going altogether), and I have never found a locked box filled with dirt and stones a romantic mode of travel.

I prefer the Concorde, with its speed and lightness, to the dark hold of a ship. I prefer the stewardesses in their sleek uniforms, and the wines served in First Class. I even have an attachment to those warm little towels, delicately scented with almond, they give you to clean your fingers after the fruit and biscuits, and, of course, I prefer taking off at dusk from Orly and landing in New York one hour, theoretically speaking, before I have even left Paris.

I could have flown the distance myself, as some sort of bird or winged creature (and I have been toying with the idea of shapechanging into a pterodactyl one of these days - what would the radars of the world make of that, I wonder?), but then I would have to give up those warm little towels and sleek stewardesses.

I also like to carry luggage with me; favorite items of clothing, books, things that are precious to me; things which contain my memories within them, and, too, I love airports.

I am enamored with revolving baggage racks, the shining, subterranean trains that whisk one from one terminal to the next and the hungry prostitutes who wait in the shadows for one such as I, hungry in another fashion. Yes, I always fly commercial and first class whenever possible and, thankfully, I have the wealth to make it possible whenever I please.

I own a brownstone in New York's most fashionable area for that sort of thing. Before the brownstone, a carriage house stood there, and before that, a tavern. I bought the tavern in 1789 for a dappled pony and 10 shillings. I am also the silent owner and major stockholder of one of the largest holding companies in the world, `de Brissault and Sons', which handles my monetary affairs, for even the undead need money in this imperfect world.

I established an economic base back in the early 15th century when trade first began to be regarded as a respectable profession in Europe. I was in living in Florence at the time, dealing in rare manuscripts for wealthy collectors like Cosimo de Medici. Until I became a merchant, whenever I desired to move among mortals disguised as one of their kind, I played the role of an idle aristocrat, the class into which I had been born, if only as a second son. The combination of old blood and old name was, and still is in some areas, an entre to the world I love best, but with the coming of the moneymakers as the new aristocracy, I changed my coat with little trouble and have emerged, six centuries later, a bit more than merely wealthy.

I have no actual hand in the firm's day to day affairs now ... how could I, I who never change and never age? ... but `de Brissault and Sons' has known my guiding hand through the years as a succession of `sons' and `nephews', all in the guise of silent partners, who are moved by no other opinion or consideration when major business decisions are made.

Thus I have done quite well financially. Not as well as others of my kind, but better than Tony, who can't seem to think beyond next Tuesday week as `the future'. I am forever lending him money, little of which he has ever repaid.

I can afford it, though. I can afford almost anything I take it into my head to desire, including Concorde flights seven days a week, should I wish, or the complete remodeling of any of my several homes in various countries, and it was remodeling that was on my mind as I walked from Kennedy to the brownstone that evening, reacquainting myself with the smells and sights of New York, making a lovely `to-do' list in my head.

I needed to contact Ronald Higgenbothum, my latest CEO at `de Brissault' first thing tomorrow, I decided, and I must see to any repairs the brownstone might require, besides updating the furnishings. It had been some time since I had been to New York, and Cabbidu, my last CEO and, therefore, caretaker of the house, had died in 1980. I could always trust him to keep abreast of even minuscule things, like making sure the maid came regularly to sweep

22

the abandoned rooms, wax the unused furniture, and dust the picture frames.   I was not as yet sure of my new man, having never met him face to fang, as we say.

I stood outside the brownstone for several minutes admiring the brickwork and wrought-iron railings, and noting a fairly recent coat of paint on the front door, before fitting the key into the latch to enter this home I had not lived in since 1927.

Setting my leather carry-all down on the Italian tile of the hall, I saw that Higgenbothum was keeping my property as competently as had his predecessor.

The chandelier, all genuine Parisian crystal, sparkled.   The tigerwood railing of the spiral staircase gleamed.   The marble flooring of the foyer shone softly in the glow from the chandelier high above my head, a tender aura of its own emanating from the old stone, brought 100 years before from Italy.   No dust lay on the heavy oak and mahogany furniture, no smears on the elegant Florentine mirrors, no ashes in the fireplace.

No fresh flowers on the mantlepiece either, for I had not wired Higgenbothum to expect me, but at least the funeral corsages from Helena's lying-in were not still scattered about the room, as I had been unreasonably dreading might be the case.

Standing in that hall, I recalled parties in this house, with sweeping crinolines, and, later, ticking beads on white foreheads and bootleg gin.   Dimly I heard Helena's voice weeping from the overhead landing, "Why can I never warm you?   Why do I wrinkle and gray, while you do not age?"

Dear Helena.   Out of love I had stayed too long and she had begun to know me too well, to question me too closely.   It was a relief to me when she finally died of the influenza in 1927, for I have never been able to destroy

23

what I love and had had to await her natural death or leave her. Fortunately for us both, she died, sparing me the terrible pain of leaving, and her the agony of living out her old age without me.

I entered the parlor, where her coffin had lain for the wake, her ghost at my side, and crossed to the fireplace, pressing lightly a small lever positioned behind the mantle. The wall swung in without sound, and my bedroom, hidden, silent, protected, opened to receive me home. I might enter, but just as in life she had never been allowed inside this room, so now Helena's ghost must wander elsewhere while I slept.

Here there was dust, inches thick on the bookcases, drifted lightly against the bed's sturdy legs. Spiders had made nests in the corners of the ceiling, webs between the oak press and the

armoire. The linens on the bed smelled musty, but were not damp.

Tomorrow, I promised myself, I would clean the room thoroughly, but tonight, I was too weary.

I took fresh linens from the oak press and striped the oilskin cover from the feather mattress, smoothing out the sheets, carefully, lovingly.

Things, properly cared for, can last an eternity. Things outdistance mere mortals in life. They are not as ephemeral as love. They are safe, comforting, enduring.

If not for possessions, trundled with me through the centuries, I would have been a lost creature long before I met Mae, my Mae; my sad and sparkling Mae, who brought me into love again, and into terror.

But for me, at that moment, Mae did not yet exist.

That morning, the dawn falling through the stained glass of the parlor windows, I had yet to meet her. My life was still mine alone, and I was about to embark upon that great adventure that is sleep to us.

I closed the lair door behind me and fell instantly asleep on the huge four-poster bed with its immense headboard touching the ceiling ten feet above me, brought across the ocean from de Brissault chateau, long ago.

So very long ago.

****

Vampires do not dream. Perhaps we do not sleep. Our dreams are our memories, yet somehow more.

In that state, which even we call sleep, lacking some closer term to what it actually is, we relive fragments of our lives,
walk and speak again with those long dead, long turned back to dust, and now, perhaps, reborn in other bodies.

It is another kind of feeding; a species of regeneration.

On that first night of my return to America, I slipped into my memories to find myself in the rectory of our village church, the young and indifferent priest I had once been gazed through my eyes again at the woman, a dying child in her arms, who had come to me for succor and for a miracle.

****

The mother stood before me with her child bundled in her arms like a load of fragile sticks, wrapped in a blanket.

"She be wasting away, Father," she said, stoically

25

enough, though tears leaked from her eyes as from a slow, bleeding wound. "The Wicca Woman tells me there be nothing left she can be doing for her."

"You must stay away from that witch. God is offended when we seek any help but His. Holy Writ so assures us, Mistress," I said severely, though I knew such admonitions did little good.

This woman would take her child to the Wicca as readily as her milch-cow, and as often, in hopes of a cure, for these Wise Women were the closest thing to a doctor most villages could boast of in this year of Our Lord, 1323. They dispensed love spells and crop magic, healed both animal and human wounds with herbal poultices, and, in general, did much good.

But they also still worshiped the old gods of England, the Mother Goddess of the earth, her son/lover, and the meadow god, Pan, though this last was a Grecian import brought to the Isles by the Romans, and, I, as the village priest, had a duty to try and turn my flock from their still half-pagan beliefs as best I could: a task I was failing at pointedly, as the Bishop of this region and my father, the laird of Branshire, constantly reminded me.

The English were the last to be Christianized in the Roman Empire, and in that spring of 1323, Christianity continued to be infirmly rooted among the common people. They danced the May Pole with a statue of the Virgin tottering on its wooden throne above their heads. They told tales of vampires and werewolves to their children, side by side with stories from Holy Writ and the lives of the Saints as preached by myself each Sabbath in the old church.

Most priests, and many more monks, were drawn from this same peasantry. They were illiterate and untraveled, and Christianity could not be said to be that

26

much more firmly rooted in the clergy.

My companion in the village church, Brother Luke, who kept the sacristy swept and the altar items polished, after a fashion, wore a charm beneath his robe to ward off witches, yet consulted the Wicca Woman often. Her love spells were said to be infallible, and Brother's loins were infallibly aroused by the mere sight of a woman. Toothless or pocked though she might be, none were as ugly or deformed as Brother Luke, and to bed one, he needed the help of the amulets and spells he bought from the Wicca with alms stolen from the Church poorbox.

Because even the clergy patronized these women, no matter what I said, no matter what I might do for this child, the mother would take her directly from my church to the hut of the Wicca Woman, just to be sure that she had done all she might to save her baby.

"What is it you think I can do for your daughter?" I asked, knowing, too, that if the Wicca Woman had given her as patient to me, the child was surely beyond even the skill of the King's apothecary to heal.

"Mistress Storn says you have a magic oil to heal mortal illnesses."

"Mistress Storn is mistaken. I can perform the Rite of Extreme Unction for your child, but that will not heal her. It is only the anointing for death, that one may approach the heavenly throne shriven of all sins," I said piously.

"Mistress Storn says her man was healed of his bloody cough by your anointing him with this oil," she persisted.

There was no point to be gained in arguing with her. She would not understand, no matter how long or ardently I explained it to her, that sometimes the bloody cough seems to heal itself, but always returns in time and

27

darkness, to claim its victim. It is the true vampire, I thought, leeching life from men and women, causing them to cough out their lives in great gouts of black blood and yellow bile. Better to give her what she came for, I decided wearily, the sooner to be left alone again, with my books and my prayer.

"Give her to me, then." I said, reaching for the bundled blanket. "I will anoint her."

I unwrapped the child carefully, not wishing to increase her pain with sudden or harsh movements. I was a cold man, perhaps, but not a cruel one; a poor priest, certainly, but not one without compassion.

As her face emerged from the dirty folds of wool and into view I realized that whatever her sickness was, the child was not in pain.

She was very small, this baby I had baptized six years before, a tiny, malnourished doll, lying silent in the cradle of my arm. Her skin was mottled with dirt and illness, the flesh shiny and stretched tight across the bones with impending death, her nostrils faintly blue, her breath barely hitching along through parted purplish lips.

And cold. Her flesh was so cold. An inch above her body, the air seemed to shimmer with icy particles, numbing my fingers instantly.

She stared up at me mute and lethargic. She had eyes the color of a summer sky in Northern Wales. For a moment I thought them transparent, as if I held already a dead thing in my arms, a new corpse which would not lie down and be still, and for that moment, I shook like Old Man Tarrus who begged his food from door to door and slept on the hard benches in the church nave.

She felt my trembling and smiled, a smile tinged with a bitterness like frostbite.

28

I drew a deep breath and hurriedly traced the sign of the cross on her forehead and her eyes closed, the smile faded into a spasm of lips and thin cheeks. I carried her into the chapel and laid her down on the cloth covered bench near the altar, feeling now only a terrible repulsion for the girl, a deep desire not to have to touch her again, and a faint shame that I should be so lacking in charity.

"She will not eat nor drink," the mother said beside me. Her fingers twisted among the fringes of her shawl, like thin, brown worms, restlessly and pointlessly moving. "She lies about all the day and never cries. Her flesh grows colder with each passing night, until my husband can barely sleep for the chill of her body between ours. It is not natural, Father Anselm. Mayhap she is bewitched? Mistress Bowen has a grudge against me, for my man is a better cowherd than hers. Mayhap she has bewitched my baby?"

She stared hopefully into my eyes. Here was an answer to her child's illness. Here, perhaps, was the cure, as well.

"There is no such thing as bewitchment," I answered sharply and she drew back into her shawl, dropping her eyes to the floor in disappointment. What had she wanted me to do, I wondered in exasperation. Burn Mistress Bowen in the pit where diseased animals were destroyed, with a placard reading WITCH about her neck?

I kissed the stole and put it about my neck, muttering a prayer in Latin for forgiveness of my impatience and disgust with the superstitious peasant women and ugly, be-horned monks I found myself surrounded by in my life as their servant and God's and turned my attention to the woman's daughter.

29

The child was dying. Would die, I knew, and within a matter of days. Of what, I did not know, but certainly not of bewitchment.

The ability to bewitch another, I thought, preparing the oils so that I might administer the last rites to the child, would mean that man does have some control, after all, in what happens to him during life. This was the fallacy of magic, and perhaps its sin as well, for in truth we have no control, no say in our ultimate destinies as men. God alone, I believed, could right the wrongs other do us, or turn another's favor toward us, or heal His children's afflictions. If He chose not to, it must be because He was disinterested, indisposed, or just busy elsewhere with His many more important problems of kings and countries. At 33 years of age, I had been a priest for 12 years and my faith was no longer strong. It was merely stubborn.

"En Spiritu Sanctu," I intoned, and the mother lifted her head again, leaning close to watch me with eyes like silver coins, her tears so natural a part of her now that she no longer noticed them as they made their way down her chin and into her shawl where it rested against her cheek.

"Now she will be well again," she smiled when I had finished the anointing. She took the child back into her arms and said gaily, "Thank you, Father. My husband will bring you a fine calf for your kindness. She is our only bairn, you see."

I did not see, children being of little interest to me, but I nodded with priestly understanding and smiled.

I was uncharitably anxious to be rid of her and most delighted to see the back of her skirt as she passed through the sanctuary door into the dust laden street. My fingertips still burned with cold from touching the child. I could not imagine how her parents could share their bed with that icy flesh pressed between them.

She died four days later, just as the sun was rising.

The father built a small coffin for her, smaller than would have been needed had she died even a week earlier, for her body was shrunken like fruit left in the sun from which all fluid has been leeched out.

I sang the funeral mass on a dark afternoon with the rain drizzling down like chill tears upon my face. I did not expect the calf the mother had promised, for my magic oil had failed to save her child, but in the early evening, after the funeral party had marched, keening and wailing, back to the village, the father brought the calf to the small dwelling, appended like a dark mole upon the cheek of the church, where Brother Luke and I lived.

It was round little thing with a red coat and white spots on its face, planting its four feet stubbornly in the ground and tugging backwards on its leading rope. The man patted its head
and asked me sadly if I preferred him to fatten it a bit more or did I wish him to slaughter it immediately.

If not for Brother Luke's greedy eyes as he gazed on the animal, I would have told the poor man to take it home again, for it looked to grow into an exceptionally fine breed animal and he could not have had so many calves of this quality, no matter his proficiency as a cowherd, that the loss of this one would not cause him hardship.

Brother, not trusting the father to return all the meat to us, slaughtered it himself and we ate well that night, although not peacefully. Throughout the meal, Brother Luke kept up a steady stream of curses against me because we did not always sup so grandly.

He berated me for having too much pride to accept money from my father, still living in the manor house overlooking and protecting the village, for giving too much

31

money from the poorbox to the poor, for spending my time with books, instead of going to court and begging a better living from the King for us. Finally, having eaten too much to continue longer with his familiar refrain, he retired to his straw mattress in the corner of the kitchen, snug against the fireplace.

Once he had begun to snuffle and snore, I went out into the darkened streets, carrying a fine portion of the meat to the hut of the dead girl's parents, wrapped in the same cloth the child had lain on during the anointing.

In my revulsion, I had wastefully thrown it on the dung heap after the mother and her dying child were gone, and now I felt myself to be atoning two sins by its use as a covering for the meat ... my sin of uncharitable feelings toward the girl and the sin of being weak, of giving into Brother Luke's greed when I knew the parents would most likely go to bed hungry this night. Having fed their neighbors and the rectory with funeral meats, they had probably nothing left for themselves.

As it was fine cloth of good Flemish linen, I was certain the mother would be able to sell it for a few shillings or perhaps even trade it for another quality calf.

I had waited until Brother Luke's snores rose and became evenly spaced before coming out into the night, for I did not want him to wake and castigate me further for the loss to his stomach of this small, but rich, portion of meat, and because of the lateness of the hour, no one answered my knock at the parent's hut.

I placed the bundle just inside the broken door and returned to the rectory in the fresh moonlight, astonished at my own cold fear as I walked down paths I had known all my life, in this village that lay dead and white with sleep, beneath my father's manor house.

Tony and I had been raised in that towered fortress, I the second and favorite son of the Lord, the one destined to the Church, and Tony, the son of a neighboring Lord, less influential, who sent his first, and only born, son to the Lord de Brissault, to be trained as a knight and a gentleman.

We had run together through these same streets, in sunlight, rain and moon filtered night, throwing clods of dirt at Mad William, brawling in the one tavern, worshipping publicly in the church of which I was now the pastor, and privately at the altar of Mistress Breechem's breasts and belly in the small room behind the tavern when we were young, and I not yet a priest and he not yet the Lord of his father's lands.

Every muddy rise and fall of the street was familiar to me, all the plays of shadow and dim moonlight on the buildings were as known to me as the lines on the soles of my feet, yet I was afraid.

I walked too rapidly under the silent moon, and wished too heartily for a lock on the church door when finally I did close it behind me, berating myself in Brother Luke's heavy tones, for my lack of faith in God's promised protection of His priests.

I slept badly that night. I dreamt of tiny, white hands, reaching for me through the dirt of the grave, grasping my ankles and pulling me down into the earth. Fetid chunks of soil and rock filled my mouth and nose in the dream, so that I could not even scream in terror. I awoke, sweating and cold, to spend the rest of the night before the Host, praying both for the rest of the child's soul and the safety of mine.

When at last dawn began to slowly bleed through the stained glass window my father had proudly gifted to the church on the day I was ordained and given the name Anselm, I slept again, my head cradled by the white altar

33

cloth.

I wandered through that day and the next, hearing the whispers of `vampire' among my parishioners, ignoring their fear the better to cope with my own, for even I, who believed in none of these fireside tales, knew that something evil had begun to walk beneath the moon, across the spring fields.

Something which tore sheep into bloody messes of wool and flesh, something that fed upon the cattle, and moved closer to the village each night, as it worked its way from the graveyard back to its home.

Three nights after I had sung the funeral mass for the child, I awoke in the darkness of my bed to a sweet singing.

It was her, and although her body was yet that of a child, her face and eyes were no longer those of a bairn. Her lips were full and pouting, like the bawds that came each spring with the carnivals, her eyes so infused with hideous knowledge they might have been those of a woman of twenty who had lived her entire life as a whore.

She had died a child of only six years. She had risen from her grave a demon without age, trapped in a tiny body which would now never age, never change.

She gazed at me with eyes a fine shade of amber; they had been a misted blue before, I remembered, and the feral color chilled me.

"Make love to me, Father," she crooned, climbing onto the strawfilled mattress with me, her small hands brushing my thighs, and I, in utter shame, felt my body responding to her, this little girl, this baby child with a whore's eyes and the breath of a lion.

The fact I had buried her less than a week before did not frighten me as much as the thought that I was about to commit an abomination with her, for how could I

34

resist? My dusty faith in God had fallen into ruins in my heart.

Her lips cradled my nipple for an instant and I moaned, trying with what little will she had left me, to push her away.

"Oh, Father," she chided. "You have had women before this. Do not play the virgin with me." She giggled, those lips pressing against my chest, my collarbone, my throat, the teeth hard and pointed, unspeakable erotic, nipping the flesh there.

"Feed me, Father," she said, straddling me, bending to my throat again, and I let her stroke my body, kiss my mouth and eyes, those ripe lips always returning to my throat no matter where else they might wander. I let her take me in one rush of pain beyond belief, ecstasy beyond describing and relief beyond redemption.

When the vampire at last left me, still singing her wordless songs, I rose up, trembling, and made my way to the chapel. I fell several times, and there was no need to throw myself down before the crucifix, for by the time I reached it, I was crawling.

I pulled myself up by the edge of the altar and grasped the monstrance, its golden stem blinding in the candlelight, then screeched in pain and flung it from me, for it had sizzled into my flesh, cleaving the skin to the bone, cauterizing in its own wake, so that only dank smoke rose from my palms, smoke that stank of mortal sin.

Blood dribbled down my neck, staining the soutane I wore to a deeper black. My hands were burned and throbbing with exquisite pain, but my soul screamed in a greater agony, for I knew that in the weakness of my faith, I had committed an unforgivable sin with the child. God Himself would send His mighty lightning to cast His

35

tainted, His damned, priest from His house and, in terror of the lightening, I turned blindly and ran.

I bolted from the church, fleeing into the countryside to fall at last in a field of ripening hay, clutching my hair with burnt fingers, weeping with fear and exhaustion. I had nowhere to go, no home to return to, now that I was forever polluted by the child's kiss, forever condemned to a life without hope of redemption or recovery.

I lay beneath the green hay all the next day, in deepening dread as the sun lowered itself farther and farther to the rim of the world, but when she came to me in the night, giggling and hungry, I fell into her arms like a man coming home from a cruel journey and I let her feed, wanted her to feed upon me, lost in the songs she sang to me in the darkness.

Thus Father Anselm de Brissault died, giving birth in the sweet, growing hay to myself, living, yet not. Dead, yet not. Young, yet not.

On the night I rose up from my grave of earth and hay, she was waiting in the sullen shadows of the moon. "Kill yourself now, Father," she said with desperate hate, "so that I may die."

Although I did not understand what she meant, I walked away from her without offering a word in return.

I had no desire to die a second time, to snuff out this new not-life I had been given, no matter how unasked for it might be, for now, as vampire, I would live forever. I was looking forward to this eternal life freed of the bonds of society, of expectations, of pressures.

I would meet many others of my kind, I knew, and I believed I would make many new ones, to love me and stay with me throughout the centuries. I would never grow old, never sicken. Never be frightened again.

The child was mad if she thought that I, Michel de Brissault, second son of the Lord de Brissault, would destroy myself out of guilt or fear for what I was now.

I had not asked for her gift, but I accepted it completely. She screamed her rage to an indifferent moon as I walked away, laughing, roaring my joy into the night sky.

I never saw her again, and it would be half a year before I would meet another of my kind to explain her parting words to me, but in that short time, I came to know that even immortality has its price and its curse.

****

The night was just coming down outside the brownstone as I fluffed the pillows and smoothed the comforter. This very bed was the one I had slept in as a child, a boy, a young man. Tony had slept at its foot, as becomes the foster brother of the Lord's son.

We had played cards, sitting on its fur coverlets. We had tumbled ladies between its sheets.

It was Tony's sister, Aileen, our only link to the lost mortal world of our families, who brought us word of my father's death in 1333. It was she who brought the bed to me and told us of how my father had never slept in any other after my disappearance, so great had been his grief.

She was 40 years old at that time and begged Tony to give her the blood kiss. He did and they lived together for many years, before she met and fell in love with a sailor in Bridestown On The Sea. I have not seen her since, but I sleep on this bed whenever I am in New York, much as my love for my now centuries dead family sleeps always in my heart.

I protect its old wood and fine carving, as I protect

37

my heart, I was thinking, pulling on a pair of black boots and feeling pleased with my poetic turn of phrase when suddenly, like a cry within my blood, I was struck breathless by the woman's call.

I knew then that she could be no ordinary flirtation, no Helena, no simple meeting of minds and bodies for a time, however long or short, for I never dreamed of the time of my transformation unless I was on the eve of some great change in my existence. She could only be my fate, then, and resistance futile.

I closed my eyes and reached for her. I could feel her tears as she cried for me, falling like rain behind my eyelids and finally I could see her.

Not her face, but where she was.

A pretty room, in Art Deco fashion, the ocean outside the windows. She was sleeping. I could see her slight body beneath the sheets, pink satin and white ribbons, but not her face. I
did not know what she dreamt, lying there in a tangle of ribbons and lace, only where she was ... Miami, Florida ... and her name.

Mae.

CHAPTER 3

"You look exactly like your father," Ronald Higgenbothum said, looking at me oddly. "Yes, exactly as he did at your age. At our age, I should say."

"Did you know my father?" I asked politely. I could not recall ever having met a Higgenbothum before, but then there are so many names in seven centuries, so many faces. It is only the heroic emotions that stand out over so long a time; one's great friends or great enemies, of which, thankfully, I have had none in at least a century.

"I did not know him," Ronald said, settling himself behind a massive, glass desk, "but I did meet him once, when I was about seven years old, at a party old Cabbidu gave for the Paris office. My father was comptroller there."

"And you recall so clearly what he looked like?" I asked, fascinated by this odd conversation. I seated myself in a leather armchair with brass studs peppered throughout its arms and back. It looked wonderfully comfortable, but was amazingly similar to seating oneself on a pillow filled with bumpy pins.

"Having once met your father, it was difficult ever to forget him. His eyes were quite intense, quite different. That same fine shade of amber your eyes are, actually." He picked up the only folder lying on the perfectly appointed desktop and opened it. "My father said that Raymond de Brissault had made his fortune grow to devilish proportions on the strength of that intensity. It cowed his opponents and employees alike into taking risks they would not otherwise have dared."

"He was a brilliant man," I agreed. "I hope I have inherited his business acumen as well as his eyes."

I smiled, seeing not the pensive face of Ronald Higgenbothum before me, but rather that of a winsome lady in purple crepe de chine who had also attended that party of Cabiddu's. The old man had served a very potent wine and an elegant, rich supper. The lady and I danced until the other guests had gone or were asleep on the couches and floor, and the next night, I had fed well again, upon her willing blood.

"I am sure you have," Higgenbothum smiled in return, but his eyes were still resting oddly on my face. "I have been your CEO for long enough to say with certainty that you are every bit the businessman your father was, though I regret not having the opportunity to meet you sooner. Well. What shall I show you first?"

"Immediate cash assets, of course." I spread my hands and laughed. "The brownstone needs extensive repairs and with the cost of things these days ..." I let my voice trail off and watched him nervously pick at the top of his fountain pen.

He could not possibly remember what my `father' had looked like after so brief a meeting 25 years before, even if he had been struck by the color of the eyes, but I decided directly, watching him play with the Mont Blanc, that my next CEO would not be hired from within the company as, at Cabiddu's recommendation, Higgenbothum had been.

At last he nodded, uncapped the pen, and carefully began paging through my portfolio.

We discussed certain changes in a few of my investments and he tried to interest me in a new stock being offered for Russian McDonald's franchises. He noted each change in a thick, neat hand on pale beige paper with the burgundy Mont Blanc fountain pen.

I liked him more and more as the meeting progressed. He had an Old World courtliness and the aesthetic tastes from the ages of which I am most fond. His rather stilted English matched my own and I felt ... at home ... with him, yes, and comfortable, despite his eyes, searching me, reflecting my face in their puzzled brown irises. He wore his dull reddish hair parted in the middle and shiny black wingtip shoes. The telephone on the credenza, a replica of a gold Empire phone, did not ring once while I was there, nor did anyone enter the office. His room was silent, with peacefulness and good taste reflecting off the smooth glass and bronze surfaces.

Cabiddu had chosen his successor well and I would not like to have to kill him. There were too few mortals with whom I felt any sense of comradeship to toss even one of them away.

"That will do it, I believe," I said, rising to go, as he finished his notations and closed my file.

He, too, moved gracefully to his feet shepherding me to the door with quiet respect. He held out his hand to me and I clasped it for a moment, there by the door.

"Such a shame, wasn't it, about Marie Walker," he said, slowly releasing my hand. Whatever he hoped to see

41

in my face, all I allowed him to see was puzzlement and he was forced to continue with his game. By God, but he suddenly reminded me
of Archbishop Cranmer, Henry VIII's wily hatchetman. I nearly laughed aloud.

"She was found murdered in her hotel suite the night after the party at which I met your father," Higgenbothum said slowly. "A maniac, the police thought. Someone had broken her neck and drained the blood from her body."

"Shocking," I said, and hearing it described so, it was, even to me, her killer.

"Yes. It is said that she would have been an acclaimed actress today, had she not died. Her only film is a classic now and I occasionally catch it at the Old Film Festival in Greenwich Village."

"My father never mentioned this tragedy to me. I was at school in Switzerland at the time, but he wouldn't have considered such tales suitable for a child anyway. He was very oldfashioned," I smiled.

"It was a great waste of a very vibrant life, so my father said. She was only sixteen years old, you know." Higgenbothum's eyes were very bland now, his voice flat and heavy, but I noticed him rubbing the palm that had held mine against the back of his other hand. The cold of my touch had burned him, even through the thick kidskin of my gloves.

"Did he know her then?" I asked, quite as blandly and flatly. I had not known she was so young, but the incident was so long in the past, I could feel no shame over it now.

"She was his mistress," Higgenbothum answered. "She made the trip to Paris specifically to be with him. My mother, of course, never knew."

He opened the door then, and ushered me into his outer office. "Please contact me if you need anything while you're here in New York. You're staying at the brownstone till the remodeling begins?"

"Yes," I replied. "And there is something you might do for me. Please tell the cleaning service that I will not be needing them while I am staying in the house."

"Of course," he said.

This man might become a very large problem for me, I reflected, watching his eyes watch mine. Some unthinkable suspicion, unthinkable because mortals no longer believed in my kind, had formed in his mind when he saw me.

Why, in God's name, had he been so shaken by that murder a quarter of a century ago as to remember it all these years, and connect it with me somehow now? Well, I would move slowly with him, I mused, keep him alive as long as possible, for he had done wonderfully well with `de Brissault and Sons' in the past ten years, despite his youth, and I would so hate to lose him.

"Good bye," I said with continental politeness, and, "Good bye," he answered, swinging shut the heavy office door behind me.

****

I spent several days reacquainting myself with New York, which had, of necessity, changed greatly in the years since I had lived there and thinking of curses.

It is often said, even among vampires, that one of the greater afflictions of being undead is outliving everything and everyone who is dear to us. We are, then, cursed by immortality itself, although there are other and far worse curses upon us, some of which I shall tell you of

43

in a bit.   But, change, that king of curses for man and vampire, yes, it is painful.

More than any mortal, we are aware of the impossibility of ever holding to any familiar or loved thing for longer than a few, too short, years.   It is the greatest loneliness to watch cities grow up out of the bare earth, forests annihilated, rivers sometimes rerouted to make way for the dwellings and commerce of men, and then to watch the cities age, fall apart like old garments, and rebuild themselves only to again, begin to die.

I had been nosferatu for 667 years at that time and thought myself well-educated in this truth of transience and change, but still, there I was, wandering New York and thinking about the unknown woman in Miami, allowing myself to be drawn into believing again in a love that might, after all, be eternal.

I wanted to believe she was my soul-mate, as much as she wanted to believe there were vampires who could bestow, with a single, dark kiss everlasting life.   Yet I continued to resist the urging of my heart to go to Miami and continued to walk throughout the city.

I felt others of my kind as I moved through New York, especially in the Theater District, Times Square and Central Park.   This Big Apple, as they called New York now, with its anonymity and size, suited my distant brothers well.   They could hide here, among the garishly adorned punks in Times Square, the hookers and addicts of Central Park.   They could feed, without drawing attention to themselves, on bag ladies and society's other throwaways.

Despite my loneliness, I felt no desire to meet with any of them, to share in their hunting.   They were all young night haunts, smelling of the newly dead they were, and cruel as well.   As the young often do, they also fled from me when I neared their lairs, having even less desire to meet with an `Old One', as I have heard them call those of us with more than a century of vampirism behind us. They fear us, although I do not know why. Perhaps their makers whisper slanders against us to them.

So I continued alone, thinking of the woman. When I found myself visiting Helena's grave for the second time in a single day, I knew the time had come to go to Miami.

Better to suffer, if one must, the hot, sharp, cauterizing of a new pain, then the slow, poisonous canker of old regrets.

Again I indulged myself in the luxury of air travel, catching a red-eye from New York to Boston and then a first class flight from Boston to Miami. Upon arriving, I took a suite at the Mayfair of Coconut Grove, then established a hiding residence in the Coral Castle near Florida City.

Cloistered there in an underground set of rooms carved from the living coral, rooms that no tourist knew of, perhaps no caretaker, even, I could be safe from danger should I have need of sanctuary.

I wanted to stay with my friend, Richard Glewwe, and patch up an old misunderstanding between us, but his sprawling home had been replaced by neon-ribboned Metrorail tracks and glass highrise monstrosities, and I could not feel him anywhere within the state. Perhaps he had gone to New Orleans, a favorite haunt of our kind, if you will forgive the extravagant language, a place I meant to move on to myself, when the minuet with my unknown lady was done. In fact, none of our kind seemed any closer than Tampa, a situation that troubled me not at all, though I was faintly curious who that one farther north might be.

Faint curiosity is the best I can muster. I made no

45

attempt to find out who the creature was; I could feel that it was old, like myself, and as solitary.

The second afternoon after my arrival, when all arrangements for my security had been completed, I went searching for the woman.

I knew where she lived, roughly, and where she worked, approximately, from the night I had reached out and found her sleeping among the satin and ribbons. Because the day was overcast, and I was bored already with Miami, I set out to find her in the daylight, with no other plan than to simply take a look at her.

There were birds, wheeling high beneath storm clouds to the west, where the sun was still hours from its setting, and a moon, fattening to full, hanging in the east, not two hours past its rising, and I could see both, through breaks in the racing clouds, from where I waited for Mae to come out of her office
building at the end of this workday.

Tony would have seen them as symbolic, rhapsodized on the one, a star, bringer of light and warmth, and one a lightless, dead orb, reflecting the day's lost light into the night. One, Mae, one myself, but in the end which of us was the sun? Tony would have seen the symbolism immediately, but it was not until all was finished that I remembered the sky that day and saw it for an omen.

On that slightly chill afternoon in February, in my fisherman's pullover and slouching, Bogart hat, I thought only of Mae as I watched the crowds beginning to exit their office buildings. Perhaps it was the red Lotus I leaned against, smoking a Gauloise from a pack on the seat, clearly visible through the car's open door, or perhaps people here were not as frightened of loitering strangers as they were in New York, for no one challenged me. No one even turned their head to look at me as I watched them with my careful hunter's eye.

The women, in short skirts that were again fashionable, chattered as they dug in their purses for keys, calling to each other to rendezvous at nearby bars for Happy Hour. The men laughed as they swung briefcases into BMW's, Cadillacs with custom plates, and Mercedes' sedans. Despite wedding rings visible on nearly every hand, many looks were being exchanged, eyes flirted, hands fluttered and tentatively touched bodies not their own.

These men and women would eventually end at some Happy Hour, sipping cocktails, munching nachos and fondling knees, or home with their spouses, eating pot roast or steak, and wondering what it would have been like, to answer a look and go to a bar with an intimate stranger, rather than home to distant, too well known marriage partners.

Filled with discontent, they were all looking for someone or something vital and new, and it is this constant dissatisfaction that makes them such easy prey for night creatures of their own kind, and mine, and Mae would be just such a one, I was positive. I watched for her carefully as the women trickled down into the parking garage, yet when she finally did appear she was so unlike my imaging of her that, if not for the distinct flavor of her aura, I would have let her pass by with no more than an appraising glance or a moment's desire.

She was completely timeless, and though she would have been more comfortable still, I think, in the Roaring 20's, she fitted comfortably enough into this time in which I found her. Oh, she was beautiful, yes, incredibly so, but more, she was filled with a love of life that flared around her like the expanding of sunlight, like an entire galaxy gone nova.

Her hair, some shade of burnished gold and copper

47

like the sun's corona seen dancing in eclipse, was cut in a helmet that hugged her face, and the evening's ocean breeze lifted it in wisps about her forehead and cheeks. She was very slim, like a young boy, and if not for the overwhelming femininity of her features, might have been mistaken for one, she was so nearly androgynous.

In the next few days, as I followed her about the places she frequented, I saw men flood her immediate area, panting with mortal desires and fantasies. Delicately high-boned, skittishly high-strung, like a thoroughbred animal, she turned them all away with indifference as sleek as a compliment.

And as I watched her, slipping in and out at the edges of her life, I grew more and more intrigued, more and more curious, I, who had never been curious, to see if she also would turn me away.

Winning her, possessing her, was already becoming an obsession I thought I could remain the master of, for she was only a woman, after all, and I more than a man.

But she also had one of those minds from which thoughts escape very infrequently so that I could not hear her telepathically. Without her fantasies to guide me, how could I find the key to unlock her heart? She was the same mystery to me that human beings are to each other, and this had never before happened to me: a mortal mind closed to me, thoughts I could not enter, a heart I could not hear. She fascinated me.

I was certain of my inviolability, my mastery of self, but in nearly seven centuries I had met no one like her, not even my beloved Anne Boleyn.

Blinded by those spectacular green eyes, I failed to appreciate how like their color was to the depths of a Mayan sacrificial pool flecked beneath its surface with the gold of many offerings, and on an uncertain night in late February, I concluded that the time had come to introduce myself to her at last.

****

Mae had a schedule of sorts to which she adhered with some regularity.

Because she lived in South Beach, she spent nearly all her weeknights in one of the many clubs scattered throughout the Miami Beach area. Monday nights she stayed home, going to bed almost before the sun had finished setting. On weekends, she took public transportation, or rode with friends, to other areas of the city, or even as far down as Hollywood, Hallendale and Fort Lauderdale, but she went most often to a small, heavy metal bar that featured local groups called The Treehouse.

A friend of hers, a singer named Freddy Z, performed there Saturday nights, although I could never distinguish whether he had a regular band to back him or simply sang with whoever chanced to be on that night. He absolutely refused to share the stage with another singer, and that may have been why he seemed to have no band to call his own.

Unlike the others appearing there, he was really quite good, and watching him, I toyed with the idea of maybe going into rock n' roll myself. Lot's of money in the entertainment business, after all, and, more importantly, of all the men who surrounded Mae, only with Freddy did she seem to have any type of relationship, no matter how tenuous.

I had slipped farther down the road to self-delusion, you see. I was considering marriage with her, as mortals marry. I still had no intention of changing her. I was

49

simply thinking that I might meet her in the normal way, woo her so, and marry her, as I had done Helena and a few others, and if she was attracted to rock singers, then perhaps I should be one, the better to catch her attention.

Since she did spend nearly every Saturday night at The Treehouse with Freddy, it was there that I chose to wait for her on that particular February night, sitting at a long table, bought from some church rummage sale (I could still catch wisps of squirming children and praying women as I sat on its smooth boards impatiently waiting Mae's arrival), sipping a Peach Snap and hoping I had not made another of my rather infamous miscalculations in coming there.

Not that I doubted she would show up eventually, but because I doubted the wisdom of my being there waiting for her.

Tony was right, I thought, better to leave this alone, but I could not bring myself to leave, and so sat on, waiting.

The night was muggy, breathless. The doors at either end of the smallish room hung open like mouths gasping for air but only able to breathe in thick smoke and humidity, the smell of sweating bodies, sharp alcohol, expensive perfumes, and rich, musky blood. What the night needed was a good storm, someone near me said, and just after midnight, when she finally arrived, Freddy Z on her arm, their heads close together and her, laughing, the storm began to break, both outside the club and within my heart.

Freddy's hair was night black, hanging to the waist. Resplendent in electric blue spandex, he had a kind of dark sensuality that melded with her flashing white light to produce an exceptionally striking portrait of light and darkness. I was suddenly jealous enough to rip his throat out and present him his precious larynx and voice box as a necklace.

They passed near me to a table where he yanked out a chair for her before moving off to get their drinks at the smaller, less crowded, back bar. She watched the band perform with the same indifferent appraisal with which she responded to the men who began to approach her now that Freddy was temporarily out of the way. The band was doing a loud, painfully unmusical, heavy metal version of "The Ballroom of Romance" and Mae and her suitors acted out the lyrics.

They leaned over her chair, she shook her head, they moved away, shrugging and laughing.

She was waiting, also.

This cheered me considerably, as did Freddy's depositing of her drink in front of her before moving off with a blond of no more than 15 years, a drink in his one hand, and a breast in the other.

The bar grew more crowded, more close. I had not fed and the scent of heated blood roared through my nostrils. The band changed at 1 A.M. and again an hour later, and I watched her.

She remained, by choice, alone. Occasionally Freddy would stop by to replenish her drink, but no one else now tried to sit with her. She had turned them all away. It was time for me to begin the dance, to see if she would turn me away, also.

When Fred grabbed the microphone, catapulting onto the stage to howling applause, I finished my drink, made my way to the front, just beneath the stage, and then began to move toward her.

I let her see me, approaching through the crowded nightclub, lit here and there by bright pools of blue and smoky light, winking in and out of her vision as I came through the press of laughter, of light, of smoke, of heat. I let her know I was staring at her, that we were alone in this packed, pounding place, felt her feeling me, the bass line of the band beating in cadence with her heart, and, in the end, I disappeared like the dream I was, to reappear, the monster I am, behind her chair.

"May I buy your next drink?" I asked and she turned to me slowly, still caught in the dream and said,

"I was sleeping."

"Quite an insult to the band," I noted, sitting beside her. The others, sitting at the opposite end of the long table began to drift off.

Mortals often do sense us, in the darkness, on the periphery of their psychic vision, as it were, and turn away. Only those who desire death stay - death or the brief, blinking hope of
immortality. She watched them go, her eyes still blank with the dream.

"Just look how hard that singer is gyrating, all with the express purpose of keeping you awake." I couldn't resist the dig at Freddy, with his wildly swaying blue spandex hips and dancing hair.

She looked toward the stage, her eyes clearing, and laughed. It was a good sound, a tinkling tone made of equal parts of color and the sea.

"They're called the Lost Boys, after that vampire movie. Have you seen it?"

"No," I answered, leaning closer. "I don't like horror flicks. Too unrealistic."

And ... tiny pieces, locks of words, floating down like small clouds coming to rest in hollows of mist, scattering like mist, these words, our laughter together.

We were alone at the table, two blond heads now leaning close in intimate conversation, rather than black and blond, but still one darkness, one light.

She wore white cotton, thin and sheathing her like a tube, with rhinestones. They reflected, on her throat, her wrists, her earlobes, sharp rays of brilliance from the stage lights.

She smoked too much. I lit every cigarette for her. I swam in those eyes, forcing myself not to touch her, as once I had forced myself not to touch another of my forbidden loves, the promised of a king, Anne Boleyn.

"Last call," the waitress said, bending down to empty the ashtray. Her breast lay gently against my cheek. Toothsome and buxom, we would have called her, Tony and I, drinking at the Royal Swan. She smiled at me, but she spoke to Mae. "Freddy's last song."

I remembered another who looked much like her at the Lamb and Peacock, in 1632. I did not smile back, but my eyes told her I would be waiting when she emerged, high heels clicking on the blacktop at 4 A.M., to give her the oblivion she desired.

"Last call," I said to Mae.

On stage, Freddy was thanking everyone for being there instead of at Penrod's and admonishing them to hug a rock 'n roller whenever possible. He was looking at Mae.

"Is it so late? I have to get home," she said, looking uncertainly at the waitress, at me. She stood, sensing the darkling currents between the other woman and myself, disturbed by them. I wanted to cry out, to assure her that the waitress meant nothing to me, that my heart was saved for her, like some black and cursed jewel, an organic Hope Diamond. The savagery of the emotion frightened me and I swallowed the words, saying instead, "I'll walk you to your car. There are killers in the night." I smiled at Mae, then at the waitress, and she giggled.

Mae did even not smile. "No, thank you," she said stiffly. "I'm riding with a friend."

"I hope to see you again," I said, following her as far as the door and there bowing to her. She was so far out of time herself, she saw nothing odd, nothing foolish in this courtly gesture. She nodded absently.

A cool rain had started. She watched it fuzzing the neon sign that blared `The Treehouse' across the parking lot. Freddy Z cast a long look over me, before spreading his umbrella for her. Who was this one who had managed to capture his Mae's attention? his black eyes challenged.

They walked together, two warm mortals, into the cooling night. Thunder cracked loudly enough to rattle the glass in the ticket booth. Rain began to fall more urgently. I watched her go and vowed never to seek her out again.

Love is too risky, too shattering, even for a vampire.

Especially for a vampire, whose very existence may be ended, if one's choice of a lover proves to be the wrong one.

CHAPTER 4

I returned to New York.

I crashed about the brownstone like an out of control poltergeist.

It was not Helena who haunted me now in every room but my hidden lair, it was Mae, and she would not even respect my sanctuary, intruding there as well with her weeping and calling.

I walked round and round the city, by day and in darkness.

I came upon one of my kind mauling a child outside One Police Plaza, doing it there, in that place, to demonstrate his contempt for mortal efforts to retain order in a world vampire and human must alike share, and I destroyed him for his folly. Monsters such as he yearn to let the darkness in forever, and whoever had created him deserved it if a year had not passed since his dark birthing.

I wandered here and there, picking up women in bars, at cultural events, speaking with them only to find they were stultifying, dull, not Mae, nor even her sisters. I

55

was so certain her blood would taste like the rarest of wines, that even their blood then, pursued and lusted after by me, given willingly in darkened rooms or beneath candlelight by them, was unsatisfying and tasteless.

I spent hours in museums, disgusted with the various inaccuracies propounded by the young guides, and hours more reading in my private library back at the townhouse.

I was restless, and had I been human, might even have been termed cranky. I continued to ramble through the city.

One afternoon I wandered into Tiffany's.

I have always loved fine things, expensive things. My family was nobility, made so by Edward The Conqueror when he took England for his private estate, and I had grown to manhood with wonderful objects all about me.

My grandfather and father had both gone to the Crusades and returned from their adventures with riches not seen before in Branshire ... carpets from Turkey for our castle walls, golden objects from Egypt to adorn the sleeping rooms and great hall, jade from even further east, and spices to so flavor food that a man would kill to taste cinnamon again when it was finally used and gone. Now one need go no farther than the corner store for cinnamon, and on Fifth Avenue one can find jade, gold, Turkish carpets and delicious, Stuben glass, all the treasures won by death in my childhood, and more, available now for mere green paper or a variety of plastic cards.

Tiffany's, at least, had changed little from when last I had shopped there in 1927. It was still a bastion of civilization at its most frivolous and its most beautiful.

True, the old, refined objects I once had purchased there were gone. Silver plated ball point pens shaped like bamboo replaced the solid gold fountain pens I had bought with regularity in the years just after the First World War, and the famous Fabrage eggs were smaller and less ornate than they had been in the early years of the century, but the sales personnel was still softspoken, the jewelry even more stunning beneath clever, modern, inset lighting, the floor managers still obsequious.

I finally came to a case of diamonds and saw there a bracelet, diamond and emerald, fashioned to resemble the Deco jewelry of the 1920's ... square lacings of jewels, delicate green and red and blue fires burning within, all set in platinum. Breathtaking, oh, yes, and I knew I must have it for Mae, and knowing that, I knew I would return to Miami for her.

Tiffany's still required a name and address from any customer purchasing one of its originals. Before computerization I had willingly given mine, but now I try to leave as few personal traces of myself as possible. I went to Higgenbothum and instructed him to obtain the bracelet for me, as a corporate purchase of 'de Brissault and Sons'.

His reaction was akin to my father's when I asked him to buy me a set of hunting hounds one Christmas.

"$97,000 for a bracelet?"

"I wish it for a young lady I met in Miami," I said, a bit sullenly.

"Miami? You were there less than six weeks. It's your money, of course, but I am your CEO, and thus your financial advisor, and don't you think $100,000 for a woman you can barely know as yet, is a bit, well, precipitous, Mr. de Brissault?"

I thought of Mae, incendiary in rhinestones, and did not think so at all.

"Perhaps it is not my place, even as your CEO, to say this, but your father would never have allowed such a purchase," Ronald said primly.

57

"I am not my father," I shouted. "Just get it for me, Higgenbothum, and quickly. It is, as you say, my money."

I slammed out of his office in a most ungenteel manner, leaving him to stare bemused, at a Rembrandt on the wall over his studded leather armchair.

When night came, I shocked myself by taking two victims in Central Park. No courting, no dream of love for these poor souls. I took them with a simple brutality that frightened me. I had not killed so, nor fed twice in one night since I had been newly made. Something worse than bloodlust was upon me and I feared to face it.

I was in love.

Four days out of five, my re-livings were of that night in The Treehouse. I kept remembering her eyes, her scent, her laughter, the way her slender fingers held the English cigarettes she preferred, the sparkle of rhinestones on the flesh of her throat. Awakening from these dreams I would be in a frenzy of confusion.

I rang up Higgenbothum to enquire about the bracelet. He assured me he would bring it round personally as soon as it arrived. I roared that I had not known a corporate purchase would take so much longer than a personal one and mashed the phone down into its cradle so hard it splintered, and, of course, corporate purchases are no more lengthy than private ones.

Higgenbothum was stalling. He was up to something, but I was so close to insanity at that point, that I could not even sit and think things out rationally. In my rage, I could only determine to kill him once the bracelet was in my possession.

Three days later he came, alone in the blowing night, to the brownstone.

I opened the door for him, as nervous as a child on

58

Christmas dawn. "Let me see it," I demanded, right there in the hallway, with him still standing on the steps, snow drifting down about his ears and catching in that maddingly even part in his hair.

He was looking past me, to the staircase, the tile, the chandelier. "You have a beautiful home," he said wistfully, drawing the flat box from his pocket.

I snatched it from his hand and opened it carefully, drawing the bracelet up and out from its velvet bed. It literally dripped its multicolored fires over my fingers. A tiny white gold medal affixed to the clasp announced its status as a Tiffany original.

I sighed with happiness and some of the crazy tension of the past weeks drained away. I always feel better when a decision is taken, even if it may be the wrong one. "You haven't been inside before?" I asked, prepared to be a good host, now that the bracelet was in my hands. I even reconsidered my earlier resolution to terminate him as I tucked it back into its white and blue velvet box. "Let me give you the sixty pence tour then. I have some lovely art pieces I know you would appreciate, Ronald."

"No, thank you, not tonight. I would like a word with you, though, if I may."

"If it's about the bracelet," I said, leading him into the parlor and seating myself on a crushed velvet banquette that had once graced the lobby of the Armitage Hotel in Key Larraine,
Florida during its somewhat horrific heyday, "I'd like to apologize for my rudeness to you."

"It's not about the bracelet." He shut the parlor doors as if to give us privacy from my non-existent servants and family. I turned to look at him and saw that he was standing before the carved mahogany doors exactly like a man holding a gun in his hand, minus the weapon. I stood

59

also. Time stretched out, as it sometimes does.

He was sweating. Melted snow and sweat ran down his cheeks and into his overcoat collar.

"I know what you are," he said and his voice did not tremble.

"Do you?" I smiled pleasantly.

"I've been watching you." He was sweating, but not frightened. Determined, yes, but not afraid. His hands did not shake.

"You, yourself? Or some private detective?"

"Myself. Alone. I followed you from the office that day you came to tell me to purchase the bracelet. I followed you all afternoon and most of the night."

"What a perfectly extraordinary thing for you to have done. Whatever possessed you? You don't seem at all the incautious type. But, have a seat, Ron. Drink?" I moved to the liquor cart and poured him a straight scotch. He took it, then seated himself in a wingback.

"Your eyes," he said wearily. "You can't imagine how unique those eyes are. I couldn't get the resemblance to your `father' out of my mind. My father always believed your father killed
Marie Walker, you know. I have always remembered those cold, amber eyes, looking at me down the dinner table that night at the party. They were eyes quite capable of murder. But also, perhaps, great love, and when I saw you, I saw those same eyes. Those utterly, unmistakable eyes."

He leaned forward, moving the glass back and forth between his palms absently, not taking his eyes from mine. The condensation from the icy glass left wet patches on his black leather driving gloves, like splotches of fresh blood on dark cloth. I wondered if he could see Marie Walker reflected in the amber depths of my eyes, head bent back in ecstasy, a single drop of blood shimmering on one white

60

breast.

"I did some discreet, oh, most discreet, I assure you, investigating after our first meeting and found your `father' had `died' in a boating accident. The body was never recovered," he continued after a moment.

I nodded.

"He had inherited control of `de Brissault & Sons' from his `uncle', Josiah de Brissault. Josiah `died' while on a hunting trip in Mexico. One of the last people to see him alive was Ambrose Bierce, the horror writer, who a short time later disappeared in that same area. Josiah, though, did not disappear. His `body', dressed in his distinctive hunting outfit with its solid gold epaulets, was found several weeks after Bierce's disappearance; was found, in fact, by a party searching for Bierce. The face had been torn off by some wild beast. The Mexican police never connected the two men, one vanished and one dead, but I think I have."

"So you have, Ronald," I nodded. Bierce had braced me, just as Higgenbothum was doing. His had been a convenient body for my disappearance, which I arrange every 50 years or so, as circumstances dictate.

"Before Josiah, there was his `father', another Michel. He `died' in a snowslide in the Alps. The body was, again, unidentifiable, other than by the clothing and jewelry found on or near it. The head had been crushed between two blocks of ice." He stopped again, taking a slow swallow of the whiskey. "Every one of these men were in their fifties when they `died', and none looked older than 35 by all accounts and what contemporary photographs exist. I felt that if I continued back in time, I would only find more of the same; faceless bodies, missing bodies, unidentifiable bodies. I felt that I had gone as far back as I needed to, especially once I made the connection

61

between Ambrose Bierce and Josiah.

"It is all true, isn't it?"

"Tell me about your Sherlockian efforts of the past few days," I smiled.

"I saw you in Central Park," he said with finality. He might have been informing me that the company was bankrupt, so intense, and yet impersonal, was his tone. "You killed those men just as Marie Walker was killed."

"Why didn't you call the police?" I asked, getting up to pour myself another drink, this one a blood colored wine in a fluted crystal glass. "That is proper procedure when you see murder done, is it not?" I swirled the wine slowly about and he watched it with wide, unhappy eyes.

"You must understand," he pleaded, laying aside his Scotch and holding his hands out to me as beggars in medieval times had done. "I wouldn't have followed you but for what I had learned about your `father' and `uncles'. You are not some psychopath acting out a fantasy. You are no common, garden variety murderer, Mr. de Brissault. The police can't touch you, and oh! I am doing this so badly!, but it must be done, I must say it, you are a vampire!"

The final four words came out slowly, thudding down on the carpet between us. He had an astonished look on his face, as if he had not believed he would actually say them, could not believe he had dared to think them.

The room itself relaxed.

So he did know. Somehow he had made the intuitive leap from Josiah and Bierce, from the missing bodies, the mutilated faces of my history, the memory of Marie Walker, to this, his secret knowledge. Seeing me kill had been the bridge by which he had made that leap to his horrified destination, and don't journeys end with lovers meeting?

62

I found it quite wonderful that a twentieth century man should actually have come to believe in what his culture taught him was inconceivable, foolish and a bit mad.

Any other man, even seeing what Higgenbothum had, would attribute my method of killing to madness or perversion. He would not have thought `vampire', but then he would not have known of Bierce as Higgenbothum did, of Marie Walker. Seeing me kill, then, this dull, detail oriented, stolid man, with his perfectly parted hair and shiny wingtips, had believed, and believing, was now come to exact something from me, as Bierce before him, had done. Yet amazingly, I was not angry. I did not feel threatened.

This reaction of mine was more surprising to me than his discovery of me. Others had done it in the nearly seven centuries of my existence. Others would do it again in the coming seven centuries. It was this almost fraternal feeling toward him that surprised me.

I was intrigued, positively fascinated, that Ronald Julius Higgenbothum, MBA, Ph.D., CEO, avowed agnostic and logical, stolid family man, had uncovered my secret, and I was a bit proud of him, too, for doing it.

I moved to sit in the wingback directly before him and leaned forward, taking his outstretched hands in mine. Our faces were very close.

"What is it you want, Ronald?" I whispered.

"Why, to be like you," he whispered in return, eyes still wide and sweat nesting in the hollows of his temples.

"It is not a good life, Ron. You cannot die (a slight untruth, but only a slight one, as he would discover should I change him). You will watch your wife grow old, while you do not. Only a fool takes his wife with him into eternity, Ron. You will eventually have to disappear, to begin again elsewhere. That is

63

not easy, either, as you know, for you managed to ferret me out, didn't you? You will have to feed, once in 48 hours at a minimum, and early in this life, more often, for the bloodlust will come upon you and you may not be strong enough to confine yourself to animals or one human a night."

His face paled, but his steady yearning eyes did not change.

"You will have few close friends, either human or vampire. It takes centuries to develop such friendships. I myself have only three, and one of these I have not seen since your country's War Between The States. You will have no allies in the human world; Dracula is a fiction. There will be no devoted human to watch your coffin as you sleep, Ron. You will have to kill. Can you kill, Ron? Your conscience will not die with your body, my friend." And oddly, I did feel him my friend then, wished for him what he wished for himself, wished for him sweetness and a gentle love for the deep of night.

"It is life," he said simply. "Eternal youth."

"I'll think about it," I answered, releasing his hands and leaning back into my chair.

I studied him carefully. He spoke of eternal youth, yet despite his still few years, less than half a century of them, he had never had youth. You could see that clearly in the set of his lips, the bleakness of his eyes. As a child, his father had probably begun grooming him for a top management position with my company before he was out of diapers; dragging him to the dinners, the parties, throwing him in Cabbidu's way at every opportunity.

He spoke of something, then, that he had never had, something he yearned for, but something which being un-dead could not give to him.

We only bring with us into eternity what we were

64

and possessed in life. Time is the novitiate of eternity, as the Catholic Church teaches, and what we are at our death, we remain.

"I'll think about it," I said again.

"Yes, of course." He drew a deep breath, groped for a hat he had not been wearing, and rose to go, shining the palms of his gloves on the crease of his trousers as he stood. "I didn't expect you to, ah, bite me, or however this thing is done in real life, immediately. And, well, I hope you know I shall never tell a soul what I know, even if you refuse my request. I know you can, you would, kill me, and I have a family I must think about, you see."

"Ron, I am not a movie monster, for God's sake," I said irritably. "It is true I killed Bierce when he came to me, accusing, condemning. But you are not threatening to impale me with a stake, as he did."

I might have added, but did not, that Bierce also wanted me to sign over control of `de Brissault and Sons' before lying down obligingly and letting him stake me to the barren Mexican soil.

"I would never do that," he cried. "I will never betray you, Mr. de Brissault. I have been your CEO for a decade and if you choose, I will remain your CEO for the rest of my life. I have always served you. Well, since graduating the university, anyway. I was raised to serve you and that will never change, no matter what you decide."

I stood, too, and placed my hand on his arm. "Sit down, for Christ's sake, man. Have another drink. You look a bit weak in the knees. I am not so frightening as all that, surely? Of course not. Now, sit, my friend."

He sank down into the wingback and I made him a fresh drink. "Now. Tell me the truth this time. Why do

65

you want this? The future is uncertain, after all. Where will my kind feed if your kind blow themselves up in a nuclear exchange, and we survive, which as a race, we shall most certainly do? Most men today do not find life so precious as to cling to it. The majority do not even respect it any longer."

I was truly enjoying myself and this exchange. Oh, but this was refreshing! The man did not love me, expected no love from me. He did not, apparently, even like me much. The most that could be said was that he admired me for my home and business, and suddenly I knew his motivation. "It's the money, isn't it?" I asked, seating myself and handing him his freshened drink.

"You have a fortune. Anything you want, you can have," he said, his words rushing out of him as if they could not wait to be heard. "You have seen, ah, what you have seen through the centuries! I envy you what you have seen almost as much as I do your wealth. You have had the time to see and live and build up a fortune and it grows greater each day. You've set it up so cleverly not even I could trace all the holding companies and dummy corps back to `de Brissault and Sons', or to you individually. Why, if you had been as careful about disposing of your previous identities as you've been about covering yourself in business, I could never have found you out, never have ..." He stopped and blinked in confusion before resuming, "I would, of course, stay on as CEO of `de Brissault and Sons', even as a vampire, as long as you thought it wise to continue," he finished primly, not in the least deflated by all his words.

"Of course," I agreed dryly. "And you would no doubt invest everything you have in the company as well. Perhaps I should gift you with a partner's share of stock, too." I was being sarcastic, but he was too good a man,

66

too simple, to see that. A small worm of shame crept about my heart, but this making of a new one is not a thing lightly done. I must be sure. I must believe it would benefit us both, since I could not leave him, a cuckoo in a hostile nest.

"Oh, no," he protested. "I have some wealth of my own. Simply let me invest with you and that will be enough."

"You could do that anyway," I said, moving back to the banquette and picking up the velvet box. I opened it and pictured Mae's face when I gave the bracelet to her. He did not answer. "I am certain you do that now anyway," I prodded gently.

"Yes, but I will not have the chance to see it blossom to millions in a normal lifespan, use it to travel and explore and learn all the things I am unable to see and learn now because I must work each day until my death just to pay the bills. If you had any idea how much money my wife spends, it would age even you. And, as you say, the future is uncertain. I could be run down by a taxi tomorrow crossing Fifth Avenue."

"That uncertainty is what make life sweet, Ron. It gives a man impetus to make his life meaningful, knowing that he dies so soon, and at any time."

"It is what makes life meaningless," he corrected me urgently. "Death is what sours life from its very inception. No matter what a man accomplishes, it dies with him, or with his children."

"Not necessarily," I said. "Think of Michelangelo. Of Mozart."

"They were special men," he cried passionately and I was delighted. A vampire cannot exist without passion. Passion for life, for living, is the only thing which can overcome that first harrowing year of darkness.

"I am only an average man," he shouted. "When I am dead, another will take my place as CEO. My accomplishments, such as they are, will be improved upon, or discarded as outmoded. Whatever money I may have accrued will be squandered by my wife, my children. I will be like Marie Walker, forgotten, having accomplished nothing, when I might have done so much. Please, please, if there is any compassion in you, if being what you are does not preclude pity, then pity me. Give me what I ask of you." He dropped his face in his hands, exhausted, drained at last, by his words and his yearning.

I moved to him and stroked his head softly, as a mother does a child who weeps. "You do not understand what you are asking for," I said gently. "You do not know the rules of the game you seek to play."

"You can teach me," he said, raising his eyes hopefully to mine.

"If I were to do this for you," I said and his face brightened like a small boy's at his first circus, "we would be inseparable for the first year. You would have to take an extended leave from the company, follow me wherever I might go, do whatever I told you without argument, without hesitation. Do you understand? Your continued existence would depend on it."

"I understand what you are telling me, but why?"

I went to the fireplace, turning my back on him. I touched a portrait of Helena painted in 1899, set in the center of the mantle between two vases of yellow roses. She was wearing a white lawn dress and large hat with fruit spilling from its rim. I thought of Helena and Mae and Tony. And I thought of loyalty.

I thought of Ronald offering me loyalty, no matter what my decision. Loyalty beyond merely keeping my secret between us, for who would believe him if he should wail it from the World Trade Center's roof?

I had heard the clarion of his thoughts clearly the moment he cried out Marie Walker's name and he would serve me in all things if I would do this one small favor for him, save him from her meaningless death, those thoughts had screamed.

Loyalty, unlike love, often lasts, as possessions do, for an eternity. I still did not know if I would change him, but I knew that I wanted to make him immortal. I wanted him by my side for however long he might wish to stay. And I knew I must be honest with him, make myself vulnerable to him, and then let him make the decision for himself.

I turned back to him and he was watching me with the hungry eyes of a lover.

"Why? Let me tell you of what it is to be undead. Because you have asked for this changing, you probably will find your first reaction to be a wonderful joy when you wake from the dead to our unlife. But I did not ask for it. I was horrified and frightened and disgusted when the bloodlust came upon me and I had to destroy my first human being. The vampire who made me taunted me at our parting to commit suicide and I did think of it often in the following months, once the thrill of knowing I would live forever wore off and I came to realize the price for that immortality.

"I overcame the urge to destroy myself, by turning my thoughts to my family, by watching out for them, protecting them as best I could, despite the distance I was forced to maintain from them. But what will overcome that urge for you when it comes, as it will, when the darkness closes in and you are drowning in the blood of your victims and you realize suddenly that you will never

69

see the sun in a cloudless sky again, never can look to God for comfort again?"

"I do not care about the sun and I have never believed in a personal God," Ronald said firmly.

"We have enemies," I continued, as if he had not spoken. "Other vampires. Sometimes a human, though that is rare now. And The Other Immortals. They will try to destroy you, especially during the first year, when you are weak and unschooled."

"Others?" he asked.

"Yes, there is another race of Immortals and they hate us. I will tell you of them someday. Tonight is not the time. All you need to know of them now is that they will seek to destroy you if they become aware of you." I sighed and turned again to the portrait of Helena.

"Then they will destroy me if I am not strong enough to survive. It is a chance I am willing to take," he said slowly. "At least, as a vampire, there is the possibility of immortality. As a human, there is none. And you have just said you will be with me, to protect me and teach me."

"Yes, I would be with you, if I should do this for you," I agreed. "But not for unselfish reasons. Not to protect you. To protect myself. For if you die in that first year, I, too, will die."

He was silent. The room filled with a heavy tension again. I turned to him and saw his eyes widen with shock.

"You see," I said, gliding to his side, beginning to weave my glamour over him. "You ask me for immortality and in giving you the chance to be immortal, I must expose myself to the possibility of final death."

I reached out for him, laying the back of my hand against his cheek, as lovers do. He did not flinch away

70

from its cold.   He did not speak.

I leaned over him, took his face in both my hands, and kissed him full upon the mouth.

"How much do you love me?" I whispered.   "Do you love me enough to protect us both for that first year? To deny your desires for freedom, for release, perhaps for death, for 365 full days?"

His eyes were glazed, but he suddenly stood, shaking off the glamour, passing my final test.

"I do not love you," he said, "but I will protect you. I am a man who has never dishonored a bargain.   Your company has done so very well under my leadership because others in the business community know they can depend on my word.   I give you that word now.   I will obey you in everything for the first year.   For your sake, I will never place myself in a position of danger, neither will I destroy myself until the year is passed, should that desire ever come to me, which I doubt."

"Go home, Ron," I said quietly.   "I will think about what we have talked about."

"I understand," he said, just as quietly.   "This cannot be an easy decision for you to make.   I did not realize, well, you know ...   the vampire movies never even hinted at such a thing as this.   In fact," he said smiling a little, "they have it reversed.   When Van Helsing killed Dracula, the taint of vampirism was removed from Mina."

"It is a well kept secret," I agreed with a small smile of my own.   I ushered him through the parlor doors.   "I will contact you with my decision in a few days."

"That will be fine," he said, as if we had spent the past hour discussing a new stock opportunity.

I took him to the front door, opened it.   He glanced again with longing at the chandelier, the staircase, the marble flooring, as he had done on entering.

71

"You have a beautiful home," he said again.

"Good night, Ron," I said, holding the door for him.

"Good night, Mr. de Brissault," he answered, passing out into the snowfall, which had become quite heavy.

I went back into the parlor and sat on the banquette, taking the bracelet from its box.

I listened to the car slam, the engine start, heard its purring BMW sounds as it disappeared down the street, carrying Ronald Higgenbothum away to his home, his wife, his children, his mundane and mortal life.

I sat with the bracelet held now against my lips, now reclining from my fingers, but I was not thinking of Mae.

I was thinking of Ronald Higgenbothum. Thinking of business arrangements and friendships and loyalty, and at length, sometime after three, when the night is thickest and the air coldest, I stood beside his bed and awakened him.

"I have come for you," I whispered, and his eyes were white in the darkness.

CHAPTER 5

"I really don't like this club much," Mae said, as I seated myself beside her at a table fronting on the swimming pool; plastic cups floated in the pale blue water, napkins scummed the bottom. "It's always so crowded and they don't even have a live band."

With the ocean only a few yards away, the swimming pool seemed an obscenity, one more reason not to like the place, and I said so.

She did not seem surprised to see me after my absence of several weeks. She held her cigarette out to be lit as if we had seen each other just last evening; as if we saw one another regularly, here on the terrace of what was being called South Florida's hottest nightspot. Next week, or next month, some other club would be the hottest, but tonight it was Penrod's, with its muscle beach and kiddie area, it's polluted swimming pool, and Mae, looking like a teen model in scarlet and gold.

"Yes, it is decadent, isn't it?" she exhaled vigorously, both words and smoke tumbling out, spilling into the still air between us. "Decadent. That's one of my favorite words. De-ca-dent." She drew the word out, sounding each syllable as if they were plump strawberries she was savoring. "It's such a lovely, such a, well, decadent, word, isn't it?"

"Oh, certainly," I agreed, signaling the waitress, who ignored me. She was one of those who knew I was dangerous, one of those with psychic vision. She would have nothing to do with
me, not even so small a thing as taking my order, and I applauded her silently. If I had not been so caught up in Mae, I would have tried to woo her, just for the sport of it.

"Sex, I suppose, is one of your favorite words," Mae said carelessly. "It usually is, with men. Oh, I'd like you to meet a friend of mine. Sex is certainly one of his favorite words. With a face like his, you can see he rarely lacks for it. Waldo, this is ... " She turned to me and raised her eyebrows, wriggling them like Groucho Marx.

"Michel," I said, rising, and holding out my hand to be polite, although I did not feel polite, nor even civilized. "Michel de Brissault."

Waldo took my hand and applied just enough pressure to assure me he was not a weakling. I caught vague thoughts from his touch, like mildly unpleasant odors, all of them astonishingly carnal.

He was patently Cuban, although when he spoke it was without an accent. Dark skinned, dark eyed, he might have been Freddy Z's cousin, right down to the sullen sexuality that permeated the air around him. Handsomer than Fred, taller, well-built where Fred was slightly pudgy, I might have understood why Mae was here with him had she been a normal woman, but Mae was not normal, and she never went anywhere with any male except Freddy Z in his spangled spandex.

One thing was quite clear to me, though, as I restrained myself from crushing his hand in mine; physically I was not Mae's preferred type.

I am tall, yes, with excellent musculature, but I am blond, my hair tied back in a small ponytail a la Steven Segal, though I have worn it this way for almost seven centuries, my high, too pale, cheekbones planes of shattered light and dream and, at times, later throughout the night, I would hear from Mae, like a radio suddenly cut off in mid-sentence, the beginning of realization as she looked at me, the odd way the light reflected from my skin, in my eyes, "Not-human, not-human, not ...", these thoughts occasionally colored brilliantly with subliminal sexual longings.

Physically, she found Waldo and Fred erotically attractive, yet she desired me, and subconsciously recognizing the danger in it, she also feared me, so that already she was beginning the process by which mortals assure themselves that what they have wished for cannot possibly exist. Vampires are not real. They are the product of Victorian sexual repression, modernized for twentieth century consumption in Lost Boys and Graveyard Shift. I, therefore, being real, was not a vampire, yet she was drawn to me, blond hair, white on white skin, and all, and would not allow herself to know just why.

"Waldo's currently recovering from a broken heart," she said in a light conspiring tone, pulling me away from my thoughts, and his, of his sleek brown body covering Mae's slight, white one, which I already considered exclusively mine. "I thought Penrod's might cheer him up, and do you know? I was right. He came with me, but he's leaving with someone else." She laughed.

"I wouldn't have left you here alone to find a taxi home," Waldo said, smiling shyly, "but if Michel wouldn't

75

mind ... "

"Not at all," I assured him. "I'll see to it she arrives back home safely."

"Great," he answered absently, no longer present with us now he had been released from his responsibilities to Mae. "Great. I'll see you at work, then, Mae. Tomorrow. Don't drink too much, heh?" He shook my hand again, and this time I felt not only polite, but positively well disposed toward him.

"Great gloves," he said, staring down at my hands. "Say, where are you from? Your accent is odd for around here."

"Europe," I said. "That's where I got these gloves."

"Great. Great," said Waldo, and rubbing his hand, he moved off into the crowd heading for a Cuban lady whose coloring could only be described as vivid.

"He's sweet," Mae said fondly, "but I lied. He lacks a heart to be broken. Are you sweet, Michel?"

"A lady I once knew well, but not well enough, was fond of calling me Sweet Michel," I answered, signaling another waitress. This one obligingly came over to the table and I ordered a Pink Gin Fizz.

"What was her name?" Mae asked, smiling a child's smile at me. "Was she prettier than I am?"

"Anne," I said. "Anne Boleyn. She was a great love of mine, but no, not prettier than you."

"Oh, just like that queen back in England," Mae cried joyously, lifting another cigarette to be lit.

"Just like her," I said.

"He doesn't even know who he's leaving with yet," she laughed, gesturing after Waldo, who was now talking with a blond girl who towered over him by several inches. Mae sipped her drink and winked at me over the rim of the glass. I toasted Waldo with my drink and she laughed again.

Mae loved to laugh, as Anne had, and my heart clinched with dread for a moment.

I had not lied to her. Anne Boleyn had been a great love of mine and that relationship had ended very badly indeed.

"I was cramping his style fearfully, although he's far too sweet to ever say so. I was preventing him from `getting lucky', as Fred says." She tossed back her drink in a way that reminded me of Tony and that, somehow, made me feel better. "Let's walk on the beach. It's so noisy here I can't hear myself scream."

Standing at the waterline, lifting her scarlet muslin skirt up around her thighs and splashing in the surf, she looked like a pagan goddess, or a child. The ocean seemed, as it always does on moonless nights, to be a black, sentient creature. It licked worshipfully at her calves and made her laugh again.

The sound of the nightclub was far away, though the smell of its smoke drifted down to us. A couple were necking in the sand. Beyond them a boy stared pensively out to sea and urinated into the foam at the water's edge.

"Do you like the ocean, Michel?" Mae asked, throwing herself down on the beach and cradling her head in her arms. She could not wait for my answer lest it prove too inane. "It's so magical. All life begins here."

"Began here, Mae," I said, sitting beside her.

"What?"

"Began here. Millions of years ago." Tony had told me that, during one of his scientific enthusiasms.

"Don't be so literal, Michel. There's more to living than facts, you know. There's magic, too. I never feel alive unless I am near the sea. It is my magic, my friend,

77

my hope. When I am beside it, I believe in immortality."

She lay on the beach, unspeaking, and at length I realized she had fallen asleep, her fists wrapped around the sand, like a child's.

So she had found me banal, after all, I thought, and retreated into her dreams. I sighed, and watched the moon rise over the blackened sea.

****

The phone was ringing as I slipped the latch to my room at the Mayfair Hotel.

"Michel," Ronald Higgenbothum said, sounding breathless and quite done-in, "do I have to bite them in the neck?"

"What are you talking about, Ron?" I lit a cigarette and stretched out on the bed. I had never before had a fellow vampire call to ask me the proper mechanics of feeding. I should have anticipated it, though; Ron was such a meticulous sort. The love of fine detail was ninety percent of what made him such an outstanding CEO.

"I mean, must I bite them only in the neck? Can't I bite them somewhere else?" he pleaded.

"Good grief, Ronald, don't you ever go to the movies? Of course you can feed elsewhere if you choose. Any major vein or artery will do."

I began to regret leaving him alone in New York even for the few days it would take him to process his extended leave from `de Brissault & Sons'. I would not have convinced myself that it was safe to do so if I hadn't been so mad over Mae and now it seemed as if he had managed to find himself trouble before his body was barely cold.

"What have movies to do with it?" he asked

irritably.

"Didn't you see <u>Once Bitten</u> with Lauren Hutton? The femoral artery, on the inside thigh is an excellent site, especially on women, as you can take them during lovemaking and with no fear on their part. I've never cared for the tartness of adrenalin in the blood myself, although Tony claims it's like the addition of carbonation to wine and finds it quite delicious." I stared at a seascape on the opposite wall and thought of Mae. What would her blood taste like? Strawberry wine, no doubt.

"Of course I saw that movie." He sounded aggrieved, as if he suspected me of treating him lightly and I was, despite my worry for our wellbeing. "I took my kids to it, years ago. But I thought you didn't like horror movies?" Now he sounded betrayed and I laughed.

"I love the silly things," I said, still laughing. "Just as Tony is enamored of literary vampires, I am enchanted with celluloid ones. Now that is a secret, Ron. One which only my closest friends know."

He sighed. "But, to feed there, doesn't the, eh, victim, have to be a virgin? Wasn't that the entire point of the movie? That Lauren Hutton needed a virgin? Where in New York am I to find a virgin, Michel? Other than my daughter, and I have my doubts about her, even if she is only 13."

"Mythology, Ron. Mythology. You can bite wherever you choose, despite your victim's sexual history." I snubbed out the cigarette. "Anything else I can help you with? It's almost dawn and I've not had a very productive night." The truth was, I had not even fed, and my mind slipped and slid from exhaustion and hunger between worry over him and longing for Mae.

"Well, there is one thing more I've been wondering about," he said in that hesitant, apologetic tone that both

79

exasperated and charmed me.

"Yes? What is it?" I said, and wished my words sounded less sharp, but I could hear him hemming and hawing down the line from New York and my exasperation was greater than his charm. I snapped, "Come on, man, I'm beat. Out with it!"

"This matter of crosses," he said, sounding terribly dejected. "I went to pick up a prostitute tonight, but she was
wearing a cross, so I thought I'd better ask you first about, well, about ..."

I laughed again, but this time it was a tired laugh, a sound more like despair and I shut it off quickly. "Higgenbothum, you're amazing," I said, with not a little admiration for him and the surprising amount of imagination he seemed to have acquired in death. "You don't even believe in God."

"Yes, I do," he said. "I just don't think I believe in a personal God. But I thought there might be some inherent power in crosses, something that might, well, burn me, whether I believed in it or not. Something that might harm you as well as me."

"How long since you rose from the dead?" I asked him, lighting another cigarette. It tasted like horse dung liberally mixed with Mexican straw.

"Forty-eight hours," he answered, his voice decidedly woeful now.

"And you haven't fed at all yet?" I asked in sudden alarm.

"Just little sips from my wife while she sleeps."

"Well, stop that nonsense right now, my friend. You infect her with each `little sip' and increase her lifespan exponentially. You don't want that, Ron. Believe me, you do not want her around your neck 50 years from now."

"I do believe you." He sighed again. "But I just can't seem to figure out this matter of feeding, Michel. What happened to that bloodlust you warned me about?"

"I'm puzzled about that myself," I admitted. "You should be so hungry by now you'd attack Arnold Schwartzenegger if he came within a hundred yards of you with a stake and a hammer. You must have been an inordinately passionless man in life." The sun was starting to lighten the cracks around the blackout curtains at my window and I felt heavy with the need to sleep. But I also felt heavy with dread. "The thirst should have taught you all you need to know to hunt. Ron, I want you to catch the next plane to Miami. Alright? I want you here with me. Now. Good night, Ron. I want to see your face when I wake up in a few hours. Understood?"

"Wait," he wailed. "What about the crosses?"

"Ronnie, what if you were Jewish?" I began to bellow with laughter again. This was so ludicrous. Had any vampire I ever made been so helpless? It was hysterically funny, but frightening, too. It was imperative that he come to Miami immediately where I could keep an eye on him.

"Well, actually, I wasn't even raised Catholic," he was saying, "but in the movies, you know...". He fetched up a truly soul-weary sigh this time. Being undead was more complicated that he had thought it would be. It did not fit neatly into his spread sheets and corporate annual reports. It did not have clear cut rules like it did in the movies, except the one, never
mentioned in any movie or novel, the one we, who create the New Ones, call `Fear Year'.

I felt a sudden pity for him and for myself. His dilemmas forced me to remember a time when belief was integral, when even great sinners, who scoffed publicly at

81

God, would yet appease Him privately, especially as death drew near, or age, or financial misfortune, explaining themselves to Him, excusing their acts to Him, bartering for His forgiveness, arguing their rights as those who had been redeemed by His Blood.

Blood.

It always came back to blood. Henry VIII had been such a man, and Tamerlane, and that oddest of Russian czars, Peter The Great.

I remembered them all, and I remembered, too, a priest who seared his hands grasping a monstrance in hopes of atoning for his sin with a child vampire who had come to him singing in the night.

"More mythology, Ron," I said and rubbed my watering eyes. "Religious objects used to have a kind of power over us, but that was a long time ago. Before technology. Before cotton mills and steamships; perhaps even before the great plagues of the Middle Ages that destroyed the Church as a secular power. Before crosses and Stars of David and evil itself became mere symbols. If they had any power at all, even then, it was because of the faith of those who wielded them. You can only be hurt by something like that now if you believe you can, for your disbelief, in this age can outweigh even the most ardent faith of a believer today. Maybe it was always that way. I don't know."

I was very tired now. I remembered how effortlessly Mae had slept in the sand.

"Oh, how you wish for a good, faithfilled vampire hunter now, eh?" Ron chuckled. A weak joke, but it drew a smile from me.

"Something like that, perhaps," I agreed. "But, did you hear me, Ron? Catch the next plane. I mean it. Don't try to fly it yourself by shapechanging. You're far too weak for that. Take a private Lear if you want and charge it to the company, but I want you here when I wake up this evening. Bundle yourself up well and avoid direct sunlight as much as you can. You understand?"

"OK, yes, I'll be there. Thanks, Michel. I'll try not to bother you with this kind of thing anymore."

He was apologizing again and I wished he wouldn't. He was, in the only way I would ever bear one, my child. I loved him, I realized, and that made me regret my teasing of him.

"Before you ring off, Ron," I said quietly, "I'd like to apologize to you. I shouldn't have created you and then left you alone up there, even for a few days. I am sorry."

"It's all right," he said softly. "You left because of the woman. I know what obsession is. I was obsessed with you, remember? And I have been careful, Michel. I don't want to die anymore than you do."

"Thank you," I said. "I'll see you in the morning then. Go find yourself a small animal and feed before you catch the plane or you'll be too weak to take a sick grasshopper by tomorrow."

"I will," he said. "Good night, Michel."

I set the phone back on the hook and got up to undress.

It was odd. He had not loved me before I made him. I had not loved him, yet bound now by the darkling kiss and our shared vulnerability, we did love. Would Mae still love me, when I had changed her? I wondered and then shuddered.

It was the first time the thought had consciously entered my heart, and I did not beat it back as I should have even though it terrified me. I let it roam about inside me as I made up my bed in the closet.

It was there with me, as was Ronald's accusation of

obsession, as I pulled the blanket over my head and settled into sleep, to dream of the only woman I had ever considered myself truly obsessed with ... Anne Boleyn.

******

On that, my first night back in Miami with Mae, I slipped into my memories to find myself in the gardens of Hever Castle, and the Lady Anne wandering like a ghost among her roses, those harsh, tiny headed flowers, made so insubstantial by the lowering summer's evening fog.

Sir Thomas Wyatt, her cousin, and, some said, her lover, sat on a bench among the roses, watching her with anxiety in every line of his pointed face, in the tenseness of his shoulders, the twisting of a white rose in his hands, the quivering of his mustache.

Tony, through whom I had met Wyatt and his captivating cousin, like to laugh at that poor, quivering mustache and, in truth, there was not much to it, but the man was a fine poet and there was, indeed, much to him.

"I fear for her, my Lord de Brissault," he said to me now, and the re-living truly commenced.

"She has recovered well from the Sweat," I observed blandly, reaching for a blood-hued rose to present to the Lady Anne when she should deign to officially notice my presence. These flowers, being cultivated, were no danger to me. It is only a wild rose that renders us motionless.

"She will not recover from him," he answered sullenly.

"No, she will not, and why should she? He is King. He can give her what you and I cannot."

"I love her ..."

84

"As do I, but he offers better than we can. A crown, my dear Thomas. And the means to avenge herself on those who have slighted her, blasted her hopes of marriage with young Percy, and called her foolish, when not naming her whore."

"You speak of the grazier's son, Wolsey, yes, but vengeance is a dish best eaten cold," Wyatt gloomed. In that time, you must understand, this saying was not yet considered a cliche; rather it was an adage to remember and live by. I would cringe at its use in conversation today, but back then, I agreed heartily with him, nodding encouragement for him to continue.

Sweat, like tears, beaded on his cheeks. A drop of blood beaded on his fingertip. I wished he would not tear at the stem of the rose so. Its thorns were sharp as tiny fangs and I forced myself to look up into the evening sky, away from the blood and the hunger it roused in me, despite an earlier feeding.

The day, like Anne's mood, had been hot, overcast, and heavy, perfect for a vampire like myself wishing to visit his lady love in the late afternoon.

Mortals believe vampires are constrained from moving about in the light, just as they believe we must sleep on a bed of our native soil. In both cases, these misconceptions are useful to us, especially the belief that we melt or explode or burn or whatever it is they think we do in sunlight, as it serves to protect us as we move among them.

Like an albino, our skin is sensitive to direct sunlight; so, too are our eyes. We can bear the sun, though not easily, nor for prolonged periods. Cloudy days are very comfortable, and in England, there are many cloudy days. We prefer the night, but are not banned from the light, as a friend of mine, who, unlike Wyatt, was a very poor poet, once wrote for a play he was producing in Paris in 1750.

I was watching the sweat dribble from Wyatt's mustache and thinking of these things when the Lady Anne swept over to us like an empress in her yellow velvet, her hound, Urian, padding patiently after, his bullet-shaped muzzle sweeping the air in a hopeful search for threats to his mistress.

Many said Anne was a witch. Was her animal not called by one of the names of Satan? they whispered. Did she not have a sixth finger on her right hand? No, her left, wasn't it? None of these gossips knew for certain. Perhaps it was both hands. Maybe both feet as well. Wolsey was the most powerful man in England to think her one of Satan's Tarts, but he was not alone in his belief; in this one instance, he had much company among the nobility and the common people.

Men either loved her to the point of social madness or hated her enough to wish her done to death; women almost without exception, despised her. There was no middle ground with Anne; she desired, and gave, no half measure in anything. She would have made an outstandingly wonderful vampire and I worshiped the very rustle of her feet as they moved on the graveled path toward me.

I saw that her color was sallow in the uncertain twilight as she drew near, and thought it a good thing the King was not there to see her. Her fight with the sweating sickness had left her overly thin, shrewish, lacking in that fire and light Hal so loved and that made her so different from his rigidly pious, older-than-he, wife.

"God's nightgown, it is close today," she sighed, wiping her neck with a silky piece of something. "I almost believe I am ill again with all this sweat trickling about my ears."

Wyatt was silent and she made a face at him.

"My Lord," she said softly, turning to me and extending her hand to be kissed. "How do you this day? It has been long since you came to visit."

"Well, as always, but better still now I am with you again," I murmured, bending over her long fingers. On each, not forgetting the thumb, rested a gem set in gold. Henry's gifts all, except for a tiny amethyst on her right little finger (the left one being that with the nub of an extra finger growing out from its side).

The amethyst was the gift of another Henry, the young Henry Percy, who would be the Fifth Earl of Northumberland when his father passed on and who Anne had hoped to marry. She had been judged by Wolsey to be too common for a future earl to wed and banished from court and separated from Percy who was married to another against his will. I knew that amethyst's origin, though few others did, and my heart always hurt for her when I saw it.

I set my lips to her palm and she shivered. The smell of her blood beneath the thin flesh was intoxicating. She smiled, arching her thinner black brows and touching the tip of her tongue to one lush lip. Anne was an incorrigible flirt, but I did not mind at all.

People said, and say still, four and one half centuries after her death when they should be worrying about more contemporary matters, that she went after Henry with cold calculation, plotting his capture by holding him off with a nonexistent virtue. They whispered that she was no true woman with hot blood running in her veins, for if she were, how could she possibly resist the advances of our shining, golden Hal? They hissed that she and she alone was twisting his mind and heart until he must, for her, put away his lawful wife and child and deny the authority of the Church and Holy Father.

The truth is, and this comes from one who was there, remember, that had there never been an Anne Boleyn, there would still have been a divorce. Henry needed sons and Katherine had given him only stillborn and short-lived ones throughout the many years of their marriage.

And Anne was not cold. She burned, a living, white flame.

They said, and say still, that she manipulated her way to a throne, this woman too common to marry the future Earl of Northumberland, but I, who knew her and was burned by that flame, never believed it. She was, simply, a flirt. I do not believe she ever envisioned to what her flitting smiles and glittering eyes would lead when first she captured Henry's attention, not until they had led her too far to withdraw, and then she grasped all it was within her power to take, as any woman would have.

And I, caught also by those eyes, that smile?

I did not contemplate changing her, giving her my Kiss, although I loved her to the point of madness, and not only because of that first year of danger.

Anne reveled in life, loved it with every cell of her body, every thought, every instinct. She was always reaching out for life, grabbing it in huge handfuls like a greedy child with sweetmeats, tucking it into the pockets of her skirts, and hiding it beneath her pillows, to keep for a time when there might be too little of life left for her, for a time when she would be old and men would not eddy and pirouette about her, made subservient to her strange beauty by their lust.

I would have spoiled her had I made her one of us. She had no desire for eternal life, only for a life well lived, well danced, well sung, in the present. Forever meant nothing in the face of today. She had no need of the vampire's only gift.

"How cold your hands are, Sweet Michel," she cried now, withdrawing her own from mine, but that husky voice was filled with sexual promises and temptations. It drove me quite silly.

"My heart can barely beat when I am near you," I apologized. "My extremities suffer, therefore, from a lack of warming blood."

"Shall you die for me then?" she laughed, pleased at my poetry of expression. Wyatt looked even more miserable.

"Most assuredly," I answered solemnly, crossing my heart, like Tony and I had done as children whenever we wanted my father to believe some especially outrageous lie.

"Would that the King might feel so," she shrilled suddenly in one of those mood swings that frightened even mighty Hal. "Why does he delay sending for me? I am well. I have been well for these seven days past. I even sent Dr. Butts back to him so that he may know I am recovered. Has he another doxy on his knee, do you think?" She turned on Wyatt with the fury of a wind newly blown up in the English Channel, throwing herself on her knees before him and clutching his legs.

The night had completely fallen now, and over his shoulder I saw the servants placing torches outside the main doors of Hever Castle. Her mother stood watching us from a circle of darkness where the torches did not reach. With my preternatural sight I could see how rigid and disapproving her face was as she glowered at us, at Anne, screeching at Wyatt as if she were a common fishmonger's daughter and not the promised of a king.

The newly rising moon caught Anne's tear-streaked cheeks in a stray beam of ghastly orange. For a strange

89

moment, she seemed afire there on the black gravel path.

"Tell me, Thomas," she wept, shaking his body. "You are newly come from Court. Tell me, of a truth. Has he another whose duggies he loves to kiss?"

"You know how affrighted he is of illness, Anne," Wyatt soothed. He lifted his hand to smooth the waist length, black hair, but did not quite dare to touch it. His fingers caressed, instead, the air a mere breath above her neck. "You will soon be back at Court, Sweeting. There is no one else for him; how could there be?"

"There could not be." She pronounced the words as an incantation, and poor Thomas shuddered. "I am a fever from which he shall never awaken. Never," and laughing, her hand on her white throat as if it pained her, she disappeared within the manor house.

Her mother lingered a moment more, still watching us, then turned to follow her daughter through the heavy oak door.

Wyatt looked at me and said, "You see, My Lord, do you see what I fear? How she runs to her destruction on the legs of her emotions?" I could only shrug, clap him companionably on the back, and take my leave.

Anne was recalled to Court, but not until Christmas was almost upon us.

The Italian, Campeggio, sent by the Pope to conduct a hearing into the King's Secret Matter, had arrived earlier that fall, but Henry's annulment from Katherine still looked as far off as it had in 1523, five years before, when Anne had first dared to tell the King she would not be his whore, only his wife.

As if wearied by the delay, hoping to make his position unmistakably clear to the Pope and his errand boy, Great Harry gave her luxurious new quarters next to his,

90

and a smaller, rival court began to form about Anne. Myself and Thomas Wyatt were a part of that sparkling band.

I was an especial favorite of the ladies who loved to `ah' over my `exquisite muscles', my `extraordinary height', my `yellow eyes and yellow hair', and my `mastery of the dance', but Wyatt, with his poetry, was even more sought after by the ladies than I.

Wolsey still hated the Lady Anne, though even he had come to believe in her virtue, cursing it at every chance to whomever he could persuade to listen to his lamentations. In that year of 1529, there were not many who dared to listen, other than the Spanish and French ambassadors. I once tumbled him across the receiving chamber after overhearing him depreciate her to a Flemish diplomat. Henry nearly rolled from his audience chair in laughter at the sight of staid Wolsey, his somber gown about his ears, his garters showing, lying stunned against the wall, for Wolsey was falling from favor with the King as surely as those who helped him to his divorce were rising.

Henry's court was so large, his hanger's on so numerous, that I felt myself well hidden by the crowds as I, too, hung on, haunting the winter balls, the spring jousts, that dying summer's masques, lingering for a look from Anne, a casually spoken word from her, that radiant jewel enthroned at the center of all our combined youth and radiance.

Tony came to court in the fall, shortly after Anne herself returned from a forced retirement at Hever while Campeggio's court of hearing sat, but left within days, saying the atmosphere boded ill for anyone involved, even peripherally, in Hal's folly. Although she obviously enjoyed my company, Anne grew to speak with me less and less as her tension mounted, so that I, in turn, spent less and less time at court, as my obsession with her grew, and with it, my jealousy.

I began to travel, returning at times to see her. In 1531, while in France, idly seducing one of King Louis' mistresses, I heard of Henry's final break with Katherine at Windsor; how he left her alone in one of his castles during the Summer Progress, he and Anne completing the seasonal round together.

Anne was now queen; she lacked only coronation and a marriage to be legally recognized as such, and I, hearing this, admitted at last that she would never be mine. Now she was indeed, as Wyatt had written of her ... Caesar's and untouchable.

It was not until the fall of 1532 that I again returned to England and chanced upon an opportunity to speak privately with her, in an oddly deserted corridor of the palace at Whitehall.

"What say you, Sweet Michel?" she asked, drawing the cord of her dress through her hands in nervous tugs and pulls. "Do you also think this granting to me of the title of Marquis of Pembroke be Harry's way of saying he will not play at this divorce game longer, that I am to be cast aside after these many years, as was my sister, Mary, before me?"

"I am hardly in His Grace's confidence," I said, "but Mary received no title when the King tired of her. Why do you ask me this? I have not even been at Court for over a twelvemonth,
Anne." I held my hand out to her, but she ignored it, her eyes darting wildly down the corridor behind me, then back to my face.

"It is said you know people too well, that their very thoughts you hear. I have heard you called magician of a time, here and there." She smiled without mirth, fully

92

aware of the peasant women who called her Witch.

"Those are unfortunate accusations," I said lightly. "I shall have to avoid Spain, lest I find myself slowly roasting at the auto de fe."

And I would have to avoid the King's Court for an even longer time, as well. There was no Inquisition in England, but there was still Hal, bluff and godless, and like all godless men, dangerous, especially to those he considered sorcerers and heretics.

"And I have heard it said," she continued as if I had not spoken, "that you are as astute as our Archbishop. That ye be a priest once. Tell me what this sudden elevation betokens to you," she begged, suddenly digging her fingers into my surcoat sleeve.

Only Tony could have told her I had been a priest, and I silently damned him. Kings and priests have all the answers directly communicated to them from God Himself, or so people were wont to believe then. So Anne believed, and here she was, this tiny, white and black woman who I loved as I had never loved another in my entire existence, asking me for answers I could not give her.

I had consciously kept myself separated from Hal for the past three years and knew his thoughts no more than she did. He had one of those mortal minds that is always shouting. Being close to him was like standing next to a foghorn as it bellows to the sea; very uncomfortable. I had no answers, no reassurances to offer her that would be truth, yet a vampire, for sheer length of living, does become astute at understanding human motivations, and seeing that she would not be jollied, I choose my words carefully, basing them on what I perceived Henry's motives to be from what I knew of him as a king and a man.

"I believe he gives you peerage to stop the tongues that say he marries a common grocer's granddaughter," I

93

said carefully, hoping this might sooth her. "I believe he means to honor you, Anne."

"Is it so then? Of course it is," she laughed. She ceased to dig at my surcoat, petting the cuff of the sleeve instead. "That is just what he said to me," she cried, tilting her eyes up to mine. "`I do it to honor you, Sweetheart.' You must come to see me elevated, Sweet Michel," she said more calmly, brushing my cheek with her lips. "I command you, as your future Queen, to attend. I shall look for your golden eyes among the crowds that will be there to see me made a Marquis."

I bent to kiss her hand but she moved stiffly down the corridor away from me. Light from a mullioned window bisected her neck at the shoulders and I shivered at the sudden, ugly picture that came to me ... Anne, her head rolling down the hall's flagstones, her body walking on without it.

My wandering route out of Whitehall took me past the chapel where Henry sat, enjoying one of his daily Masses, and I stopped for a bit, to hear the words of consecration that I had once spoken in the village church of Branshire.

The King sometimes attended Mass four or five times in a day. I suppose it helped him to feel filled enough with His grace, privy enough to God's mighty secrets, to be able to stifle his conscience over the wrong he was doing to Katherine and his daughter, Mary, and the schism he was causing in the Church.

A man like that, I thought, might twist his conscience to encompass any atrocity and I suddenly wished I were in Egypt with Tony.

But in spite of my misgivings and my desire to leave England immediately, I did stay long enough to see the King create Anne Marquis of Pembroke. She had asked me to, and truly I would have done anything she asked of me, but mostly I did not want her to look out over the crowd, composed in the main of her enemies and not see those golden eyes that loved her, among the blue and brown and green ones that hated her.

This granting of title to her did make me uneasy, for all my blithe words to Anne. Those who hated her twitched with joy at it, for she was the first woman to be given a man's title in her own right, and a certain clause on the charter of awarding, that which stated the title to be hereditary only for those children `legally begotten' had been omitted.

Thus the gossip that sprang up so rapidly that she had finally given into his lust and bedded the King and now, in satiation, he was ready to be rid of her with this casting-off gift to her and any bastard she might bear him. No one seemed bothered by the unreasonableness of this gossip. The illogic of a king divorcing his wife to marry a younger woman so as to beget a male heir, then casting away that same woman before a possible heir could be born, did not occur to them.

Oh, yes, the talk ran through the palace that August like ale down a drunkard's throat as the day of her investiture approached, but on that day, no one could mistake the look in Henry's eyes when she appeared at the entrance to the hall for the ceremony by which he would ennoble her. That he was still in love with her was too clear to those who had hoped to see indifference as he looked upon her with his tiny, pig-set eyes.

She entered the Great Hall of Windsor Castle to receive her peerage clothed in a crimson velvet gown that matched in color the ermine furred mantle of rank that would be placed on her shoulders. Her elegant head was held with cool dignity at the end of that long stem of a neck, her eyes were arrogant as she swept the French ambassador, the Dukes of Norfolk and Suffolk, with her gaze, a queen's gaze, and she not yet a queen. They did not soften when they chanced to find my eyes.

Anne was arrogant, as integrally as she was sensuous, and for the first time I saw what had troubled Sir Thomas years before in the rose garden.

The strain of this waiting game she played with Henry for a divorce that was still as distant as it had ever been, was changing her, stringing her out. The sensuality was disappearing into her arrogance, the sweetness souring into shrewishness. It made me immeasurably sad for her, and frightened, too, for I could see that the King was also changing beneath the strain and the uncertainty. His eyes were often cruel now, where once they had never been anything but open and joyous.

The Bishop of Winchester read out the patent of Anne's new nobility, the coronet was placed on her head, the mantle of rank about her shoulders, and the deed was finished.

I did not stay for the feasting, but left for Holland that same hour, to stay with another of my old friends, the Countess Ana Schvetcholtz, and to try to forget Anne.

Ana had been transformed in 1430 and was yet new to our life. A woman in her late 40's when someone (she has never told me her story) fed upon her, she was a ribald old bitch, always chasing young, young men, grabbing for male asses and thighs if they came within reach of her long hands, keeping each of them with her until she bored of their conversation or their lean, muscled bodies, and betook herself to find a new dalliance. She loved the catch and the chase equally.

I loved her, as I loved Tony, and as she loved me.

96

I always enjoyed visits at her castle, but was never very sorry to leave; the parties she held night after night would have wearied even a French king.

I heard from a Spanish ambassador attending one of Ana's soirees, that the King of England had married his concubine in a hole-in-corner affair and then declared himself head of the Church in England to legitimize his secret marriage. No one but Henry, of course, could possibly accept its legality, but it was not conducive to a long and prosperous life to voice one's opinion too loudly in England now. The Black Crow, the ubiquitous `they' whispered, was pregnant.

I hoped, for her sake, that Anne would bear Hal the son he was obsessed with siring. I feared he would divorce her otherwise, and Anne would be no more easily put aside than she had been wed. I also prayed, after my fashion, that he would
divorce her, so I might have her at last for my wife.

Anne did not birth a son, although she did bear Hal an heir, and I sent a velvet christening cap to her when her daughter, Elizabeth, was born in 1533. I never received an acknowledgment
for my gift, but then perhaps it never reached her. International relations between France, England and Spain were not good at that time and mail moved slowly across Europe if not carried in some court courier's pouch.

I was not much bothered that she did not send me thanks for my gift though; I was far more interested in pursuing a pink and gold milkmaid through the hills surrounding Ana's chateau. No one milkmaid in particular; Holland was too full of these delightful wenches for a man to limit himself to one. They were also too beautiful to kill (most of them, anyway), so I contented myself, for the most part, with little sips now and then of their rich,

97

milk-fed blood, and I did not worry overmuch that I had not even a message of thanks from Anne.

I would hear of her, or from her, eventually. If she bore Henry no son in a year or two, he would discard her, and then I reasoned, I would have my chance to woo and win her.

And then one night I did hear her. I dropped the calf I was feeding upon and sprang to my feet, caught in the web of her panic.

I could see her quite clearly, laughing hysterically, screaming with rage and frustration and fear, close to madness, locked in a chamber of the Tower. She was not calling me; she had, perhaps, long ago forgotten me. She was howling for life, and I, who am Death's bosom companion, heard her.

I had loved her for years, did love her yet, and I could save her, could give to her my dark and immortal kiss. I became the hawk and soared through the night to her. I became the wolf and ran through the night to her, but I am neither wolf nor hawk. I am vampire, and move more swiftly than either of these. Before the sun had thought of rising, I came into her tower room as a beam of moonbright.

She knelt on the flagstones, her back to me, her hair tumbling like black water to her waist. No one kept the death watch with her and that, more than anything else, enraged me with a terrible sorrow.

"Anne," I said.

Her head jerked at the sound of my voice. She was facing the door and knew that no one had entered, that nothing human waited behind her. She turned slowly and stood, steadying herself with a hand on the bedstead.

The hysterics were gone now. Her thoughts rippled through me, telling me before she spoke, that

98

tomorrow she would die, but her courage, as great as her beauty, had won out over the terror. She faced me calmly, with the dignity of a born queen.

"My Lord," she said with a tinge of irony, and curtsied.

I kissed her hand, and she did not draw back from its cold this time as she had in the rose gardens of Hever while Thomas Wyatt, wretched in his love, looked on.

"You are as chill as the tomb," she whispered, turning my hand over slowly within her two. "As icy as the death wherein I shall lie this time tomorrow. What are you, my Lord, to come to me as cold as my dying? What manner of demon have my lips kissed of a moment at Hever and Greenwich?"

"My sweet Anne," I said. "Look upon the gift I bring to you." I allowed my fangs to elongate, so there could be no mistaking the escape I offered her. She paled even further, as dead white as if the headsman had already drained her blood out onto the straw.

"God's Holy Breath, no," she whispered. "I cannot."

"Anne, you will live," I pleaded. "I love you and would take you into eternity with me."

"No, Sweet Michel," she said, taking her hand from mine. "I will die."

I let her pull away. I would not inflict my existence on her without her consent, her desire. If she found being undead too repulsive to be borne, she would destroy herself and me with her. I could only be her friend now; if not her lover and her savior.

I could, at this, her end, be the one who saw the death watch through with her. I went to a chair and sat, and she came to lay her head upon my lap.

"This is the same room wherein I awaited my

99

coronation," she whispered. "How quickly the time has come when the King has tired of me. I believe he first grew dissatisfied after the night in Calais when at last I gave myself to him. Perhaps he had expected to find a goddess in his bed and woke to find only a woman no different from Katherine." She lifted her head and stared beseechingly up at me.

"My father was a-hunting at Windsor when they arrested me, did you know that? No, of course, you could not know that. He was hunting stag while his daughter and son were being imprisoned in this place of traitors, and I am told, slyly and with such malice, by my keepers that he knew of the arrests before ever they happened and contrived to be away at Windsor so as not to be contaminated by our evil fates. How weak he is, my father.

"I never believed he would have me killed," she said earnestly, laying her head upon my knee again. She spoke of Henry now, and I stroked her hair, as Wyatt had been unable to do. "But I perceive that as the others have died, so shall I. At least he has promised he will not burn me. I could not face the flames, dear Michel. But ... poor Norris, and Weston, and Brereton, to die so terribly for me. And my beloved brother, my Georgie, to die for the sake of his wife's jealousy of me. Do you know what Henry said to me once, not so long ago?"

"No, Anne. Tell me."

"He said he had always loved me for my variability of mood. `But now,' he said, `you have only one mood. You harangue me like a fishwife. It is no miracle I cannot make a son with you.' But, oh, Sweet Michel, how he hates me that I did not give him a son, when truly, how could I when his member would not harden enough to seed me with that son?"

100

"Anne," I cried. "You did not say so publicly?"

"Not I, but George. At his trial. That comedy of a just hearing held by our peers of this land."

"God's death, my darling," I said sadly, drawing her up and into my arms. "No wonder he hates you. You have told the world the King is no true man. What colossal foolishness."

How I loved her, though, in those last hours before dawn. I had never loved her so much, or wanted so badly to give her the blood kiss, though she might hate me always for doing so. Yet there was my own desire for existence. Even for love as strong as this, I could not so foolishly endanger myself.

I did try to persuade her, telling her she would be able to take a fine revenge, such a one as not even she could dream of, upon the man who had betrayed her, and who would now kill her as well, but she was firm. Only as the sky began to lighten did she turn to me with a trace of madness and say, "If there can be such demons as yourself, my Lord, then can there not be ghosts?"

"I do not know. I have never seen one," I answered truthfully.

"Can there not be haunts as eternal as you? I will be such a one to Harry. I will never let him go. In every woman's kiss he shall taste mine. In every dark night, he shall hear my voice upon the wind. In his death, he shall turn to see me waiting. I will blight every marriage he turns his hand to, for he will marry, again and again, in his search for sons. His lability of conscience will demand it of him. I will destroy his children, should his potency return in some other woman's arms, and I will obliterate his offspring completely, even until my daughter is Queen. I swear it," she whispered, her lips brushing my ear, her breath searingly hot on the ice of my flesh.

101

She rose from my lap, clenched her fists, raised them to the window where the new day was breaking forth and cried, "I swear it. Such is the power of my love, now turned to hate."

The bolts of the door rattled back.

"Good bye, Anne," I sighed and became a mouse, slipping out easily through the legs of the man and woman now entering to prepare her for her execution.

My last sight of Anne was of her face, set in sallow calm, her eyes like burning ebony stones, standing beside the dawn washed window.

When Henry VIII died, after four additional attempts at marriage, they say he called to Anne, as if she stood waiting among the hangings of his bed. When his coffin was being transferred to its place of burial, it fell from the carrier and his blood ran black across the stone flooring. They say a dog, resembling Anne's dead Urian, licked the blood and smiled a foaming smile. There are always those who look to spread such tales, but still, it is very like the revenge she had sworn to me and the stories may well be true.

What is certainly true is that his only legitimate son, borne to him by Jane Seymour, who he married within days of Anne's execution, wasted away and died before attaining his manhood. Harry's first born daughter, by Katherine, Bloody Queen Mary, swelled and died, without issue. She was hated by the people for her religious excesses and her marriage to Philip of
Spain, and was unmourned by the crowds who roared their joyous acclamation of Anne's daughter, Elizabeth, queen.

Like her mother, Elizabeth refused the Kiss from me, although she did allow me to bleed her once when she had the smallpox. In doing so, I saved her life, and brought myself much grief. But that was another re-living, and in another daysleep I would find myself with those memories. For now, I was awakening in my closet bed in the Mayfair Hotel, and in my half-sleep I realized that I had never been obsessed with Anne as I was with Mae.

The thought scared me so badly that for a moment I almost screamed, but then I awoke fully and could not remember what had so frightened me.

I did not remember until much later, when Mae herself became my monster and my terror.

CHAPTER 6

I should have been more attuned to myself.

Like the sun and moon, both hanging opposite one another in the same sky that first afternoon, the dream of Anne was an omen of desolation to come, and I did not see it, refused to recognize it.

Each night but Monday I left Ron alone in the hotel room, and each night I returned to him impossibly dejected and incredibly elevated from the mere hours spent with her.

Days passed, became, somehow, weeks, as night after night I met Mae in the clubs where she chose to spend most of her free life. Like a queen, she seemed to expect my presence at her side and was rarely accompanied any longer, even to The Treehouse, by Freddy Z.

Waldo I saw not at all during this period, although she spoke of him sometimes, as one does of a brat brother and she began, too, to talk incessantly of vampires.

She was reading Anne Rice's <u>Vampire Chronicles</u>, swallowing it whole, reading all three volumes back to back and anxious for the fourth to be published. She read while we drove about the beach from club to club, she read at the table while I went to collect our drinks. She would sigh over Lestat, teasing me that I looked like him (which I most assuredly do not!), become indignant over Armand, feel pity for Louis, as if they were real people who lived in her apartment building, people she spoke with whenever she went into the basement to do the laundry, or while soaking in the jacuzzi on summer nights. Just as Mae's sensuality was ambiguous, so, too, was her maturity.

At one moment she was the most exciting woman I had ever known, a woman so sensuous and hunger-engendering even Anne Boleyn would have faded into insignificance beside her. At the next, she seemed as young as the vampire who had created me, bequeathing the amber eyes of her bloodline and her terrible hunger.

And beneath all the kaleidoscopic masks and changing forms of Mae, there was the brittle, doomed core of her, reaching for comfort where there could be none, pursued by death, and a total inexperience of what she really was. Not that I knew her any better than she did herself.

Constant proximity had not opened her mind to me. I never knew what she was thinking other than for a stray thought or two escaping at uncommon times, usually when she was very tired and beginning to doze in the car seat as we drove around and around Miami.

Those thoughts, half buried in dreams, gave me no help in identifying her, categorizing her, and so my obsession with her grew with each passing night.

The psychic separation from her was more painful for me than my self-imposed physical distance. I never touched her for I thought if I could refrain from even so small an intimacy as not
brushing her fingers when I lit her cigarettes, or a casual

106

hand upon her arm as we walked, I could refrain from the largest and most dangerous of intimacies: the taking of her. The changing of her. The transformation of her.

To say I was fascinated by her, seduced by her, yes, even as Ronald Higgenbothum had said, and I denied, obsessed with her, is to say nothing that approaches the truth of what I felt for her. She was a continuing and puzzling discovery.

"I don't, of course, believe in vampires," she said one night over Pink Ladies, and I knew that this, at least, among the morass of lies she feted herself with, was true. She had had ample opportunity to recognize me for what I was.

The too-white skin, the fantastical eyes, the slightly old-fashioned speech, the odd hours I kept, should have told her clearly what I was; the vampire lover come to take her into eternal life, if she had wanted to know, but she resisted that knowing. She did not believe in the undead. They were only a favorite fantasy.

"That is their greatest shield," I said solemnly, "the disbelief of mortals."

"And that is a cliche," she answered, just as solemnly. "I'm sure I read that exact phrase somewhere not long ago."

"I believe it was first used concerning Satan," I agreed. "A demon of another sort altogether."

"Do you think, then, that vampires are demons?"

"I don't know what they are. I don't, of course, believe in vampires," I answered, bringing the conversation round full circle.

"But there must be real vampires," she insisted.

"You just said you don't believe in them," I laughed.

"I don't. But logically there must be real vampires," she argued. "Man is incapable of visualizing

107

anything that does not exist."

"I don't think that's true," I objected. "Man invents things all the time that people a thousand years ago couldn't have imagined. Computers, gasoline driven vehicles ... ", and I knew better than she just how true that was, having lived most of the past millennia myself, rather than having learned of it from historical novels, as she had.

"That's entirely different," she said firmly. "Those things are built on the ideas and inventions of the men before them. Da Vinci invented submarines on paper in the 1500's. Someone else, centuries later, invented them in water. I am talking about spiritual things, unprovable things. Man can't imagine on a spiritual plane that which does not exist. How could anyone imagine a being such as this ... something that does not die, does not change, that can shapechange and lives on the blood of its fellow men? If not for the murder, of the creature's soul and other human beings, a vampire might be only a fantasy of what man wishes to be: immortal, eternally young, powerful. It is murder that speaks for its having once existed. And if it existed once and is immortal, then, voila! it exists still."

And what could I say to that?

"What do you think is the meaning behind the vampire's fear of garlic and silver?" she asked on another occasion as we walked the glittering night beach, a broken shell coated with sand in each of her long-fingered hands.

"Oh, I imagine those things probably represent some sort of allergy the poor, benighted creatures suffer from," I said, remembering with distaste the way my nose stuffs and my chest contracts whenever I accidently eat garlic. The sensation is remarkably similar to a violent hayfever attack.

Silver, the beastly stuff, corrodes my flesh like acid

and the wounds do not heal without scarring as all other wounds do. But to harm me, the metal must be pure, and fortunately, most people in past ages could not afford pure silver, while in this day, most people prefer to buy gold, thinking silver of little worth, so I bear few scars from contact with it.

"An allergy. How funny you are, Michel," she laughed. "They're dead, how can they have allergies? No, I am sure you are wrong."

"As I do not believe in your vampires, it is very likely that I am wrong," I agreed amiably. "I don't think about them much, you know, Mae, unless I am with you. But I am hypothesizing that it must be an allergy since steel swords never do them any damage, nor bullets either."

"I'm sure you are missing the symbolic energy behind the silver phobia," she declaimed, a chemise gowned, rhinestoned, university professor with sand on her hem and shell grit sparkling between her fingers. "Silver is a pure metal. Vampires are impure, therefore, they could not possibly be killed by something impure like steel. It's symbolic. You see? If steel were pure and not manufactured, it would work as well as silver."

"Well, I don't recall ever reading that a vampire could be killed by silver, Mae. I think you are confusing them with werewolves and some types of ancient demons, but I do see your point. You are talking about a symbolic allergy, yes?" I stroked a non-existent goatee as if I were Sigmund Freud, who did, in fact, used to stroke his beard in just that manner during our sessions together. It really was an irritating habit the man had and it used to drive me quite mad. "But this would still not explain the garlic, nor why a

109

pure metal like gold cannot harm either werewolves or vampires. No doubt the truth lies in quantum mechanics."

She threw her shells at me, laughing, and ran away down the sloping, wet sand.

I followed, laughing too, but wondering what Tony would think of her theory, which was, after all, interesting and not one I had ever thought of, certainly. But then, I rarely bother
to try and analyze my vampirism. It is enough to live it, century after century, without trying to understand it, too.

****

"We cannot know if our children will live to manhood, nor if we ourselves will live to old age," Mae said, watching the bits of waxed paper, dead leaves, and other pieces of debris blow down the dark street at our feet. "We cannot even be sure of love or life or health. Only of change and death."

Walking beside her, I was silent. In these clumsy words of her own, she was saying what Ronald had said when he asked me to make him nosferatu.

"Looks are fun, as a friend of mine said the other day, but they don't last. Look at you, so tall and slender. So handsome with your blond hair and amber eyes. One day those laugh lines will be wrinkles and liver spots will destroy these patrician fingers. Oh! how can you bear it?" she cried, stopping in the light of a lamp and grasping my hands. "How can I bear it?"

It was the first time any physical contact had been made between us and for a moment it stunned me, the feel of those warm palms with the blood pounding through them, holding so tightly to my cold hands in their calfskin gloves. "Tell me how to bear it, Michel," she pleaded.

"Mae," I began, but she spun away from me, her fear palatable, like an extra layer of clothing, a mourning dress, put on in agony.

"Vampires are the best of myths, because they touch that part of us that does not want to believe death and age are real," she said and smiled, to let me know her moment of terror was passed. "Do you believe in ghosts, Michel?" she laughed.

"I have never seen one," I said slowly, filled with the eeriness of having spoken those same words to Anne Boleyn in the pre-dawn darkness of her execution day four centuries ago.

In this pre-midnight darkness of early June, Mae had the same near hysterical gaiety, the same sparkling curtain of nerves about her as Anne had had, that same fated aura.

"Come on," she cried, tugging me toward the Lotus. "I know where there are simply dozens."

"Where are you leading me, wench," I laughed, allowing myself to be pulled along, heady with the touch of her fingers, so long denied, so long resisted. Now she might touch me forever and I would never have enough of it, I thought giddily.

"The Armitage Hotel down in Key Larraine. If you drive like a dragon, we can be there by midnight." She dug in my coat pocket for the keys, like a child searching for sweets in her father's overcoat.

Mae had that ability, to make me feel innocent with her, to make each experience a part of a child's game. I was flustered with her, enchanted with her, new, somehow, when I was beside
her. I had not laughed so uninhibitedly in too many centuries; not since Sonia, and thinking of her cut my

111

laughter off abruptly.   If I had not laughed so wonderfully since Sonia, I had also not thought of her terrible end in two centuries and I did not want to think of her now.

Mae finally grasped the keys and pulled them jingling out to dangle before me.   "Unless you're afraid of ghosts?" she teased.

I took the keys from her and unlocked her door. "As long as you don't want to pass the night there," I said, willfully
forgetting Sonia and Anne and all the others over all the years.   "I hear the Armitage only accepts platinum cards in this incarnation."

"The last time I peeked over your shoulder, you had one of those," she said smugly.   "And a corporate gold VISA and American Express and Carte Blanche.   Your company in New York must do very well."

"Humph," I said, closing her door.   "You should have been a spy, lady."

"I love it when you talk so old-fashioned," Mae said, as I slid into the driver's seat.   A dreaming look passed over her eyes.   "Wench is so medieval."

"I am medieval," I said, with what I thought was just the right touch of lightness.   "Early medieval."

****

Mae also had that rare ability, infrequently seen outside of contemplative convents, of being able to sit in perfect stillness, without speaking or moving, for long periods of time.   Her silence was never uncomfortable; it drew you into her circle of peace and consoled you somehow.   Throughout the long drive to Key Larraine, she did not speak once.   Nor did I.

But like hers, my outward stillness concealed inward

112

thoughts that shambled and pinged and would not be stilled.

I felt that only I knew how utterly false her serenity was. The longer I knew her, the more apparent it became to me that Mae had no peace, had never had, and feared she never would. I wondered, during that headlong rush into the night to a hotel I had once helped build through `de Brissault and Sons', once danced in with Helena, what had made her so unsure, so haunted, and it was then that the idea came to me of invading her dreams as a way to unravel the mystery of Mae.

I was always thinking of her, constantly trying to analyze her, as I had never done with anyone or anything. I tried, in moments like these, to find what it was that made her so unnerving, so alluring, to me. Perhaps, I thought, as we drove the empty bridges to the Key that night, it was a sense of being doomed which she reflected like an undercurrent of dark water all about her.

Something so bright as she could not die old and peaceful in her bed, but must burn out in a flare of heat and shock, like a sun exploding into space, and a man would not care if his own heart should be destroyed in that explosion, if once he might hold her briefly to him, penetrate to the core of her dreams and her body.

It is part of the myth that vampires do not have sex. While we do not procreate as mortals do, we are sexual beings for we are manifestly physical creatures. We eat and drink and smoke, dance and make love, fight and kill and touch, as humans do, but we have a command over our bodies they do not. Wounds heal of themselves; small ones instantly, more serious injuries quickly. We cannot die except our necks be broken or our bodies consumed in fire. Sex is as important to us as feeding, for it is our last real vestige of humanity, our last common link with life.

Mae attracted me sexually. She attracted me in ways I had thought myself too jaded to desire any longer ... clean, innocent ways. I wanted to possess her completely, and afterward to fasten the bracelet about her wrist like a diamond and emerald handcuff. I had been carrying the bracelet with me all those weeks, waiting for the proper moment to present it to her.

On the drive to the Armitage, I realized that there could be only one proper moment: the moment I claimed her as mine, that moment I finally admitted to myself that I was going to change her, make her one of us.

And yet how could I come to such a decision when she was, at her core, untouchable, inviolate? How could I be certain that she would not find a way to kill herself that first year, and me with her, if she found life as a vampire intolerable?

I could not change her, nor even decide to, until I knew her deepest heart, knew if the risk to myself was worth the possession of her. Perhaps in her sleep, in her nightmares, she would cease to be unknowable.

The hotel sprang out suddenly from the night, blazing with light, a particularly hellish effect being created within its tower by a bloody lamp smoldering in the highest window. I parked the car.

"That's the Tower Suite," Mae said, tilting her head out of the window to look up at its fierce glow. "It's $1,200 a night. I've always wanted to stay there. It has a reputation for suicide."

"Delightful," I grunted, opening my door and stepping out into the warm, sea-fragment night. I had heard the tales of this place, of course. My company had financed the construction and lost money on the deal when the Hotel Armitage, as it was known then, found itself unable to remain open to paying guests for more than a few years at a time.

Ghosts, maybe, suicide, murder and disaster, certainly, had haunted this beautiful structure throughout the century of its existence.

We strolled through the cut glass entrance doors into a lobby that looked exactly as it had in 1895 when Helena and I had come here on our honeymoon. It felt vaguely disagreeable, to be there, to see it so unchanged. Even the night clerk behind the massive check-in counter looked like Raul, with his wet, slicked hair and clipped black mustache. The unchangableness was unnatural, I thought, almost nasty, and suddenly saw myself as aberrant, my continued existence as something bizarre and odd and not beautiful by any means.

Unaware of my discomfort, Mae strode up to the night clerk and he smiled with delight at her.

"My friend hasn't seen the hotel since it reopened," she said. "I know you're not supposed to let people just wander about, but do you think we might walk a bit around the ground floor and the swimming area?"

"I'm sure no one will mind at this hour," Raul's clone gushed. I gritted my teeth. "We've put all the original furnishings back, just as they were when the hotel first opened
in 1890," he continued, handing her a brochure which she accepted as if she were a queen receiving some poor, but heartfelt gift from a peasant. "That round carpet, just there, was the first one installed in the Armitage." He pointed to the carpet in question, a still lush oriental with vines and overblown roselike blooms twined throughout the pile. Mae went to it and stood on at its center.

"It's so soft," she cried to me with pleasure, rocking from toes to heels. Raul smiled upon her, a favored child.

"The brochure gives a history of the hotel and our

115

prices, of course. We hope you'll decide to spend you next vacation with us," he said, his voice as unctuous as his smile. He turned to the cabinet behind him and began to root about for other brochures. "We have both indoor and outdoor tennis courts, a polo field, two golf courses ... "

I took Mae's arm and guided her down the nearest hall, away from him and his sales spiel. His voice faded out behind us.

"Isn't it wonderful?" she laughed. "Imagine. All the original furnishings."

"Not all," I answered shortly. The other men who fawned over Mae made me feel almost humanly jealous. "I have a velvet banquette at my townhouse in New York that came from the Gold Ballroom."

"Do you? How did you get it?"

"My father," I said. "He helped to finance this monster."

"Don't you mean your grandfather?" Mae asked. She was staring at the elevator. "Let's go up to the fifth floor. There's a hotel museum there."

We stepped into the elevator, which was also just as I remembered it. Small and coffin-like, with diamond cut mirrors lining the walls, a hundred Mae's reflected back at me, each elusive, distorted.

She did not notice my lack of reflection, being busy with the pamphlet Raul had given her, or busy, perhaps, deliberately ignoring the mirrors, empty of any face but her own.

"So where are your ghosts?" I asked, trying to be in a less apprehensive humor, despite Raul's wet, slick hair and smile, and my gnawing fear that she would look up, find herself alone in the mirrors and I would suddenly be faced with changing her or killing her.

116

Even then, so late in our game, I was unsure which I would alternative choose if forced by circumstance to make an immediate decision.

"There are sure to be scads of them on the fifth floor," Mae said, leafing through the booklet. "That was where the psychiatric wing was when this place was used as a VA hospital in the 50's."

"Of course," I said.

"Oh, Michel." She made a face, denoting patient, long-suffering, but still she did not raise her head to look into the mirrors. "There was an awful fire and because the ward was only for the violently, criminally insane, all the doors were locked
and they all died. They all burnt to death because no one could get in to help them and they couldn't get out. Michel, this pamphlet doesn't mention that." And now she did raise her eyes from the brochure, for the doors of the elevator were sliding open and the mirrors directly in front of her were disappearing with them into the walls.

"Of course," I said again, entering the shadowy hall of the fifth floor with relief. Not a ghost in sight, I thought, but I was wrong.

On the wall directly in front of the elevator door, hung a photograph taken in 1890, on the day the Armitage had opened for business.

The three men who had financed the building of one of Florida's most luxurious and, undeniably, most ill-fortuned resort haven, stood with arms about each other's shoulders in front of a semicircle of political and societal bigwigs. A face not unlike Al Capone's grinned from behind mine, staring out at us, from the center of the photograph.

I froze in apprehension. How could she not realize now, after the elevator filled with its lead crystal mirrors

117

and this photograph staring at us in cold sepia, what she had invited into her life? I made the only decision about her I had ever been capable of making in that instant when I thought she must surely begin to scream in horror, the same one I had made after speaking with Ron that night in the Mayfair, in those long seconds while she stared at the photograph, growing paler and paler. And then she sighed.

"Is that your grandfather?" Mae asked, touching the print of my face behind the non-glare glass. "You look exactly like him. A not uncommon genetic occupance, for traits to skip a generation," she said lightly, and waltzed away down the hall.

****

Later, as we stood by the pool, the ocean visible not twenty yards away, I drew the bracelet out of my pocket where it had rested all those nights past, and made my commitment to her.

I clasped it about her wrist and she looked down to see what gift I had brought her in this strange night.

"Thank you, Michel," she said quietly. "It fits this place exactly."

"It fits you, Mae," I said, feeling foolish and tender and quite stupid.

"How perfect," she said, looking at the full moon just gliding down past the tower with its gruesome light. "Such beautiful rhinestones to give me in this place that flowered in the rhinestone era."

"They're not rhinestones, Mae," I said. "They're real."

She never even looked at me.

****

"Why doesn't this brochure mention the gangster massacre or the fire or the suicides and all the ghosts?" Mae asked Raul, who ceased immediately to smile.

"There are no ghosts in the Armitage Hotel," he said, tightly, and closed the guest book with a testy little snap.

"You have no idea what has walked these halls tonight," Mae said reflectively, fingering her bracelet. "Perhaps I do not either."

****

The next night, being Monday, Mae stayed at home and I came to her in her dream.

I sat on my bed in the Mayfair of Coconut Grove, Ron sleeping beside me in the armchair, an open book on his lap and listened until I heard her heart, beating soundlessly over the night city, then allowed my senses to sink into its measured beat, until, at last, I faded with her into her sleep.

She was standing on a high balcony overlooking a city of highrises and dark lights. The bracelet shown on her wrist, sending shards of multicolored fire into the night.

I approached her slowly and felt her awareness of me, though she did not turn. I placed my hands on the curve of her body where shoulder becomes neck, and she trembled.

"I am sleeping," she said.

"Yes, Mae," I answered, bending to kiss that curve of shoulder and neck.

She turned to me, taking my face between her palms and kissing me with a fervor that spoke of

119

desperation and fear but not love.   Not yet.

"Don't leave me, Michel," she cried, throwing back her head to expose the soft, lightly tanned underthroat and spiraling away from me.

"I will never leave you, Mae," I whispered.   "But you will not stay with me an eternity.   You will leave one day."

"Only to go down into death," she vowed and held out her hands to me.

They were covered in blood and she screamed.

CHAPTER 7

Two nights after I tried, unsuccessfully, to understand Mae through her dreams, I found her at Penrod's.

It was a little after midnight and Waldo was with her. She greeted me coolly, for in some distant chamber of her heart she knew that what had happened between us was not merely a dream and she felt violated by the experience, but she still wore my diamond and emerald handcuff.

She also wore a shiny grey, double-breasted suit with heavily padded shoulders and a tight, minuscule skirt, with white stockings and grey, French-spike heels. She seemed armored by her clothing and makeup, which was heavier than I had yet seen her wear, by the chunky, square steel earrings locked tightly to the lobes of her ears and even by the bracelet I had given her.

I sat silently while she chattered to Waldo, who, I could see, was just this night finally perceiving Mae as the beautiful woman she was and not merely the co-worker whose body he coveted in his automatic and indiscriminating lust. He had no intention of leaving her for me to drive home this time: he eyed me with the same animosity with which I glared at him.

And she was using him, too, to save herself. I did not need to hear her thoughts to know what she was thinking. If she gave herself to Waldo she believed she might yet escape whatever fate awaited her with me, but it was too late for that now.

I knew the truth at last, even if she did not. I was too caught in her not to take her, and I would do so by violence if there was no other way. I had never felt this before, not even with Anne, and the rage built within me as I watched her touch and fawn over Waldo with his alternately silly smiles for her and glaring grins for me, until at last, seeing there was no chance of engaging her attention and fearing I would kill him if I did not get away from them, I rose from the table and left.

I did not seek her out for many nights after that, though it pained me not to, but I wanted her to come to me freely and out of desire. I wanted her to love me as her pleas in the night had promised, and I had the time to wait. For as long as I felt she had not yet committed herself to Waldo or Fred, I could be patient.

During those nights, too, I reminded myself that it was not my original intent to change her, I had not come to Mae in order to gift her with the blood Kiss and the not-life it bestowed. I had come to do exactly what I had somehow done by invading her dream ... drive her to the arms of life, lived typically, for a usual span.

The wisest of every course, I argued to myself, as I again slipped in and out on the edges of her life, was to leave her, return with Ron to New York, or head out for Europe, or even go down to New Orleans or out to Los Angeles. It would be better for Ron, too, who sat alone in the hotel room, never going out, even to hunt, until I returned from my nights with Mae to accompany him. He would have me to teach him this existence if we were to go away together and leave Mae to her life.

But just as it was too late for Mae to escape me, it was also too late for me. I had fallen into the trap set by what gods there are for those who swear never to love again, and I could not release her. I burned at the thought of her in Waldo's bed, or Fred's arms, and followed her, helpless to stop myself from what I knew must happen if I found her with either of them.

On the eighth night, she did come seeking, and found me on the beach, far from the lights of Penrod's, but not so far she couldn't easily find me.

The sea was black like liquid obsidian, the moon an upturned, orange Cheshire Cat smile, hung low on the horizon to lick at the sea. She sat on the wet sand in an elegant cream creation of beads and bits of glass, the cloth molding to her breasts, and drew her knees up to her chest, like a small, repentant child.

"It's so beautiful," she said.

It would have been banal coming from anyone else, this praise of the sea and the moon for their infinite and immense variations in such common and finite words, but that timelessness which clung about her could change any banality, any cliche, to a fresh truth. With her the words, the sea, the sickle moon, became something new, even to me, who had lived so long and seen it all, the end of times and kingdoms, pass and come again, to pass away once more.

It was as if, in her fantasies, she had already come halfway to being a vampire. It was as if, she, too, had already lived the centuries, seen the world change, renew and then destroy itself to become something it had never been, become something it would, nevertheless, always be. She would have fit so well at Augustus' court.

She would have fit even better at Caligula's.

Henry would have loved her. Perhaps there would have been no Anne Boleyn, no Katherine Howard, had there only been a Mae Remotti dancing at Greenwich before Great Hal.

If there had been no Helen, Agamemnon, Achilles, and the others would still have sacked Troy for the prize that was Mae. Casanova and Don Juan would have been defeated by this child-like being sitting in the sand, her knees cradled against her chest, her face alight with obsidian sea and orange moon and how then could I resist her?

"Michel," she said, "I am sorry." And I was well, and finally, lost in her.

****

Later, as midnight turned to the dark hours of early morning, Freddy Z stopped by our table at The Treehouse.

He nodded, nearly civilly to me, but with his dark sensuality wholly and exclusively ablaze for Mae as he dipped his head close to hers so that she might show him her jeweled cuff. As their cheeks nearly touched over the bracelet I had given her, he lifted his eyes to meet mine and I understood him completely, saw through him as sharply as light spears through clear glass.

He was not frightened of me, though he recognized my darkness. He had his own private shadow, one I have recognized in few mortals; a whirlpool of black magic erupting out of his soul. In my childhood, such men were commonly alluded to as alchemists; in the time of the Renaissance, they were called sorcerers. Now they are

124

called magicians and credited with psychic abilities and the power to cast spells.

Psychic or not, he knew I was not what I appeared to be, but he did not fear me. He had faith in his own darkness, in its ability to protect him from hell itself. It was only Mae he feared for, and watching her with him, I saw that she cared equally for him; that, perhaps, they even loved one another.

I understood very little about Mae, but as I looked at Freddy and comprehended him, I saw him as an eternal. A black bookend, matching the white of Mae, and myself caught between the two of them.

Our life is one of unthinkable being; a life of incredible beauty, brilliant savagery, a life draining on through the centuries, pulsing slowly throughout the eternities. There is no one eternity, but many, and each, a perfect replica of the last. For a man like Freddy Z, that life would be as natural as breathing now was to him. And I knew he would be the first she would desire to transform when it lay within her power to do so, and I was jealous, hatefully jealous, and terrified for her.

His head came up slowly and our eyes clung together.

"You should take Mae home, now, Michel," he said softly, as the last screeching sounds of Lita Ford's duet with Ozzy Osborne, `Close My Eyes Forever', died out in the club's too tightly packed room.

Mae looked from my face to his, and stood. Freddy moved close to me and, still softly, said, "Don't hurt her, dude. I don't know what you are, but whatever it is, it ain't quite real. Just don't you let Mae get caught in anything messy; anything she don't want, or can't get out of later. Just you make sure of that, my man."

I laughed, and he knew it was not in derision of

125

him, though he could not know it was from relief. Two mortals, in one year, confronting me with my secret, would have been a bit much to cope with right then.

****

I had not been into Mae's apartment before. Not with her permission. Not bodily.

The building itself was architecturally known as Architectonia and I wondered how she could afford to live there on a secretary's salary. She had decorated her three room flat in the style commonly referred to these days as Art Deco, though the term had meant merely black, white and chrome geometries when defined in the 1920's. Mae had green and pink quartz wall sconces, bamboo and wicker furnishings, live miniature palms on the terrace, geometric shapes heaving out of the halls and around corners.

An old print of the Armitage hung over a heart shaped fireplace. A lamp, shaped like a fat egg held in the hand of a black porcelain woman stretching languidly to the ceiling
illuminated the living room with a soft, egg-shell white light.

She poured a sweet, pink wine for us both, then sat, legs twined beneath her on the couch, while I sat in a wicker rocker, my legs extended straight out before me, head resting back against a small pearl colored pillow. A kitten, too young to be wary of me as adult cats are, rushed out from under the bookcase and scrambled up her chest, trying to suckle at her throat.

"Don't do that," she said sternly to it, as if it could understand English. "You know I don't like it." But the kitten continued to try and find nourishment from the blank expanse of throat she would not allow it to access,

126

wriggling and struggling in her arms, small nose seeking the warm flesh. She set it firmly down in her lap, holding it by the scruff of the neck.

"Is that how you would greet your vampire, Mae?" I asked, laughing at the look of distaste on her face as she wiped away the animal's saliva.

"It's disgusting to have something nuzzling at your throat," she grimaced delicately. "Not even a vampire shall feed there, unless he is my lover."

"Other women save their maidenhead, Mae," I said slowly, my eyes falling half-closed. Through my lashes she wavered in the smoky light, as she would have had she been a dream.

She smiled. A secret smile.

"I have saved both," she said strongly.

Deliberately she stretched out her arm to me, holding my eyes with hers, and sensuously laid the kitten's muzzle against the soft skin at her wrist. "This is all any vampire shall have of me," she said. Her eyes dimmed, looking at thoughts I could not wish to see. She continued to faintly smile in my direction, but I no longer existed for her.

"Unless he is my lover," she repeated, her eyes focusing on me again, challenging me, reaching for me.

I stood and moved to her, sailing on the drowsy light, and took the kitten, yowling in frustration at being disturbed, from her wrist where it had been content to suck a bit of flesh up between its teeth in exchange for the throat it coveted but was denied. I would not be so easily satisfied as that warm little animal.

"I will be your lover, Mae," I whispered, rushing in upon her, blotting out the glow of the lamp. Across her face only my shadow now rose.

"Shall you then?" she asked dreamily. "I wondered

127

if it would be you."

I pushed her down onto the couch. My strength is terrible, even in gentleness, and her eyes opened wide as if her kitten had suddenly become a jaguar.

"You're such a child, Mae," I said in wonder, tracing the line of cheekbone and jaw with my fingertips, for suddenly her heart was opened to me. Suddenly, I understood.

It was not eternal life she sought so desperately in her vampire fantasies, but eternal love; that very thing we ourselves dream of hopelessly as the centuries pass. She had been afraid to love, afraid of its dying, its ending, its falling into dust and old rose petals. She had saved more than her maidenhead for me, although she did not yet know it was me she had cried for: she had kept her heart locked safely in ice and fantasy, for the lover she did not believe would come.

This was her siren call, her seduction of me and the others who pursued her. She was forever untouched, believing her lover only a phantom of humid nights and fire strewn dreams, remaining forever locked, forever a mystery to the men who flocked around her.

"You frighten me, Michel," she said. "I had the strangest dream about you one dawn."

I trailed my fingers down her throat to the slope where neck and shoulder meet, the small, creamy patch of flesh where I had kissed her in her nightmare.

"Daydreams are always strange," I said softly, watching her eyes, so brilliantly green, even in shadow. "What did you see?"

"I saw blood on my hands," she whispered, shuddering, "and a dark face in a white night."

"Do you want me, Mae?" I whispered over her words, overlapping our two passions, her fear, my gentle

128

lust, mingling them so she might have thought they were her words haunting those still inches between us.

"Take off your gloves, Michel," she said, almost silently. "They are too much like a mask."

"Do you desire me, Mae?" I murmured, tugging the gloves off quickly. "Do you?" I persisted, my lips to her ear, my hand upon her breast where I could hear her heart through my palm, ticking as rapidly as her kitten's had.

"No," she whispered.

"Yes," I whispered.

"Yes," she sighed, turning smoldering eyes drenched in tears to me.

"You love me, then," I said, stretching myself out upon her body.

"Yes," she mourned.

"Though I am not what you wish me to be?" I persisted, my hand drawing slowly up her thigh, bringing the flimsy white material up to her waist, holding her eyes yet with my own.

"Yes," she said, the upturned meaning of my words escaping her. She thought me only a man, now, when her demon lover had at last come for her.

"Don't be afraid," I whispered, then, my lips against hers. "I will never hurt you."

"You are cold," she wondered, resting her hands on the small
of my back, "but your flesh burns me."

And so I took her, there in the shadow of her dreams, as men have always taken their lovers, and left her sleeping at dawn secure in her belief that we had been completely consummated in love.

Before I slipped the door closed behind me, I saw the kitten, curled on cushion of the rocker, idly licking its one white paw. I picked it up and fondled the small ears, then carried it back with me into the bedroom.

Oval mirrors in which I could not see my face, reflected back to me sea shell sconces on the salmon walls, white wicker furniture, and Mae, sleeping amongst satin and ribbons, and in that lightening room, I bent over her wrist and nipped it gently.

Barely a scratch and she barely stirred, but her blood made me dizzy for a moment, so that I trembled on the edge of a nearly uncontrollable desire to feed upon her. At last, panting a little, I drew back from the craving.

She was mine now. She had given me her promise and I would now fulfill mine; the promise she did not know I had made to her when I clasped the diamond and emerald bracelet about her wrist.

She might leave me in the years to come, but I held to the belief that this one time, love might truly prove immortal.

Whatever it is that makes us what we are, perhaps a virus, as Tony was fond of theorizing, now lived in her. Soon I would take her again, as vampires have always taken their lovers, and her transformation would be final, our consummation complete.

I laid the sleepy kitten down by her bloodied wrist where it lapped contentedly, purring loudly, and then I left them, before the sun could climb too high.

****

Back at the Mayfair, Ron was reading another book on occultism. The room smelled of human flesh.

"Did you have someone here tonight?" I asked him, rather more angrily than I should have done.

"Only room service," he said quietly, tilting the book at me. I would not let him leave the room by himself and he had to ask for his books to be delivered, the motion seemed to remind me, but gently and with no reproach. "Have some champagne, Michel," he said, gesturing to the cart where an opened bottle of Cold Duck resided in a silver-chased ice bucket.

"Don't let anyone in here again, Ronald," I said. "You never know who you are talking to, what they might really be. You're too young yet to know the smell of an Other. I'll bring your books from now on, or better yet, we'll go to the library or the bookstore each night after we hunt, if you'd prefer."

"Alright," he agreed calmly. "Did you bring me anything to eat tonight, though? It's already light out, you know, and too late to hunt."

"I know," I said miserably. I opened the sports bag I had brought up from the car and gave him the Doberman pup I had stolen from the yard of a rich man's house in the Grove on my way back to the hotel. "This will soon be finished, Ron," I said gently. "Soon she will be with us, and we will all hunt together."

"I'm not angry and not feeling neglected, Michel." He tore the throat out of the pup with practiced ease and began to drink the new blood. He was finished in only a few seconds and as he wrapped the corpse in a garbage bag for me to dispose of in the coming night, he smiled shyly and said, "I'm very anxious to meet your Mae. It will be nice to have someone else with us."

Dear Ron, I thought. How could I have ever guessed that such an innocent, good soul was within that CEO's body? I smiled weakly at him and patted his hand before moving to the windows to pull the black-out curtains tight. Falling onto the bed, trembling on the edge of sleep with the smell of an unknown human in my nostrils, I suddenly wanted to tell him how much he was coming to mean to me, but the re-living began and I could not find my voice. Instead I slept.

If I had not been so tired, so full of Mae, so full of guilt over leaving Ron alone each night, I might have been more suspicious of that odor of human. I might have insisted on the truth from him, for I did half-suspect that he had had a man or woman in the room that night for more than a few minutes; that he had sought, in his loneliness, even the comfort of conversation with someone from room service.

But I didn't insist, and by the next evening when I awoke, all I could think of was Mae, waiting for me, waiting for the fulfillment of my promise.

****

Night came and came again.

Mae moved through the discos and the clubs like a dream, emerging from shadows like a gasp. Already her features had begun to refine themselves, the eyes to darken to the amber of our bloodline.

I watched benignly as she danced with Waldo at Club Nu and strangers at Club Deco. She was mine, and none of these mere men could now compete with me for her love.

The night after I had first nipped her, I again took her home.

She stared at me in the dimness of the bedroom, the ocean rising outside the french doors and I waited by a pink Deco Lady, holding high a rounded mirror in which I could not be seen.

"What do you want, Mae?" I whispered into the cool, almost dawn morning. "Tell me. Anything you have ever wanted from a man, from me, tell me, and I will be that fantasy for you."

"You are my fantasy," she answered. "Love me. Take me, as you did last night."

"Is that what you want?" and when she did not answer, standing mute in the darkness, "Tell me. Is that what you want? Am I now all you will ever want, no matter what you may discover me to be in time to come?"

"Yes," she breathed, and her eyes closed, her head fell back as I rushed in upon her, light fading around us to ink.

I left her seriously bitten in the crook of the elbow just before dawn.

And so the nights came and went.

We drove to several clubs a night, always ending at her apartment. As her blood became more and more mine, less and less hers, she developed a shimmer to her skin and a grace to her walk that should have been impossible in one already so shimmering and graceful. I was so proud of what I was creating in her that I began to take Ron with us as we cruised the clubs and beaches and he gave his heart to her as unquestioningly as I had.

Fred watched her Changing with narrowed eyes, and on the seventh night, he leaped on-stage to howl out his rendition of `Love Bites' from the Creatures of the Night album. After he had finished, he told the audience, so stuporous on cocaine and whiskey they could not have been less enthused, the song was for `his Mae', but his eyes were fastened on mine, and in them I saw a sad malevolence.

Leaving The Treehouse, he stepped out to bar my way, saying, "I think I should take Mae home tonight, Michel."

I pushed him aside with as little force as I could, sending him crashing into the nearest table. Other women

133

squealed, covering their mouths with painted fingers, but Mae stood frozen, her eyes not seeming to see what was happening.

Fred began immediately to struggle to his feet and I leaned over him nose to nose and whispered, "Do not tempt me, little man. But for her love of you, you would already be dead."

"Like you?" he growled and I laughed.

"Truly dead," I assured him. "Forever dead. Not like me, at all, my friend, for I live, as you see. I live and she is mine."

Behind me, Mae stood still and glazed, like a figurine of finest china. Ron stepped forward and laid his hands on Fred's shoulders as gently as he had once caressed his computer keyboard. Fred held my eyes a moment longer and then waved us away with an admirable display of defeat, but I did not believe in his capitulation.

His faith in his private darkness was too perfect. He would not let her go so easily and I knew this night must end with Mae completely transformed or I would risk losing her to his misplaced zeal to protect her.

"Go back to the hotel and wait," I said to Ron. "I will be home after I drop Mae at her apartment." I spoke casually, and Fred, still on his knees, weighted by Ronald's hands, collapsed into himself in true defeat.

****

"I have always been so logical," Mae said, proving again that a person's concept of his or herself rarely approaches the reality of themselves as seen by the others with whom they are
intimate.

"Yes, Mae," I smiled.

"You are all sensuality, all physicality. You seduce me through my senses and not my intellect. That is why you frighten me so, Michel. You open windows to desires I have never dreamt slept within me. I wish you hadn't hit Fred tonight."

"I'm sorry," I said, though it was hardly true.

"Yes, I know that you are, or perhaps you aren't, but I can't seem to feel that it really matters. I have changed so since we met. You have become the center of my life. I am sure I am in love with you, but that is not all.

"Have you never had a feeling, oh! a knowing, that something big and bright was coming, just around the corner of the next hour, coming only for you?"

"No," I said, quite truthfully.

"That is how I feel," she sang, and whirled about the room, her arms wrapped around her shoulders.

"Come and sit beside me, Mae," I said. "I want to explain something to you."

She came obediently, like a child doing its best to please a distant, little known, adult relative, but eager to return to its play.

"Mae, your fantasies of vampires ... "

"Oh, I know they have to stop," she cried gaily. "I know they're silly. Juvenile, really. But don't think I haven't noticed how you try to fulfill even those for me, through your
little nips never really hurt, thank goodness."

"Mae," I said slowly, "when you want something very badly you often attract that something to you."

"There are no vampires, Michel," Mae said patiently, as if I were a trifle insane, not enough to worry about, but still mad
enough that I must be handled with gentle, feminine logic. She patted my hand reassuringly.

"If there were ... " I answered, then stopped sighing. How was I to explain to this child-woman that not only were we real, but that I loved her and would take her with me into a world she had never conceived of even in her most feverish dreams of fire and bloody kisses? How, indeed. "If there were vampires, Mae, their life would be very different from what you imagine," I said limply.

"More beautiful that I could imagine," she smiled. "More sordid that I could envision, perhaps."

"More lonely, yes."

"Oh, Michel, I don't need that fantasy anymore. I have you now to fill these lonely, empty places in me. I know you have not said you love me. Men don't like to say it, I've heard, but I believe you do love me. I would feel it in your touch if you did not."

"I love you, Mae."

"Then we'll not worry about the vampire thing. I'll never mention it again, I promise. I only needed it because I was so afraid of dying without ever having loved and yet afraid, too, to
love. Loving was always more important to me than being loved. "

"Yes, I know." And, God, how I hoped it was true enough for us both to survive her transformation.

She sat beside me, smiling timidly, waiting for me to propose. She was thrusting her thoughts at me like concentrated radio waves. They spilled out of her like strands of colored
ribbon. She wanted to marry me. She wanted to birth a little boy with blond hair and eyes both gold and green.

And for a moment I considered it, considered asking her to marry me, living with her as I had lived with Helena. In time she would cease to want the child, so busy would I keep her with love and travel and the acquisition of

136

expensive things. But the consideration lasted only a moment ... it was too late for such sunlit dreams.

"Mae." I grasped her hands and kissed them both, each fingertip. Mae, you are such a child. Here, give me your bracelet. Do you see these diamonds, these emeralds? You thought they were rhinestones."

"Are they real, then?" She was suddenly pale, gazing at the jewels made pallid by the brilliance of her skin.

"I told you they were. You knew that they were, inside your self, within your heart, you knew. Where nothing remains hidden, but may always be denied, you knew, and you have always known what I am, in that same secret heart."

She stared at me, allowing herself to actually see me for the first time, as Waldo had seen her for the first time the night at Penrod's when she had tried to flee from me and whatever our relationship was becoming.

"Perhaps I don't want to hear this," she said quietly. "Perhaps I have changed my mind." She walked over to the balcony doors, swinging them open, to look out at a yacht anchored offshore, its decks ablaze with torches.

I followed, moving slowly after her. She stood there, very still, hugging herself against the damp and the wind as earlier she had embraced herself in the dance.

"There is nothing left to hear," I said gently. "Your heart has already heard and made your choice for you."

"If you want something badly enough?" she whispered.

"Diamonds can appear to be rhinestones."

She would not turn to face me, so I put my arms about her waist from behind, pinning her hands to her shoulders, and kissed that same slope of neck and shoulder, as I had in her dream. She trembled like an ash tree in a mid-winter storm.

"It is time, Mae. For the unveiling, for the final truth, for your Changing."

Even in that last minute of her life when she knew it was
all true, knew what was coming and was terrified of it, she did not struggle.

How easily she gave herself, though in sudden cruelty that she had forced me to this, forced me to love her, I bit hard, fangs sinking into her throat the way another man might take a mistress he both loves and hates with a violence of forgotten kindness.

She cried out a little, like a kitten mewling, but then her head fell back and cradled itself in my shoulder, and what is sweet in this bitter Kiss came to her in mist and pain and blood and the welling of her heart until its pulse was all the sound we could hear, she and I joined by its savage beating, through her blood flowing into my mouth, both beat and blood, into my body, emptying from hers, being replaced by drops and rivulets of my blood, the beating of my immortal heart.

Mortals say the vampire's kiss is sweet on the surface and bitter beneath, for they fear to live forever unrestrained, forever an outsider. How lonely, they cry, to be a vampire! I should never want to be one, they insist, all the while wishing in their hidden places that they, too, might be given this dark kiss of immortality, this aloes gift. Yes, we are lonely, but so are they, and Mae knew now, lying in my arms, completely mine at last, and I so completely hers, that the reverse is true in dying.

In pain we die and are born again into eternal life ... from great bitterness to greater sweetness, in a space of moments, of heartbeats, measured and quick, slowing and

138

dying into
nothingness.

She slumped at last, a feathered being, and we slipped to the floor, lovers still entwined, rocking gently, reluctant to release our kiss, the sounds of her life ebbing away with the tide outside the balcony doors.

And when her life, that fragile, flowered thing closed, I held her yet awhile, watching the fire on the water and the gulls wheeling against the moon, far out to sea.

140

CHAPTER 8

Night came and came again.

Sequestered in a stone room beneath the Coral Castle, I sat beside Mae and awaited her waking.

The hurricane lamp shone on the faintly wet walls. Lightening walked over the coral above our heads and thunder shook the air of the chamber. It was not a cheerful place for her to awaken to, but I could not keep her in the room at the Mayfair. She was, after all, dead, and I would not expose Ron to the possibility of discovery by some maid or room service dolt accidently finding Mae's body stuffed in the closet or under the bed.

The time between death and rising varies for each of us. Mae's body had been prepared for the change by my initial bites, yet she lingered long in death. I could not go more than two days without feeding or I would become weak, and that weakness would breed recklessness when I finally did go to hunt, yet I fed only on the first night. After that I sat beside her on the damp coral floor of the chamber and waited.

I wanted to be there for her when her new and feral eyes opened at last.

And the night came and came again.

I slept my sleep of memory and dreamed of Anne's daughter, Elizabeth, weakening into death, finally allowing me to bleed the smallpox poison from her through the arch of her foot. How haughty she had been afterward, knowing that a trace of immortality circled in her veins.

I saw again, too, the dead on the Italian fields of battle during World War I. Both Tony and I had fought in the two world wars, throughout France, Italy, Germany, for our England.

On another night I drifted with Helena through a speakeasy, Tommy Catania following in my footsteps, babbling his stories of murder and gin. He admired his boss, Al Capone, but he worshipped me.

On the fifth night, I woke from my reliving of the day of Tony's death, to the sound of a loud, heckling, beloved voice.

"Well, it's true then. God's nightgown, I could not believe it when Anthony summoned me, but here you are. Michel, my love, you are a fool, and worse, you have become unforgivably careless."

"Ana," I said stupidly.

Behind her Tony materialized, a shy wolf's grin lighting his face. He had Ronald Higgenbothum firmly by the elbow. Ron looked awed in the presence of these two Old Ones of whom he had only heard, and that sparingly, from me during pre-dawn ramblings over Cold Duck.

"Dear God, you have not fed," Tony shouted the moment he saw me. "Have I not said it before, Michel, that you need a keeper?"

He released Ron's arm and blundered across the small room to me, wrapping those big bear arms about me

142

and lifting me from the floor in his embrace. "And have I not said, Countess Ana, that God looks out for fools and vampires in love?" He squeezed me once more, then set me down carefully, as if he thought my bones would break from being breathed upon too heavily.

"God surely has enough work without being responsible for the idiocies of vampires in love," Ana said tartly. She turned to look at Mae, lying on her coral bed. "Has she not awakened yet?" she asked softly.

"No," I answered, rubbing my eyelids weakly. "Not even a false awakening."

"Find him food, Anthony," the Countess barked. "Someone strong. Mind you don't bring back some drunk from the beach, either."

"Yes, Ma'am." Tony bowed to her, his smile returning, a joyful, very mischievous one this time. She was the only one in all eternity who could order him about and he enjoyed it thoroughly. I watched them, feeling amused through my weariness, and filled with love for them both, my oldest and closest friends, even if I did see them only once in a century or so.

Tony left, kissing Ana resoundingly on the cheeks, waving to Ron and me.

"Now. What is this nonsense, boy?" the Countess asked, sitting down beside me and enfolding me in her pudgy, jasmine scented arms.

"I love her," I said. The petulant whine in my voice disgusted me, but I was weak with hunger and could not help myself. I began to weep onto Ana's bulging chest. She cradled me and cooed as my mother, an elegant, haughty woman, had never done.

Ron stood awkwardly near the entrance to the room and I could see him there out of the corner of my

143

eye, his sympathy and his helplessness to help expressing themselves in his hitching
from foot to foot in silence.   It made me giggle through my tears.

"Love is not an excuse," Ana said severely.   "And stop that giggling.   It grates my ears worse than your weeping.   Come, sit up and listen to me, now.   Love is not an excuse and it is the worst of alibis.   I have loved thousands of men, my child, and a few women.   Literally. If I had changed every one of them, this world would be nothing but vampires and we'd all be starved into insensibility by now.   Not to mention the very real possibility of dying forever if I'd chosen the wrong little mortal love to transform."

Ana held me away from her comforting bosom and searched my eyes to see if I had understood what she was trying to tell me about my Mae.   How was I supposed to answer her?   The heart is illogical.   "She loves me," I muttered, dropping my eyes from hers.

"She is very beautiful, Michel.   That will last.   Her love for you will not."

"You said it was Tony who summoned you," I said, twisting away from her.   I might have well as said, `Let us change the subject, Countess', for she sat back and folded her hands in her
lap.

"You summoned us both, Michel.   Tony and I came to New York to find you, as did Richard Glewwe, but he remained there with his new wife.   He's staying in your brownstone, awaiting our return.   Richard's wife is a mortal, I might add as proof of
point."   She eyed me closely again to see what effect the news that Dickie was waiting in New York would have on me.   She knew how much I loved him and how I missed

him as the years bled on and on. I had not seen him since 1864 when we quarrelled over a woman. Apparently she saw nothing in my face to encourage her. She motioned for Ron and he obediently came and sat at her feet.

"Once we were in New York," she said, resting her hand on Ron's shoulder, "Anthony found the mortal wife of this, your other new one. Your accountant had nipped her so often she was nicely scented. No doubt one of the Others will find her before long, destroy her, and then come for you and yours here."

"Ron is not an accountant," I said sulkily.

"Whatever he was," Ana said loudly, "he is now a vampire and so will be this woman. Have you gone out of your mind? You make no new ones in more than a century and then you make two in six months? You neglect your first child in the pursuit of this second one, and neither train him nor prepare him for this not-life you have given him and are responsible for now?" She held her arms out to me beseechingly.

"Ron begged me for the gift," I shouted, springing away from her proffered embrace, my hands balling defensively into fists. "He begged me, do you hear, Ana?"

"How you came to change him is not important. It does not negate your responsibilities to him. How will you ride rein on both of these new ones? And why did you not bring your little clerk with you to this dank hole, so that he might feed you and you might keep your life by watching out for his?"

"How did you find me?" I repeated, trying to unclench my fists. She was my friend. She loved me. I kept reminding myself that her attack was only worry and launched against me from care for me. "And you know why I left Ron at the hotel. It was safer for him not to be with me, in case one of the Others found me here too weak

145

to protect myself and Mae, much less him."

The Countess sighed heavily. "His wife in New York told us that he had come to Miami on business. It was easy then to home in on your distress call, once we knew where to look."

I had been sending a distress call? I shook my head, trying to remember if I had felt threatened or in need of help during the past few days. All I could remember was Mae, being always lost in her, needing her, desiring her, obsessed with her, anxious for her. Always Mae.

I shook my head again and Ana reached out to delicately smooth my hair. "We are here now," she said.

Love, so much love in her voice, and I shut my eyes, leaning again upon her bosom, wanting to sleep more than to feed, which is how it is when we wait too long to hunt, but at that moment Tony pushed his way back into the room carrying an unconscious male, about 18 years of age.

"Feed," he commanded, making a tiny cut in the boy's throat with a fingernail, so the smell of fresh blood would arouse me. "When she wakes, do you want to be so feeble you cannot care for her needs?" he rumbled.

I sat up, brushing the tears from my cheeks, and humbly accepted the gift of blood and life and strength from Tony's hands, as he had once accepted them from mine.

"This is a mistake, my foolish brother," he snorted, motioning to Mae.

"There is nothing to be done, now," I answered. I was voraciously hungry and already the boy's body was near death. I stood to make a clean snap of his neck.

"Of course there is something to be done," Ana said. "You can destroy her now, before she wakes. You will have enough to do keeping yourself alive with your

146

other new one to protect. Kill her now, as you have just killed the boy."

In the sudden silence even Tony looked at Ana as if she were a stranger.

We are not human beings, after all, and do not kill our own, unless greatly provoked or lost in madness. But of course, until Mae awakened, she was not one of us. She was a dead body until that moment of waking and could be finished off without danger to me.

"I will not destroy her," I shouted. "She will certainly cease to love me, to that I agree, but that day is centuries in the future. Until then I have time to prepare for her leaving. Now she loves me, and now is my time. She will not disobey me or place me in danger; not while she loves me. It is only for a year, Countess, after all," I finished scornfully.

"Only for a year. You delude yourself again, as you have done before. Look at her," Ana cried, sweeping her hand regally over Mae's sleeping form. "She has great beauty. She will leave you within that first year for another to love. Such a woman is cursed by her beauty, cursed by the need to have it reaffirmed again and again. Had she grown old in the normal course of things, she might have stayed with you, though she would never have been faithful to you. As her beauty faded, so would her need for other men to attest it. You have given her the power to remain always as she is now, and you cannot hope to hold her, Michel. No. Not even for a year. And when she flees you, her inexperience will cause her to make mistakes, mistakes that may kill her. If she dies, you will die. You know this. Why do you deny that you know?"

I knew Ana was wise. I knew she loved me, as Tony did, with loyalty and friendship that could not be dimmed by either centuries or momentary quarrels, but I

147

could believe only in Mae's eyes, full of love for me, her easy acquiescence to my every whim when she had been alive. I must have faith that she would still be so, now, in not-life, if only out of gratitude for the immortality I had given her beauty and if only for a year's time.

Ana saw my repudiation of her and turned away from me, pulling her veil over her face.

"I am frightened," Ron said and dropped his face into his knees drawn up tight against his chest.

"Do not be, little one," Tony said. He patted Ron's hair with a hand that was larger than poor Ronald's head. To him, my slim, short CEO truly was little and Tony meant no insult to his dignity.

"Why do you care so much that I have created her?" I asked sullenly. "You are not upset about Ron. Both you and Ana seem pleased enough with him. And let us not forget all the new ones you have created over the centuries. Did I ever scold you for those children of yours? You have never been afraid of the Fear Year and now you preach to me of its dangers?"

"Have you forgotten Caroline?" Tony's voice was low and sifting through it were tones of both pity and anger. "I will not even mention Sibby, who tore your friendship with Richard to fragments, nor Sonia, only Caroline."

No, I had not forgotten Caroline Wingard of the Atlanta Wingards. In 1864, following the confrontation with Dickie over Sibby Monroe, I had fallen in love with Caroline beyond sense, transformed her, and become certifiably mad when she left me two years later for her first lover, a plantation owner out by Charlottesville.

Tony had taken me to Europe, nursed me through it, given me his friendship and company unstintingly, and when I was healed of her, extracted from me a promise that

148

never again would I fall in love with a mortal woman to the point of transforming her. "With you, my little brother," he had said, "it is not the Fear Year that is dangerous, it is love itself."

Tony had been the one to send me to that neurotic psychoanalyst, Freud, half a century after Caroline abandoned me. I would have promised him anything to get out of having to watch Freud incessantly pull his beard while I babbled of everything but the true reason for my madness: my immortality and the impossibility of immortal love.

"This is different," I exclaimed.

"I can see that," Tony said dryly. "Why could you not love her as you loved Helena? Or Sibby, for that matter? If she had stayed with you instead of going with Richard, you would never have changed her."

"They were different. They would never have found happiness being as we are. But Mae, Mae was made for the night, for the shadowy way we live. She was made for me. If you had only seen her when she was alive, you would not argue with me now."

"All right, brother-mine," Tony soothed. "Now you must sleep for awhile. You are still weak with lack of blood. I'll watch your lady for you and if she stirs, I promise to waken you immediately."

I moved closer to him. "Be sure Ana doesn't try to destroy her," I murmured and was immediately ashamed of my stupidity. Ana would never have done such a thing behind my back, and Tony did not dignify my statement with an answer. His eyes shifted away from mine and I dropped my eyes in shame to Mae's face, which suddenly twitched.

Her amber eyes opened to the flickering hurricane lamps, the weeping stone walls, Tony towering over Ron's

149

hunched form, Ana sitting wrapped in her shawls like a medieval nun, and myself, standing as if struck to stone, the body of the boy sprawled at my feet as if kissing my toes.

"I am hungry, Michel," she said simply. "Michel, I thirst."

****

I did not need to teach Mae to hunt. She knew it in her core, like a genetic trait only now become evident. She did not need me to teach her to kill. It came too naturally to her, so that where once I had been proud of what I was creating, now I shuddered at what I had made.

Oh, she was always cautious, even the first time, when she was weak with hunger and most likely to have been reckless.

The men she lured in the clubs, flashing lights and alabaster limbs enticing them out onto the dark streets, or the darker stretches of beach, came without resistance, died without struggle.

We slept in the Coral Castle. It appealed to her with its aura of desertion and tragedy, just as the Armitage had appealed to her in life. Ron was far too fastidious to sleep among sweating coral and Ana moved into the suite at the Mayfair with him, complaining of the smell of human that infested the room night after night when she returned from hunting, but Tony, Mae and I remained beneath the earth and rock of the Castle.

Mae never returned to her Art Deco apartment, and I often wondered what would happen to the kitten she had left behind. Tony had transformed his dogs as soon as they were fully grown and the Afghans had been with him since 1660, but Mae apparently forgot her kitten entirely.

I could not, and one night, about a week after her waking, I entered her apartment for the last time and set the animal free on the beach. I hoped a child would see it, desire it, give it a home. It was a cute little beast and would live a longer than normal lifespan because of the taint of immortality it had acquired licking Mae's wounds.

I have an obscene amount of ready money available, for the undead are a materialistic lot. As I have said, things last through the years that wear out relationships and human emotions, but Mae wanted no part of my fortune just yet. She preferred to steal her clothes from expensive shops in the Grove and Bayside, her jewelry from her victims. She would often select a woman for death simply because she coveted a ring or necklace the poor thing was wearing.

Though Ana would not speak to her, Tony was as quickly enchanted as Ron and I. Mae would stretch her cat's body lazily and his eyes would glaze. He was ensorcelled by her, but frightened of her also. Tony, who had never feared anything, not even death, was as afraid of this tiny, delicate girl as he was enamored of her.

And I, I was beginning to admit, was also fearful of her, for Mae was one of those freaks of life: a being without conscience.

During those early weeks I told myself she was amoral. When she had been alive, her humanity was a facade she had worn to fit in with other people and this masking of her true self had been what made her mind inaccessible to me. Now that she was dead, she no longer needed to shape herself to any human conception of appropriate behavior and she could be and act as she truly was. At first, I could not admit that what she was, was evil.

151

I had to believe that she was merely amoral and had not yet learned that vampires have rules of behavior just as mortals do. I had to believe that she would learn and abide by those rules, or I would be admitting that she could as easily kill one of us as a human victim.

Ana left during the second week of Mae's awakening, but Tony stayed on and we became a foursome with Ron, flaring through Miami's nightlife like black fire.

In the third week, we ran into Waldo at Penrod's. Mae had always been a good dancer, but now her body seemed to have no limits, as indeed it very nearly did not, and soon the entire crowd moved away from them as she and Waldo flashed among the lights and the music, now apart, now closer. She was seducing him with movement, intoxicating him with a clarion of sexual promise, and infatuated with her skill, I didn't see that she was promising him even more ... life eternal, youth unending, madness and blood and heat and night, and the dance, forever.

Caught in my pride over her skills and with keeping my eyes on a slender boy who had been batting his eyelashes at me for the past hour like some actress in an old and atrociously bad film, I did not immediately follow her when she left, Waldo's hand grasped tightly, leading him with it as if on a leash. It was Ron who said, nudging me with a forearm like a sapling branch, "Something is different with this one. Perhaps we should go after them."

I nodded, remembering how she had once thought to escape me using Waldo as a shield. The boy could wait. Mae, capable of anything within my imagination, could not.

They had walked down the beach, away from the lights, into the emptiness. As Tony, Ron and I drew near, I could hear her voice, tangling with the wind and the waves, crooning, whispering, "Come with me, Waldo. Be with me. Forever and forever."

152

"Forever," he answered like a man wishing in his sleep, and she reached up to open his shirt, exposing the brown flesh to the hot, white moonlight.

"Forever," she growled and sank her fangs into his throat.   Tony lunged forward, but I put my arms around his waist to stop him and the very incongruity of my attempting to hold him did.

"Let her feed," I said tightly.   "Then I will destroy him."

"If you do," Ron observed, "she will hate you."

"Not enough to kill herself to spite me," I said. "No hate will ever be strong enough for her to do that."

"Perhaps enough to kill you outright, though," Tony said helpfully.

Mae and Waldo had fallen to their knees, the waves lapping about their thighs and as he fell backward into the sand, I leaped forward, grasping Mae by the neck and tossing her to Tony.   She clawed wildly at Tony.   She shrieked at me, an unearthly sound that was heard only in the mind and not with the ears, chilling flesh and curdling brain, then she rested in Tony's arms, unnaturally still, watching.

Waldo's eyes were empty, but he was not dead.   He focused on me slowly, his ecstasy passing to terror at the sight of my face, and I broke his neck with savage satisfaction.

Mae observed, standing as still and silent as stone washed in pearl dust, rage like boiling lava spilling out of her very pores.

"We're going to New York," I said to her, kicking Waldo's body into the sea, where it rolled at the tide line with ticking regularity.   "I cannot trust you here."

"You have taken my pleasing Waldo from me, but I

will have Fred," she warned. "I will change Fred."

"I will kill you first," I shouted, my own rage billowing up at last. "Do not think you are so safe in my love."

She laughed. "Will you then? Will you kill me, my Michel? I thought it might be you," she whispered contemptuously and another chill coursed over my flesh to hear those words, once spoken in desire, now unleashed in anger, spat at me by this woman I had loved enough to dare everything for: my love and even my existence.

"But not until the year is over will you kill me and perhaps by then I shall be stronger than you, eh, Michel?" She laughed the biting white laughter of hate.

"Can you not stay with me alone for just a little while?" I pleaded, my fury gone, the fear of losing her returned.

Tony, ashamed of me, turned his face to the sea and watched Waldo lolling and ticking in and out among the waves. Ron studied the moon's face carefully.

"For awhile," she agreed softly. "I do love you, Michel, but I am lonely without my friends." She came close to me and I could smell Waldo's blood on her breath as she kissed my cheek and stroked my face. "I would have my friends with me, as you have Tony and Ron."

"Later, then," I answered, as gracefully as possible, knowing it was, after all, inevitable. "Let me take you to New York, to Europe. Let us have some time together before you increase our family."

"Yes," she said. "A year for ourselves. I would love to see Europe." She wrapped her arms about me, now smiling a warm and loving smile, and like Waldo, I accepted her embrace without thought of the dangers there, simply grateful that she was smiling upon me once again.

CHAPTER 9

Mortal, living, alive, Mae had never seemed completely human. She had had a timeless spirit, a fey delight; she had seemed a being from a dream, or a fairy from some hidden forest that grows only sleep.

Now, immortal, dead, living without life, she was completely monstrous. Gone was the woman who had seduced me into love and in her place was a changeling, a creature from some distant, cold galaxy. She killed without remorse from the very first. She fed without pity.

It was terrifying to behold her on the hunt, ablaze with darkness and her endless thirst, a forgotten goddess returned to the world to punish her faithless followers.

And I could not yet admit all this. I could not allow myself to acknowledge her monstrousness. I must love her still, and as blindly as a peregrine, hooded before the hunt.

I had lost perspective on Ron, as well, during the nights I had left him alone at the Mayfair. I did not know how he had spent his evenings with humans in our rooms,

155

talking with them, learning from them all the things he had never had time to learn in life.

University professors and occultist quacks shared champagne with Ron each night while I courted Mae, leaving only their scent behind for me to come home to each dawn. I did not know that he had made one special friend, a priest, who would follow us to New York.

But it was in New York that I first willfully turned away from my new knowledge of Mae and it was there I would meet the man my fortuitous neglect of Ron had brought to us, Father Ray.

****

Tony, Mae, Ronald and myself arrived at Kennedy Airport just before dawn put a finish to the night that had seen Sweet Waldo die.

I would have hijacked a plane to get Mae out of Miami and away from Fred, but my money made it unnecessary. I chartered a private Lear for us and despite the luxury of the flight, we were worn out from the night and the intensity of our emotions by the time I unlocked the door of the brownstone.

Richard was standing in the hall, adding water to a vase of silver hued roses.

For a moment, neither of us moved. Perhaps he was remembering old quarrels, old hurts. All I remembered was how I had loved him and found that love still vibrant beneath the patina of the years of our estrangement. Then he held out his arms, smiled, and I ran to embrace him.

His girlishly beautiful face was no older, for we do not, of course, age, but it had hardened somewhat in the

years since I had last seen him. As our physical strength is heightened by our
transformation, so, too, are our emotions. Loves, hates, angers and desires all increase, and the heart of a vampire is a holocaust of feeling at every moment. Thus I knew that our argument over Sibby Monroe in 1864 was still painful to him and he was uncomfortable with me yet because of it, as I was with him, yet yearning to be quit of it, as I was.

"I have missed you," I whispered into his ear and by the tightening of his arms about my shoulders I knew he had missed me as much.

"Michel," he said, stepping back from me, and I could feel how cautious his happiness at seeing me was, as if he expected blows to follow my embrace. That hurt me and the absurdity of our discomfort suddenly overwhelmed me.

"Dickie," I howled, and burst into loud, joyous brays of laughter that had never failed to elicit an answering laugh from him back in the times when we had fought together at Shiloh and Gettysburg, and on the unnamed battlefields of minor skirmishes throughout the South.

"You have forgiven me then?" he laughed, too.

"Have you forgiven me?" I countered, punching him lightly in the forehead, where his gorgeous black hair fell forward to his eyebrows in a silky wave.

"What did I have to forgive you?" he asked, honestly bewildered. "I stole her from you and believe me, I regretted it within the first week. Aside from the loss of your companionship, I suffered mightily from that tongue of hers. She could have flayed a lion with it!"

"She could, couldn't she?" I was laughing so hard now that pink, blood-tinged tears were squeezing out of my eyes and plopping onto the hardwood floor and the toes of his proper English oxfords.

157

"And when she aged! My God, she grew a wart beside her nose, exactly like a storybook witch."

"Well, better you took her then," I giggled, wiping the tears from the corners of my eyes with one hand while I continued to hold him tightly about the waist with my other arm. "I have always remembered her as a storybook princess. Because of the good deed you did in stealing her away, I have never had to be disillusioned of her beauty. But why did you keep her so long if she displeased you so quickly?"

"Ah, well, I felt she was a punishment upon me for estranging you," Dickie said and blushed. He looked over my shoulder at Tony, Ronald and Mae, still grouped by the door. "But it looks to me as if you've found yourself a true fairy princess this time, Michel," he said.

I moved aside, but retained my arm about his waist as I turned to Mae, standing silently between Tony and Ron.

"This is Mae," I said, and her name felt like velvet in my mouth. A blush of pride at the way Dickie was looking at her warmed my cheeks. I felt drunk with the joy of being with him again and with his evident pleasure in gazing on Mae.

"Now I know what all the fuss was about," he whistled as he went to her. He bowed slightly before her, kissed her palm and tipped her a Dickie-wink. "Anthony, old man," he cried then, straightening up and grasping Tony by the shoulders. "It's been a very long while."

"One hundred twenty-five years," agreed Tony, who always kept toll of needless statistics like that.

I smiled at my friends as they exchanged bear hugs. Mae smiled tentatively at us all, but she moved closer to Ron, as if uncertain of her place, and his, in the circle of shared time between we three older friends. I moved quickly to her and took her hand. She pulled away impatiently.

"Aren't you going to introduce Ronald to your friend?" she snipped. Then she smiled sweetly at Dickie and said, "Where is your wife, Mr. Glewwe?"

"Asleep, I am afraid. We've been married long enough for her to have decided she needn't stay up the entire night with me," Richard answered. He bent to kiss her hand again. "And this gentleman needs no introduction, my lady, though it is kind of you to watch out for him. You, sir, are the mastermind accountant who holds `de Brissault and Sons' in solvency. God knows Michel here hasn't a mind for business." He laughed, taking Ron's hand to shake, then pulling him into an embrace. Ron politely let himself be pummelled with good fellowship for one precise minute before backing away.

"Michel is a fine business mind," he said stiffly. Poor Ron, I thought, he never could take anything any other way than literally.

"It is near dawn," Tony said to break the awkward pause Ron's words had caused. "We must sleep. Tonight we shall all hunt together, and a fine feast we shall make, eh?" He started up the carved stairway to his accustomed room at the head of the stairs.

"It is good to see you again, Michel," Dickie vowed, following Tony up to the second floor landing. He hung over the banister and winked at me.

Ron followed them upstairs, their voices, though low, carrying back audibly to us until they parted at their respective bedroom doors.

"Where do we sleep?" Mae asked. She seemed depressed and wearied.

"I have a secret room. There behind the fireplace," I said, taking her hand again and leading her into the parlor.

159

I levered the door open and guided her in, telling her the history of the different objects in my lair ... my father's bed, Anne Boleyn's harpsichord, the armoire that once belonged to the Empress Josephine (I bought it at auction, never having met Napoleon or his wife), the Renoir on the wall facing the bed, the Dali over the oak press, the press itself having come from the papal bedroom in the Vatican and once having held the robes of the Medici popes, the small bust of David that Michelangelo, patronized by Cosimo de Medici for whom I had also worked as a bookfinder, had done in his extreme youth, all the odds and ends of a life lived for almost seven centuries.

Signed books from Percy Faith Shelley, Lord Byron, T.S. Elliot, lay side to corner with china knickknacks from Japan, a sketch by another of Cosimo's artists, Leonardo da Vinci, bejeweled eggs from the Court of Catherine The Great, a Ming vase, and an illuminated Bible which had once lay on the altar of my church in the village of my mortality.

On the wall above the door hung a clock from 15th century Russia, on which the face of the clock moved rather than the hands, as was common of Russian clocks back then.

"From your things, I know your heart," Mae said, caressing the gold and ruby globe Elizabeth Regina had given me.

Mae was impressed.   She was warmed and cheered. This was immortality to her.   Celebrity hunting through the centuries.   Collecting great works of art and historical places with which to furnish an immortal home, an empty heart, alone for centuries.   I reminded myself to bring Ron here, to show these things to him; he would appreciate them all, but as a man of taste does, and not, like Mae, as a child, impressed with name dropping.

We fell into bed finally, caressing one another sleepily and drifting toward our separate dreams. Just before I fell entirely into a dream of Sibby Monroe, Mae said quietly in the darkness, "You should have married me, as Richard has married his mortal. It would have been better for all of us, I am sure."

I was too far down into sleep to reply to her, so I told Sibby instead as she waltzed past me in my dream, "But I could not marry you. Marriage is not for eternity."

****

When we woke the Russian clock said it was full night outside the brownstone. We dressed formally for our dinner with Dickie and his mortal wife and neither of us spoke of those last words before sleep the night before; there could have been no benefit in doing so.

Richard's wife, Rachel, was a pretty little brunette with freckles and slightly protruding front teeth, which caused her to appear to be smiling even when she wasn't. Like all his women, she was a bit plump, with comfortable hips and breasts. A natural breeder, Mae said with a touch of cattiness later that night, although carefully out of Dickie's hearing.

Rachel had cooked a leg of lamb with sweet yams and green salad, and to please her Dickie had two helpings.

We gain no nourishment from food, but taste is a wondrous experience for us. That faculty being much more intense for us than for humans, we still retain a love of eating. The food we ingest simply dissipates, leaving no sign of itself behind, just as the blood we drink does, but I have never been able to get over my desire for the flavor of beef simmered in wine, honey cakes, and best of all, chocolate. Only blood tastes better to me than chocolate.

I ate large portions of everything, pleasing Rachel

161

greatly.

Tony ingested more wine than anything else, but he kept up a steady stream of not terribly decent stories of Egypt and his adventures there, and Rachel laughed with delight, forgiving him his lack of appetite.

Mae picked at her plate as if she had been served rat's tails and cotton balls.

The newly created ones often seem unable to appreciate these leftovers of their humanity; they despise all but the blood and the life as it rushes screaming through the veins. I did not blame her for her distaste. In a century or two, with myself to teach her, she would come to relish these reminders of when she had been human. I did blame her, though, for her deliberate rudeness to Rachel, her lack of manners.

Ronald, with his impeccable manners, helped Rachel to serve, ate with gusto and midway through dinner, leaped up to answer the door so that she could continue eating with us, rather than acting as our housekeeper.

I was far too distressed with Mae's behavior to wonder who might be ringing the doorbells, though if I had thought about it I would have remembered that no one, save Ron, had come to visit at the brownstone since 1927.

Down the long halls drifted low voices, too quiet for mortal ears to hear, and Rachel continued to laugh at Tony's tales of Egyptian nights as I heard Ron say, "You should not have come here, Ray. This is not my home. Wait awhile and I will meet you downtown later."

"I did not mean to offend," another voice replied, lower in timber, with the authoritativeness common to surgeons and lawyers and priests. "I will wait for you at ... ". The rest was cut off by the front doors closing and Tony's sudden gust of laughter. I shivered in the wake of that voice.

I strained to catch a scent, but Rachel's nearness effectively blocked any human aroma that might have been drifting into the dining room from Ron's visitor. I suddenly felt danger in every corner of my home and rose too quickly, knocking my chair over and startling Rachel. "Excuse me," I said and set off down the hall to the front door.

I could hear Ron's voice through the door and his visitor responding. I threw open the door and found myself staring directly into the white collar of a priest, a priest as big as a cathedral door and with thick, springing hair as white as an altar linen, topping a face as clear and unlined as a boy's. "My apologies," he said in that soft, deep voice. "I did not mean to intrude upon your evening."

"Michel," Ron said and then stopped. I looked into the grey-blue eyes of the priest and knew, although I could not see his thoughts, that he knew. My hand shot out as if it were not even a part of me and grasped the man by the throat, lifting him several inches off the sidewalk.

"You brought a human to my home. Worse yet, you brought a priest. You have endangered me, yourself, each one of us. What were you thinking of, for God's sake?" I roared at Ron.

"Michel, please. Please. It's not what you think. He's not what you think," he pleaded, tugging at my arm. The priest was turning a fine shade of plum beneath my grip, but he struggled not at all. His eyes, although bulging a bit, looked calmly into mine.

"He is a mortal. A priest. And he knows. He knows because you told him for whatever reason you thought you had, and now I
will kill him." I squeezed tighter and the priest's shoes kicked out a bit.

163

"Please, Michel. Let's go inside. Let me explain," Ron cried, pulling frantically on my arm now and I suddenly realized we were standing on my porch in full sight of anyone who happened to be passing by in the after midnight streets of my fashionable New York neighborhood.

My fury faded, became cold. Ron saw it and scurried to the townhouse door, throwing it wide.

I flung the priest into the hall, where he landed with a bounce against the side table, toppling the roses over in a tinkling of shattering crystal and bright water. Mae and Richard were immediately in the doorway of the dining room, with Tony and Rachel behind them, peering out.

"Go back into the other room," I growled at them and Richard immediately took Mae's arm and led her back out of sight, Tony following with Rachel in tow.

I kicked the priest in the direction of the parlor. Ron hurried to him, grasped his arm and helped him into the room, seating him in the same chair that a determined Ronald Higgenbothum had sat in not so long before, asking me to make him as I was.

I slammed the doors behind us and faced the two of them. I felt ferocious. I felt betrayed. A human, and worse yet a human who knew what I was and who probably felt himself bound to do something about it, being a priest, and who had been brought here by the one who was supposed to be most loyal to me, who should have been most loyal to me.

"Explain yourself, then," I said tersely to Ron.

"He saved my life," Ron answered steadily. "He saved me, even though he knew what I was."

I blinked stupidly. "He what?"

"He saved my life and so yours," Ron repeated. "I went out. I know you told me not to ever leave the hotel

164

without you, but that night you were gone so long and I began to be afraid you weren't coming back at all, that you were staying with Mae, and I was so hungry, Michel. Please understand. I was so hungry."

"I do not understand," I said shortly. "I never left you alone an entire night and day and I always brought you food."

"This was the first week I was down in Miami," Ron said doggedly. "I didn't know then that you would always remember me in the midst of your obsession with Mae and I was so hungry! The blood lust you warned me about just suddenly came upon me and I could not resist it!" He wiped a hand across his eyes and I realized he was weeping. "I'm sorry. I am so sorry but I went out. I had to go out. I was trying to be careful, to find a prostitute, someone who wouldn't be missed, just as you told me to do when we hunted together, but I kept getting further and further from the hotel and I didn't know where I was and then I found myself a few blocks from Father Ray's church, but of course I didn't know it was his church. Not then." He was starting to pant and beginning to lose his hold on his usually impeccable English.

"All right, Ron," I said, stepping forward and putting my hand on his shoulder. "All right. I am calmer now. I'm not going to kill your priest, at least not until you've had your say, so take it slowly. Explain to me what happened so I can understand."

He nodded and darted a quick look at the priest, who simply looked at the two of us with an expression of faint curiosity on his face.

"I was walking near his church when I saw this woman standing under a streetlamp and I called to her and she motioned for me to come over and so I did and then ... "

165

I groaned. "She was one of the Immortals," I said.

"No," the priest said. "She was a vampire. I saw her fangs. She grabbed your friend and would have broken his neck if I hadn't intervened."

"That is impossible," I said. "There were no vampires in Miami while we were there. I would have known if there were. What you saw was an Immortal, pretending, although I do not know why, to be undead."

"Perhaps so," Father Ray shrugged.

"What happened then?" I asked Ron. "This woman grabbed you and meant to break your neck, I assume. What then?"

"She had me around the throat," Ron said, shuddering. "Her lips were covered in blood and I thought she meant to tear my face off with her teeth, I really did. And then Father Ray ran out from his church and he tore me away from her and carried me, running, back into the church."

I looked at the priest, who was so much larger than Ron that I was not surprised he had been able to pick him up and run with him as if he were a football. I was only surprised that he had done it at all.

"As soon as we were inside the church, the woman stopped pursuing us. She stood at the bottom of the steps and called to Father Ray and said, `He is a damned soul, Father. A vampire. Give him to me', but he told her he would not allow her to kill me and that as far as he could see she was no less damned than I, and she went away after awhile. I never went out of the room after that. Never, I swear to you."

"I am surprised she didn't come for you in the hotel room," I said.

"I told her I would see to the vampire," Father Ray said, smiling. "She went away not completely unsatisfied."

"I don't understand this at all," I mused, going to the mantlepiece and staring up at into Helena's painted eyes. "Why did you not release Ron to her when you knew what you had rescued? Especially if you believed they were two of kind?"

"Well, to be truthful, I didn't believe _he_ was a vampire, although I was fairly certain she was," Father Ray said and this time he laughed. "It took me several weeks of companionship with him before I accepted his vampirism. By that time, I was terribly fond of him and, I will admit, very curious about you, Mr. de Brissault."

"You feel no burning desire to put a stake through my heart?" I smiled, not joking, despite the lightness of my query.

"No, I cannot say I do," Father Ray answered slowly. "That may be wrong, sinful, even, considering my vocation, but all I really desire at this time is to come to know you, your kind, better."

"Do you want to be one of us, perhaps?" I asked softly.

"No. Never. I wish merely to be your friend, as I am Ron's friend," he said firmly.

"You want to study me."

"Yes. I suppose that is true."

"You think we are evil and that I am the most evil, being Ron's creator, as it were."

"I do not know if you are evil. Perhaps you are no more evil than the forest beast who kills for sustenance. What I know is that you are not human and I would like to understand you, if you will allow me to spend some time with you."

I believed him. More importantly, I could hardly kill him now, knowing that he had saved Ron from the Other, and myself from the final death, by bringing Ronald into his

Church for sanctuary.   But that also puzzled me. Nothing in the stories passed among us about the Immortals had even hinted that they could not enter a church.   Perhaps the myth that a vampire was unable to penetrate within a holy place had risen because the Others could not.

Well, I would think about that later, I shrugged. Now I had to decide what to do about Ron's priest.

"Do not come here again," I said finally, turning to face him.   "Not without my permission.   Not without my invitation."

"All right," he agreed.

"Ron and I will come to you now and then and we will talk.   I have had human friends before, but never one who knew what I was.   I will have to learn to trust you."

"All right," he said again.   He stood up.   "I'll be going now.   I have yet to find a hotel here in New York that I can afford.   Perhaps you could recommend someplace for me?"

"Why aren't you staying at the diocese?" I asked, suspicious again.

"I am not here on official business.   I thought it better that my superiors think I was on vacation in Maine than to let them know where I was and have to answer questions as to why I came here."

I sighed.   "Ron, set him up through the corporation in one of our hotels."

"Why, thank you, Mr. de Brissault.   Thank you," the priest smiled happily and when he smiled like that, widely and unaffectedly, he looked like a child.   Against my will, I felt myself beginning to like him.

Like him, but not trust him.   It would be a very long time before I could trust him, a time that might possibly even extend past his natural lifetime.

168

He reached for my hand, meaning to shake it, but I shook my head and stepped back, and he nodded as if he understood perfectly.

I am not at all sure that he didn't.

****

After Father Ray had left and while Ron was busy telephoning arrangements for his accommodations, the others came out from the dining room and joined me in the parlor.

Tony, with his perfect aplomb, came roaring in through the double doors complaining about the cigarettes in his bedroom. "Haven't you any of those Russian Blacks?" he asked loudly enough to drown out the tentative questions Rachel was trying to ask.

"Of course," I said and we all moved to seat ourselves and begin the after dinner conversation and brandy. But the evening progressed more badly still now as Mae began a malicious game of seducing Dickie as if he were some nightclub prey she had fastened on.

He sat next to her on the banquette and lit her cigarettes for her, leaning close to caress her hand, her hair, her thigh. Rachel watched them, straining to smile. Tony sat with a grave face. Conversation faltered, fell, stopped, while I laughed far too often and at remarks far from funny, trying not to see Sibby's face imposed on Mae's.

Finally Dickie jumped up catching Mae up by the hand with him, and said, "Why don't we all go down to Times Square and walk about?"

"It's much too late for me, Richard," Rachel said quietly. "I would rather stay here and read a bit before bed."

169

"Of course, love," he said, coming over to kiss the top of her head.

Dickie already had her well trained. Their exchange had a formal sound to it that bespoke their arrangement that she not accompany him at night unless he specifically invited her to do so. I had had similar agreements with my mortal wives as well, but Mae, not yet understanding this odd co-existence of the living and we dead in intimate circumstances, looked relieved that Rachel would not to accompany us.

Mae grabbed Ron's arm and drew him toward the door, ignoring Dickie now that she had a chance to satiate her curiosity about the priest by getting Ronald away from Rachel.

We set off walking, Dickie, Tony and I in the lead, Mae and Ronald trailing a bit behind, talking of our mutual past together as human men do who have not seen one another in a long time (`Do you remember when we?', or `Remember how we?'), but soon the smell of blood from the people crowding about us began to pulse in my throat and I saw Mae licking her lips. By the time we reached Times Square, she was mad with the bloodlust and broke away from us to hunt alone.

I did not see her again until we arrived back at the brownstone where she was waiting on the steps, dangling a new diamond necklace from one hand, a ruby bracelet from the other, watching the streetlamps catch fire in the stones.

"I saw another like us, Michel," she cried excitedly as soon as she caught sight of me. "A dirty creature. He ran away."

"They almost always do," Dickie said. "They are the beasts of our kind. You should avoid them, as they do us. Sometimes they are insane and attack us."

"Nothing can harm us," Mae said disdainfully. "I

want to meet one of them. See how they live."

"They live in sewers and condemned buildings, Mae," I said. "Dickie's right. Best to stay away from them. They don't want companionship. They are solitaires."

"If he can have a cow of a mortal for a companion, then I can meet with one of our own kind, even if it be little more than a beast. After all, what are we but glittering monsters?" Mae laughed, a sharp, unpleasant sound. "Except you, Michel, you and your friends. Devils, with hearts like saints." She spit the words at me and ran into the house, closing herself in the parlor lair.

And, "What do you imagine you are?" she asked me later, just as I was falling into a sleep overlain with images of Atlanta in 1864 and Caroline standing in the muddy street before Peachtree's Haberdashery, her bare feet brown and blue with clay and cold.

"Do you think you are still human despite your death? Do you think that by living in a fine house with beautiful things, by reading books and collecting art and eating Baked Alaska and taking mortal wives you can yet be human? A man who drinks blood in the night and dreams of life from his fancy coffin? You are dressing yourself with illusion, Michel; coating a black heart with gold and forgetting the blackness beneath because you see only the shine of gold, like sun reflecting on a bottomless pit of water."

"I know what I am, Mae," I said calmly.

"You are a myth," she whispered into the darkness and pretended to be sleeping when I reached out to touch her.

What she said frightened me. I did not want to

171

think about it and I did not want to see how Rachel grew thinner and more silent as the days passed and we waited for Ron to settle out business matters at `de Brissault and Sons' before leaving for Europe.

Mae took to hunting alone more and more.

I shouldn't have let her go alone, but I could not stop her and privately I felt that if any of the Others ever tried anything with her, it would be them who would die, not Mae.

Rachel was less tense with Mae gone from the house each night, but I could see that Dickie and she would not be traveling with us to England after all. He did not say so, but I came to feel that he regretted having stayed to await my arrival in New York, and having stayed, now did not know how to take his leave without precipitating another break between us.

The spell Mae had tried to cast over him had blown away in the winds of her nastiness to Rachel, her contempt for Dickie's needing a human to bed. Although she gave the ruby bracelet to Rachel one evening in a moment of casual kindness, I found it later in a garbage can behind the alley entrance to the townhouse. Later still I gave it to Ron. Jewels and land are the best investments. God, in his parsimony, is making no more of them and a fine ruby is more valuable than a diamond.

But not wanting to acknowledge something will not make it fade away.

One week before our departure date, Mae asked me to take her to the theater. We fed first, in Central Park, then slipped into an Off-Off Broadway play, some farce that left me trembling with boredom and Mae glistening with restlessness.

As we walked away from the crowds down into the less well lit and quieter streets, a figure, darker than the alley he beckoned from, caught Mae's attention and she smiled at me.

"Now we are to be mugged," she stage-whispered. "How exciting. How New York."

She approached the alley's mouth, still smiling. A strong, black arm reached from the shadows and grasped her by the hair, pulling her into him. I saw a gun barrel glint for a moment as he motioned to me.

"Get yo ass in here, motherfucker. Shake it."

He was young, eighteen perhaps, trembling with need for whatever drug he was killing himself with, sweat beading on his upper lip, the gun held, none to firmly in his left hand. He pushed Mae into me and waved the gun to indicate he wished us to stand with our backs to the moist bricks.

"Be cooler than death, my man, and no one gets wasted," he jived nervously. "Yo wallet, man." Silently I handed him the slim lizardskin folder Mae had brought back for me from one of her hunts. Beside me, she continued to smile, like a woman at a cocktail party trapped in a corner by a boring, but important, man.

He began to rifle through the wallet, dropping its contents at our feet. "What I want with all these credit cards, asshole?" he raged, throwing the empty wallet at my face. "You better jack out with some cash, man, or I'll ... "

"I always carry the cash," Mae said softly. "You know how men are. Give them a few dollars and they spend it and then can't account for where it went."

I moved uneasily. I love killing this type of mortal. I do so whenever I can, as opposed to slaughtering innocents, but Mae did not just want this boy's blood to feed upon. She fed as much on cruelty as blood, and I was being made to realize it, consciously, for the first time. I pitied the boy, but I would not repudiate Mae by helping

173

him.

He looked at her, some comprehension that all was not as it should be slowly dawning on him. His eyes teared furiously. "Give it to me. Now," he said, but his voice was uncertain. He waved the gun at her, as much to reassert his control to himself, as to frighten her.

"I think not," she laughed, and the sound of it was like fingernails on greasy steel. "I think you're quite too cowardly to shoot anyone. I think even I could take that gun away from you."

She stepped toward him and he panicked.

The air had grown thick with shadows and emotions he had had no hand in creating, and his fear turned him first gray, then a deeper black, as the blood rushed into his face, and he fired the little revolver at her. Not once, but several times, backing away from her as she continued to step toward him, light, graceful, lithe, dancing.

Her back was to me and I could not see what he saw ... the blood mushrooming out from her white satin bodice, running in rivulets down her white, satin-clad thighs, her smile, white in
the night, but I could imagine it. I could feel it.

I could feel her exalt in her power, his terror.

He screamed and stood suddenly still, giving into the death that stalked him so gently.

When she reached out to touch him he screamed again, falling
to his hands and knees, trying to scrabble away from her over the garbage strewn bricks. "Jesus, God, no, don't touch me! You a death demon, you a fucking zombie bitch! Don't you lay those hands on me! Don't please God, don't do it!" and he somehow got to his feet, raising the gun to his temple.

Mae laughed. But this time it was the laughter of

174

larks playing in a sunlit barn, swooping in and out of the shadows and sunbars. She crooned, she sang to him, like a fire inviting a man to burn. He lowered the gun. He lowered his head.

He fell to his knees before her, as supplicants had once knelt to me, long ago at the altar of God in a village church.

Mae was right, I thought. We are monsters, clothed in satin and leather, diamonds and the dust of graves.

"You are ill," she said gently, laying her hand on his head. "You are hungry. You smell of garbage and death. Don't you want to live forever, never sick again, never afraid?"

He sobbed, once, convulsively.

"I could give you that," she whispered, stroking his sweating face, "if only I weren't so hungry myself." He shrieked then as she flowed over him, his face filling with helpless love and loathing and terror as she laid her hands delicately on either side of his head.

"Sshhh," she crooned. "I won't hurt you." And bent to kiss him, ripping his head from his body as she straightened up again, tossing it far down the alley, where it came to rest, eyes dully watching me, and I turned away then, as his blood flowed between my feet, sparkling in the far off lights of the street; turned away so that I might still love her in all the nights to come.

****

"Before we leave for Europe," Mae said, lying quiet in my arms as the dawn came, "I have a stop I would like to make."

Her bloodied dress lay discarded on the floor outside my sanctuary room, beside the fireplace. I could see it when I closed my eyes, smell, from where I lay on the big bed, its pungent odors of gunpowder and blood.

I was suddenly aware that it would be Rachel who found it in the morning. It would frighten her. Perhaps it might induce Dickie to get her out of my house before something else, something irretrievable happened.

"Not to Fred," I sighed.

"No," she answered, pulling me tight against her. "To my mother."

****

It was odd to think of Mae as having an item so prosaic as a mother. Odder still to think of Mae wanting to see this woman she had never mentioned once in the months we had known one another. I pictured her as someone like Mae herself, only older, more polished.

Mae insisted on traveling incommunicado, as she termed it, and we flew to Boston as two small barn swallows, landing in a huge lilac bush that overgrew the sidewalk near the porch of the bungalow where she had spent her childhood.

It was early, only slightly after 9 p.m., and lights shown in the windows, the smell of dinner circled in the enclosed porch. Still, the house sat wrapped in misery, shrouded in the silence of a new tomb.

Mae's mother was not prosaic, nor was she at all like her entrancing daughter. She was tiny and twisted and her first words to Mae were, "I suppose you've lost your job. Come home expecting me to support you."

"No, mama," Mae said cheerfully. "I wanted you to meet my husband. This is Michel de Brissault and he's very wealthy. Not at all the bum you always expected me to marry."

"I might have known you'd prostitute yourself to the first rich dog that came along," Mrs. Remotti said. Her eyes were bitter seeds in her face. Nothing healthy would ever grow from their gaze. A lifetime of discontent and Scotch had soured her skin, her breath, her soul. "You might as well come in and eat some supper. But you can't spend the night here, girl. I won't have the neighbors talking about me."

"Mrs. Remotti," I said, "why are you acting like this? Your daughter ..."

"My daughter, mister, has been a burden and an embarrassment to me since the day she was born. Her father left because of her. She ain't never done a right thing in her life and from the look of you, I don't imagine marrying you was a right thing either. You look like some nancy-boy to me. If you're even married," she sneered. "No more than I'd expect from her anyhow."

I wanted to ask Mae to leave then, before the hate permeating the air and the curtains and the furniture in this house burst into flame, but I couldn't. Mae had her reason for seeing this woman, for enduring the thorny words being thrust into her, and I knew what her reason was. I could not blame her. I could not ask her to forego this revenge.

Mrs. Remotti moved to a sideboard and poured a coffee mug of Pinch, tossing it down in two swallows before pouring still another cupful. Mae watched her, grim and exultant.

Dinner was an agony. The woman could think of no topic of conversation that did not somehow delineate her daughter's inexhaustible faults. Mae was stupid, she was lazy. She was ugly, worthless in all respects, and the greatest of her sins was her lack of gratitude for all that her mother had endured for her.

The horrific cliches, pouring out like sour sauce for

the overdone roast, might have been amusing if they hadn't been so painful to hear. I grew angrier and less likely to attempt to
stop Mae when the time came for her vengeance, no matter how out of control she might become.

At what seemed the midway point in Mrs. Remotti's dissertation on how Mae's father had fled from them 20 years before to get away from the eternally crying baby, the bills Mae's birth had saddled him with, and the lack of a free and easy life like that they had enjoyed before she had been born, Mae carefully laid her fork on her plate and faced her mother across the dirty lace dollies and tarnished silver with eyes as golden as a lion's.

"Those contacts don't suit you," her mother jeered. "What you doing with them? Want to look like your prissy husband there? Suit him well enough. Don't suit you at all." She gulped down the last of her Scotch and poured herself a mug of vodka, this time from a bottle at her elbow.

"Oh, but then, nothing would suit me, would it, Mother?" Mae said softly.

"No, nothing would. You been a ... " Mrs. Remotti began. She turned her eyes, bright with hate on her daughter.

Mae had always been as meticulous in her way as Ronald Higgenbothum was in his. I had never seen her change into our true form, the eyes becoming those of a cat, pupils slitted in a fury of bloodlust, teeth fanging out over the lower lip. She had continued in living death as she had been in life, groomed, scrubbed, well adorned, but now she roared in our voice, that combination of sounds like a giraffe's scream, a tiger's wail, a bear's cry, a bird's shriek, and sprang to her feet, fangs glinting in the shallow lamplight, eyes slitted like a serpent's or a yellow-eyed

178

leopard.

"Stop!" Mae commanded. "Be silent!"

Her mother stared at her, the beginning of madness creeping into her eyes, washing out the hate as sun fades color from cloth.

"All my life," Mae said, in a voice suffocating with hatred, leaning her hands on the table, those inhuman eyes and preternatural teeth mere inches from her mother's face as if she meant to kiss her, "you have insulted me, degraded me, punished me, not for what I had done or deserved, but from the perverse lies of your own decayed heart. Did you think I would allow you to continue cutting me with your words forever? Did you never think that one day you would see the faces of your alcohol soaked demons upon that of your killer? For I am a demon, come to thank you for the hell you made of my life. Without you, Mother, I might never have met Michel, never needed him, or the cursed gift he gave to me. I have become your murderer, Mother, and I will send you to a worse hell than this house."

She sprang over the table so quickly even I could not have stopped her, had I any inclination to do so. Mae grasped her mother's starkly corded neck in one hand and would have snapped it, but I also stood, pupils narrowed to those same cat slits, teeth razoring over my lips, shredding them in my anguish for Mae, and the old woman's eyes passed from horror into insanity.

"Mae," I whispered. "A better revenge is yours. Her mind is gone."

She peered into the face of her mother and laughed. I did not turn away from her cruelty this time, for it had been bred in her from the cradle by this woman's torment.

Having seen the loveless life into which she had been born, I could not even fault her now for the black boy

179

in the alley or her flirting with Dickie just to see Rachel's pain, or her careless words to me that so often wounded because they were meant to slice and tear and weaken me, as she had been torn and weakened by her mother.

"You're right," she said triumphantly, releasing the woman to slump down in the chair, drool curling over her lips and down her chin into the coffee mug of vodka. "A better revenge is mine. Now she will live out her days in a nursing home where they will forget to feed and change her, and where others will treat her with the contempt she lavished on me."

And suddenly, even as I was moving to comfort her, to hold her, she was up and gone through the roof, tearing a huge hole through the shingles and the rafters which rained down debris into the room, smashing dishes and lamps and bric-a-brac.

She was gone, dancing away on the moonlight, into invisibility, leaving me with what had once been her mother.

The room stank of feces and plaster dust and spilt alcohol, but I could summon no pity for the broken human gurgling and babbling at the table, I left, too, not caring if anyone ever
came to help her, hoping she would die there, drooling into her vodka, before anyone should come to rescue her from the ruins of her hatefilled home.

180

CHAPTER 10

Mae did not come back to the brownstone for three nights.

During that time, I paced the marble paneled halls, the spiral staircase, the gleaming kitchens (there are two in the house), the endless bedrooms, and wondered how I could survive without her should she never return.

Tony followed me grimly about as if he feared I might commit suicide; a possibility for us certainly, but only if I could find a blast furnace to throw myself into, and the despair necessary to keep me there until I was nothing but blond ash.

Dickie and his bride crept about the brownstone and nervously patted my hand or shoulder occasionally, and by the morning of the second day I allowed Ron to convince me that sending for Father Ray was an excellent idea.

We had visited the priest only twice since that first night back in New York, but I was already coming to trust him a bit, or at least, not to distrust him so very much, and

I accepted that he and Ron were friends. What I did not accept was that the Good Padre, as Tony had dubbed him with an excellent lack of taste, could help me in any fashion.

"If you want him, you have my permission to summon him," I snapped miserably, "but keep him out of my way or I will eat his eyes, Ron. I promise you. I will eat his eyes."

As it happened, Father Ray arrived that evening just after the Countess and I did not see him at all, as Tony and Ron whisked him to the dining room, leaving Ana and myself alone in the parlor.

"Michel," she said, "it is for the best if she does not return to you. Hear me this time, my child. The girl had no life in her before she was transformed, only death. The seeking of it, the desire to give it, the desire to live it. It is all she can manifest even now. Between you yet there may be a murder after the first year is finished. Let me meet her when she comes back here, as she must, and I will take her to Switzerland, keep her safe from the Others for the rest of the time left to her as a New One," she pleaded, grasping my hands with gentle, and hopeless love. "I will do this for you, Michel, because of my great love for you. Let me help you."

I buried my head in her breasts and wept. "We can only be what we are," I cried. "Mae has never been loved; how then can she love? I will protect her. I will love her. Then she will learn to love."

"No, my Michel. You have said it yourself in the wisdom of your pain: we can only be what we are," Ana said firmly. "A human being may change, may grow, but we are condemned always to remain the person we were at death. For some, like Mae, the transformation, by cutting away the natural restraints of life, brings what seems a change in personality, but there is not true change. If she had not been afraid of man's law, she would have killed, even in life. Perhaps she would have done so later in her life despite her fear of just and lawful retribution, but you, Michel, you gave her the immortality that allows free rein to her hatred, and death she is. She can be nothing else.

"And that is why, too, I do not believe you need fear the Others will destroy her. They live, and all living things shun true evil. To be safe, though, I will watch her for you. Leave here tonight," Ana whispered, rocking me against that ample body. "Leave with Tony and that little accountant of yours. Go with them to Europe. I will hold her in my castle at Brodenspee. She is young yet and her powers not fully developed and, in truth, I do not think she will miss you, nor come to look for you when the year is over."

"No," I said, pushing her away. "I will wait for her."

"She hates you, Michel," Ana sighed. "You hold her now in some restraint, yes, but later, when she feels she is strong enough, she will betray you. If you but knew ... "

"I know she does not hate me," I cried in fury. "And you know nothing yourself. I know you were considered a seer in your life as a human, but you are not truly seeing Mae as she is, and I ask you not to burden me further with your fancies."

Ana stared at me for a few moments and then she nodded, not in agreement with me, but in surrender to me. She stood and left, not bothering to look at me again.

And now, for Mae, I had lost two dear friends, I thought dismally, and turned again to the window.

Tony entered the parlor, squeezed my arm in sympathy and set himself down, remaining, morose, in the armchair, his boots on the alabaster coffee table, for the rest of the night, mud flaking off the insteps and heels, in tiny, wistful clouds, soiling the plush white carpet, so like the color of Mae's skin. We did not speak.

On the third night, Mae arrived in a taxi, long legs slipping out of the door, impossibly white hands caressing the driver's face for a moment as she paid him.

I watched her through the long linen curtains of the parlor windows. She swept into the hall like a goddess come home to Olympus after a long journey to the land of mortals and kissed me warmly, tossing a floor length white miniver fur coat I had not seen before carelessly onto the dirty hearth.

"Oh, my sweet Michel, forgive me," she called airily as she bent to kiss Tony who was lounging on the Armitage banquette. "That evening with my mother was ... well, you were there. Need I explain to you that I needed some time alone after that horrible dinner? Hmmm, and where are Richard and dear Rachel? Has she cooked something divine for our supper?" Her voice dripping with sarcasm, she grinned at me, fangs extended. "I am sooooo hungry tonight," she said.

"I imagine they are in their room," I said stiffly. "And you smell of fresh blood, so do not tell me of your hunger." I turned back to the window.

"Ah, here they are," Mae cried, throwing her arms out to Dickie as he entered the parlor. Rachel followed close behind him, her hands strangling themselves at her waist. "Hello, Rachel," Mae laughed and something in that laugh compelled me to turn back around and watch her as she now danced toward Dickie's unhappy, human wife.

"And who is this?" Mae sang gaily, as Ron and Father Ray now entered the room behind Rachel. "Why, bless me, Father, for I have sinned. I have driven my

184

mother mad and stayed out for three days and two and one half nights worrying my husband and denying him his martial rights." She laughed again, and the sound was painful on the ear, like slivers of thin glass pressed slowly beneath one's toenails.

"I have noticed something," Rachel said suddenly, apropos of nothing. "All of you have amber eyes. All but the Countess and Father Ray."

Mae's smile flickered, then became soft, seductive, much as she had looked when we had first entered her mother's house.

She released Dickie and stepped in front of Rachel. "It is our bloodline," she said, as if this were a precious joke she was sharing with a girlfriend. "What do you think your husband is, dear little Rachel? From where do you imagine these eyes came? Are we all brothers and sister from some family you have yet to meet, all except the Countess and Father Ray, of course? Well, we are a family, of a kind, I suppose."

Her laughter now was high and eerily beautiful so that Rachel stepped back, putting her hands out in front of her to ward of that sound of fairie glee.

Mae began to pace around her, moving closer with each circuit while the rest of us watched, frozen with horror and curiosity. Even the priest did not move.

"We are a family, yes, but one which only lives at night, Rachel. Surely you have noticed. Where did you think your husband went in the darkness?"

Rachel gave a little cry and tried to back away again. "What is she talking about?" she groaned to Dickie, who did not answer, and who could not meet her eyes.

"Haven't you noticed other things," Mae asked, almost absently, reaching out to grasp Rachel's still outstretched hands. "Haven't you noticed a bloodied dress

185

lying before the fireplace?"

She began to waltz Rachel about in a little circle now, as if they were dancing together, laughing together, enjoying an evening together at some intimate dinner party.

"Haven't you noticed a certain coldness in Richard's touch? A certain death beside you in the early morning? Tasted blood, perhaps, in Dickie's dawn kiss?"

Rachel screamed and tried to pull away.

Dickie moved slowly, lumbering toward the two women as they spun in an ever faster circle.

Perhaps he meant to save Rachel, perhaps he only meant to end her tortured terror, but before he could reach them, Mae released Rachel's hands and she flew across the room, her head slamming into the white fireplace marble, and she slumped, bleeding from a small cut on the forehead, quite dead, to the fine, white, persian wool carpet.

There was too much blood from that so small cut, and it was blindingly red against the fierce white of my parlor.

Mae walked over to where Rachel lay, her dead eyes staring into the night beyond the windows, knelt and dipped a finger into that red, red blood, pooling in Rachel's ear.

"Have you noticed," she said reflectively to Father Ray, "that keeping one's bloodsucking status a secret from mortals is impossible when you live with them?" She licked her finger and smiled at him. To his credit, he did not flinch back from her any more than he had from me, though Mae was far more malevolent than I shall ever be (or so I devoutly hope).

I lunged for her, perhaps meaning to break her neck and end this horrible mistake I had made in loving her and changing her, but I only grasped her neck and lifting her to her feet, I slapped her with all my strength. She tumbled

186

to the floor and lay there, in silk and lace and blood, laughing, as Ray went to the fireplace and picked Rachel up gently, reverently.

"What are you doing?" Dickie cried out in anguish.

"I will take care of her, if you will allow me, Mr. de Brissault," the priest said quietly. "I believe you have other matters to conclude now."

I nodded and Ray left the room, carrying Rachel's body as tenderly as a lover might, with Ron, weeping, stumbling behind him.

"Can we trust him?" Dickie asked dully.

I did not know and I did not care. I would leave this nightmare house before dawn and I would never return, I determined. It mattered not at all to me what Father Ray might or might not do now, for I would in Europe or Asia or Russia, where he could not follow and where the years would finally pass, solving the problem of him and his mortal knowledge.

I did not answer Dickie and his eyes flicked past me to rest on Mae.

Smiling brilliantly, she got to her feet and came to place her hand lightly in mine. "When are we leaving for Europe?" she asked nonchalantly.

Dickie stared at her in disbelief and then without a word or a look for me, he passed through the parlor doors, and disappeared down the hall. I heard the front door open, hesitate a moment, and then softly shut and knew that this time nothing would heal the break between us.

I had lost him forever and I did not know if the pain of that would ever be blunted.

"When are we leaving for Venice?" Mae asked again.

"Tonight," I answered. I felt at once sulky and exhilarated. I turned from her to the windows again.

"Tomorrow," she corrected me in a wheedling, seductive voice. "I've always wanted to see Venice. To ride the gondola's and walk along the Bridge of Sighs. But I want to sleep with you here, once more, before we go. Say you will wait until tomorrow. Say you will, Michel, for me. Oh, what is the matter, my love?"

She wrapped her arms about me and kissed my neck. I could feel her fangs, unretracted, behind her lips, pressing into my flesh. She would tear my throat out, if she believed it possible, I thought, and was cold.

I could see Tony reflected in the window pane and his eyes were half-closed, watching us, as if he meant to sleep, now, at midnight, without having fed. I wondered briefly why he and Mae reflected, while Ana, Dickie, Ron and myself, did not.

"I was worried about you," I said to Mae, when I knew I would be able to do so without my voice trembling.

I only needed some time alone," she whispered, coaxing me with kisses on my eyes, my throat. "You don't really mean to be angry with me over that cow, Rachel, do you?" she purred, opening my shirt, flicking her tongue over one nipple, and I felt as if I were again enveloped in the embrace of that evil child who had taken me so long ago on my narrow, straw priest's pallet.

Evil? I had not believed in evil for a very long time. Centuries, perhaps. I had certainly not thought of that six year old girl as evil once I had been transformed, but now I realized that she truly had been corrupt, wicked, as Mae was.

The child vampire had taken a priest but no other male in the village, or surrounding regions, that I had been able to discover in the years following. She had taken only myself, and I saw in Mae this same evil, this same desire to soil what is clean.

188

But I could not destroy her, did not even wish to, if I were truthful with myself. Evil is, after all, a seductive, beautiful thing, else one would never wish to dance with it.

I loved her yet as I loved my own existence. But I also believed in that moment that my love for her must necessarily die for we cannot love even the most beautiful of evils when the illusion has been pierced. I would then be free of her by my choice, so that the year's end would see us parted without my heart breaking at her loss.

It would be a relief, I thought, as Helena's eventual death had been, but that was not yet. Not now.

Now I lifted her laughing into the air and took her violently to our bed.

All the while, she laughed.

And while we made love, Tony washed Rachel's blood from the white marble and the white persian wool of my elegant parlor.

****

On a bright New York winter morning, we set sail for Europe on the H.M.S. Queen Diana. Mae insisted on a luxury liner and Ronald pointed out that in the protected environment of the great ship we need never see the sunlight unless we choose to go on deck during the day.

Ronald, like Mae, had much trouble with the sun. Their skins would pink up immediately and once Mae's had even begun to smoke, though she had only been exposed for a few minutes to an errant beam breaking through the clouds. That frightened me, I can assure you! This sensitivity was not fully a function of their being newly made.

Neither Tony nor I had experienced such great discomfort, and, in Mae's case, danger, when we were first

189

changed, although it is true that with age the skin seems to toughen, and even direct sunlight is not as irritating as it once was. Tony thought their reactions might be due to the presence of pollutants in the air refracting the sun differently than it had in our time, combined with an inborn difference in Mae and Ronald's flesh because they had been conceived, and lived their lives during this polluted era of artificial foods, plastic, and filthy air. Whatever the cause, neither of them could stand the sun.

For Mae, even a cloudy day was uncomfortable, and both she and Ronald were developing a positive abhorrence of daylight, like the vampires in Tony's paperback novels.

Mae wanted the luxury of a ship crossing (well, what she wanted was a first class suite on the Titanic, but what she was willing to settle for was the President's Berth aboard the Queen Diana) and Ronald, after examining the accommodations, became her unlikely ally in persuading me to it, rather than crossing by plane.

Tony, of course, was delighted with the idea, and immediately purchased an ornate, Egyptian mummy case, filled it dirt dug from the brownstone's back garden, and had it taken to the dock for loading into the luggage hold of the ship. It was placed upright in one of those cages pets are usually kept in during the voyage and huge kryptonite locks, to which I alone had the keys, were installed on the cage door.

In fact, I was the only one who did not like the idea of a cruise ship. All this might be very romantic, but how were we to feed? I argued.

Throughout the ten day crossing, Mae fed us.

She distributed dollops of immortality throughout the ship's male passengers and crew, returning to our cabin to feed both Ronald and myself.

Tony, rocking in the hold, buried in his romantic

190

box of earth, needed no feeding, for he had `gone to ground' as we phase it, and slept as a bear hibernates.

Those men Mae favored with her half-kiss, half-bite, would age more slowly than their companions, would suffer less sickness, but they would eventually die. She created no new ones of our kind; she killed no one.

"You didn't think I had the control, did you?" she teased me sometimes during the long hot days of the crossing as we lay in our darkened cabin, hands locked across the distance between our beds.

There was something unspeakably erotic about sucking life from the soft skin between elbow and wrist as I had once seen her kitten trying to do. I would find myself floating in dreams while I fed in the early dawn, her high, silver laugh cutting like a steel razor through the darkness. The couple in the next cabin would moan in their sleep at the sound of it, and Ronald's eyes would burn into my back with their avid hunger, watching me as I fed.

Mae was playing another game during those nights as well, an endless game of seduction in which she reaffirmed repeatedly, to herself, her beauty, her desirability.

She had brought no clothes with her that were not in the style of the 20's and 30's, styles that made her timeless loveliness particularly alluring.

She would appear in the ballroom in a dress of gold lame, a gold headband with beads and feathers resting over her blond bob cut, and every man there would seem to draw their breath in and forget to release it.

She strolled the deck on heavily clouded days dressed in a tight, black skirt that ended in mid-calf, cut up the back to mid-thigh, and a gray blazer with padded shoulders, a tiny, gold watch pinned to the lapel.

Men leaped from their deck chairs to seat her with colorful drinks and magazines that seemed to appear

191

magically from the air. Their women mumbled that the Remotti bitch was brazen, a slut and obvious. Couldn't the men see how obvious she was? And all the while, she laughed.

Men asked her to marry them. She blazed through the ship like a nova exploding out of control and hearts signed, hearts broke, hearts bled, hearts hoped. She told them she could never

marry, and showed them the diamond and emerald bracelet she always wore. The man who had given it to her, she would sigh, a tear stealing down one perfect cheek from one perfect eye, was dead, and she could never love again.

Hopelessly, I found hope in these words I heard her speak again and again, to some stuttering, red or pale faced man, hanging on her arm, her eyes, her lips, those words. I wanted to believe that she meant them, that she loved me, but might she not also have been laughing at me? I wondered in cold dismay. Perhaps even wishing me dead?

Yet when I knelt before her and took that glittering flesh the color of cold starlight into my mouth, the blood running off the tips of her finger to splash on the rose and blue carpeting of our suite, I almost did believe that she loved me still.

****

We disembarked the Queen Diana at London on a cold, cloud driven day in December, with the wind whipping our clothes and rain drizzling down our collars.

Tony grumbled at the weather and Mae told him curtly to go back to Egypt if he could not manage to cheer up.

Ronald Higgenbothum was delighted with

everything he saw (except the weak, clouded sunlight) and immediately bought a handful of guidebooks from a quay vendor, most of which dealt with haunted castles and manor houses.

I found I was surprisingly glad to be home in England again. I wondered if my father's castle was still standing, if it had been turned into a tourist attraction since I had last seen it in 1362.

Ronald and Mae were in complete agreement as to what constituted a fun holiday in the British Isles. Nothing else would do but we must tramp through the Tower of London and peer under the staircase where the foully murdered nephews of Richard III were buried by their murderers (or so they say), and slip into Hampton Court at midnight in hopes of seeing Katherine Howard's poor wraith running down the corridor screaming Old Hal's name.

Mae spent an entire night on the Tower green, hoping to see Anne Boleyn's headless corpse walking, though I pointed out that she was more widely supposed to haunt a churchyard miles from London where, it is said, she had truly been buried. My opinion is that her haunting ended with the death of Henry VIII, but Mae would have none of that. She spent another night in one of the old convents where ladies in white and nuns, weeping in black, are said to walk, huddling with Ronald and inducing delicious thrills of fear in each other every time a timber created or a cricket shrilled.

Anne Boleyn wandering headless, Katherine Howard screaming through eternity, ghost monks and damned nuns, now populated her fantasies as once vampires had, and she wanted, as Ronald did, to explore every haunted site in England, Wales, Ireland and Scotland.

I found it odd that she didn't care in the least to see

Stonehenge, my family castle, or the historical site of Camelot, though Ron was urgent to do so. He finally talked Tony into accompanying him to those places while Mae dragged me to France hoping to encounter Jim Morrison's ghost humming tunelessly among the crypts of that famous Parish cemetery where he rests among the bodies of literary, political and musical greats.

We had, after all, nothing but time and no need to hurry our journey to Venice, and Paris is a nice place to visit in December when the tourists have not yet arrived for its fabled spring. But I was anxious to be off for Venice, to be alone with her there and so finally, one day in mid-January, I left Ron under Tony's protection and Mae and I set off for the city of canals and history.

I hoped, perhaps, to recapture there what had been lost when I transformed her, and at first it seemed as if my fantasy might become reality.

In the beginning, because of Venice itself, it seemed possible, for the core that is this most fascinating of cities is, as Mae was, timeless, unchanging, uttering captivating, and, under the city's special sorcery, Mae again became the woman I had been ensorcelled by, the woman I had been praying, after my fashion and to whatever gods listen to the prayers of vampires, would return to me.

For that short time, I had the love I desperately wanted from her, or convinced myself that I did, and ever since, I have tried to reassure myself that it was enough.

CHAPTER 11

We detrained at the Venice railway station next to the Scalzi Church where I once attended Mass with my great friend, Lord Byron, in late afternoon.

Venice was covered in snow, her sky clouded in pink pearl. From the station doors we looked together at the Scalzi Bridge arching out over the canal, both of us remembering that time when we had not known each other, yet she had wished for me and strongly enough to bring me to her. In that moment, I regretted none of what had since happened. There was a great, loose, bubble of happiness in me that forgave her everything.

"Is that the bridge, Michel?" Mae asked. Her voice was light with happiness, too, just it used to be, and I grinned.

"Yes," I answered.

"Oh, let's stand in the exact place," she cried and tugged me by the hand down toward the bridge.

"Be careful," I laughed. "These bridges are really only flights of steps and the ice ... "

"What can it do?" Mae giggled. "Kill me?" She pulled my hat down over my eyebrows and we slickered up the stairs to the center of the bridge. "Which way were you facing?" Mae asked, determined to have each detail exactly as it had been, with the single obvious exception that she was now physically present beside me.

"Here," I said, placing her in the precise spot where I had heard her cry that second time. She sighed and laid her head on my shoulder, looking out along the length of the canal.

Venice is a city built amongst the sea. There has never been a place like it, although the Mexico City of Cortez's time might have resembled it, built as it was in the midst of a lake. I have always loved Venice and its labyrinthine streets, its softly gliding canals, its wondrous art and architecture, its sense of its own uniqueness, which not even this loud and barbarous twentieth century could change, and, in fact, I have spent a goodly portion of my existence there.

I had been anxious to show Mae this bridge where I had listened to her heart's cry, and I was anxious to show her other places, other things: the canal along which I had walked with Lord Byron in 1816, the tomb of another great love of mine, and the Lido.

I believed that this sharing of my eternity with her would surely bring her back to me. I believed it with all my strength, as once I had done as a mortal child at Christmas season when I had hoped for a suit of armor of my own, and to just as little avail in the end.

"It's so lovely," she said at last, "so clean. Gore Vidal called the light here `nacreous'. I never understood what the word meant."

"Now you do." I smiled down at the top of her head, hidden beneath a yellow thing that was supposed to

196

be a lady's veiled sweep hat, but which looked more like a $200.00 joke to me.

"Now I do," she agreed comfortably. "I understand many things now, Michel." She lifted her face to mine and I saw
tears, vampiric blood tears, glinting like miniature rubies in the corners of her eyes. "I'm so sorry, Michel," she said in the voice she had used that night on the beach when she apologized for trying to shut me out of her life, and because I didn't want to know if she was sorry for what lay in the future or what was already done in our past, I only replied, "We better find a gondola and take our luggage to the hotel. Where do you want to stay?"

"I want the finest suite at the Danieli," she stated firmly, taking my arm and steering me back to the railway station. "Higgy says it's the absolute best place to stay."

"Oh, Higgy does, does he? Well, when we get back you can tell him Charles Dickens agreed with him," I laughed.

Higgy? Well, why not. Mae could bring out the light side of anyone, even someone as stiff and uncompromisingly boring as Ronald Higgenbothum, when she choose to turn her charm on to its brightest caliber.

"Did you know Dickens?" Mae asked, after our luggage had been ferried across to the gondola station on the Santa Lucia side of the canal and we were seated side by side in the prow of a long, red and gold, motorized gondola. Night was falling down swiftly now, like a child's sleep.

"No," I answered slowly, "but I knew Lord Byron. I once rode horseback with him and that poet Shelley on the Lido before it became a tourist trap. We picnicked there and spoke of politics, not as ordinary men do, but as poets can. Just because I am seven centuries old, Mae,

197

doesn't mean I have known all the famous men throughout history."

"I know, but you've known some. You've been here before then, many times?"

"Many times," I agreed.

"Show me it all, Michel," she sighed, hugging my arm close to her small breasts. "I want to see it, hear it all."

My heart swelled with love and my gratitude, and in that instant I would have forgiven her even my murder at her hands. "What do you want to see first," I asked, smiling hugely with delight.

"My room at the Danieli," she laughed. "I want to make love with you and then I want to see St. Mark's square."

I took her ridiculous hat off and threw it into the canal. The gondolier joined our laughter as the yellow straw and lace atrocity floated away with the last of the daylight.

****

It was winter, and it was snowing, and it was night, but the Piazza of San Marco was not deserted. We stood before the huge doors of the entrance to the church and Mae bent her head back to stare up at the painting of Christ Triumphant below the first of the arches that framed the door. "I want to go up there," she said, pointing, "up there, where those horses are."

"Later," I said. "There's too many people about now and the guided tours are long since over. We can't just walk in at this time of night, you know."

"Michel," she chided me, grinning, "we're vampires. We can do anything."

"Later," I said again. The truth was that the smell of blood from the people in the square, magnified as odors are by cold, was strong enough to make me nervous.

There seemed an inordinate amount of people wandering over the snowy Piazza for nine o'clock on a winter's night and we had not yet fed. I began to play at being a tour guide take my mind off the aroma of cool, living flesh, and warm blood, and to move us farther from the main crowd clumping up in front of the church. I took Mae's arm and led her around the side of the square.

"The Church of St. Mark," I began, "is also called the Golden Basilica and it was begun in 829 when a group of nuns dedicated to Saint Zaccaria ... "

"I don't want a history lesson, Michel," Mae said, stamping her pretty boot in the snow. "I want to go up to the loggo and see the horses."

"Loggia," I said. "Later. After we feed."

The wind had shifted again and the smell of living blood was washing over us in great throbbing waves. I felt oddly out of control of myself, as if I were newly made, and feared that if we did not leave the square immediately I might do something very foolish. Mae was set on touching the horses, though, and I knew that only an invitation to the hunt would budge her. "After we feed," I said again.

"Yes," she breathed. "We'll feed together. It's been so long since we hunted together." As I had hoped she would, she began pulling me toward the canal and the dark alleys beyond the church, the horses forgotten. We left the square, walking down to the canal, choosing one of its five bridges at random.

Venice had retained its quiet majesty, I thought, its timelessness, despite the inroads of progress ... motor taxis and gasoline driven water buses sharing the canals with hand-poled gondolas, dreary Minolta toting tourists

199

whirring and clicking in St. Mark's Square despite the late hour and frost laden night, acid rain eating the five bronze horses that attracted Mae so above its entrance ... it was still medieval in its feel, and its architecture, a maze of tiny streets and narrow canals.

It was still easy to become lost there, easy to lose your way, and that night, because Mae and I were abroad in those warrens, easy to lose your life in the dark, twisting alleys.

I will not lie and say that the killing disgusts me or any of those other fables mortals wish to believe about us. I enjoy the hunt, I enjoy feeding, I enjoy what I am. I have never regretted my immortality, or wished for another life than that which I lead.

What I do not enjoy is unnecessary brutality or the nonessential evocation of terror in the victim. Mae knew this; it was why we rarely fed together, for she enjoyed too well ladling horror upon her human prey, as if it were a sauce she marinated death with, to increase its flavor.

That night she spotted a couple, a pair of mimes, both young, walking with their arms about each other and laughing, in a small street set back a good way from the canal.

Red brick buildings loomed on either side of us and the snow echoed where the boys stepped. It made no sound at all where Mae and I walked.

The two of them, slightly drunk, singing a bit, speaking of some girl with friendly rivalry, reminded me of Tony and myself long ago, outside the Wet Roe, another tavern in another city, another century. Despite my hunger, I suddenly felt pity for the boys, and wished them safely gone to some other street.

"Not them, Mae," I whispered, but she was already upon the boys, with a twist of her eyebrow to me, luring the taller one with her amber eyes and long, white hands, to follow her into a doorsill.

The other young man stared after his friend without moving and I took him quickly from behind before he could focus on what was happening in the shadows of the doorspace and raise a scream of protest.

Mae grasped her painted mime by his thick, black hair and sank her teeth into his throat before his daze of wonder at her beauty could become terror. I knew she extended him this
kindness for me, and I was grateful once again, wilfully forgetting that she had taken him despite my wishes.

Afterward we made a hard, cold love, standing in the doorsill and I tasted the blood of her kill from her lips, as she did my own from mine.

****

"Mae, come down from there," I hissed.

The gilt bronze horse mounted above the first arch, but below the second, on the facade of the Basilica, gleamed in the soft electric lights and Mae, mounted on the fourth one, the one farthest from me, glowed like a ghost upon its back.

"Not until you tell me about the horses," she teased.

"Someone will see you," I said. "Come down here and I'll tell you about them."

"What will your someone do, Michel?" she pouted. "Arrest me? There's no one out now anyway. Tell me about these horses. I do so love horses."

It was the type of absolutely absurd statement Mae like to end an argument with (she had never seen a live horse in her entire life), but I succumbed. She was right. The square below us, at nearly two on that winter morning

201

was deserted.

"They were originally cast in Greece, or at least that's what the history books say," I began, settling my buttocks carefully on the ice ledge of the loggia. A fall wouldn't kill
me, but it would certainly make me uncomfortable for a few days while the broken bones repaired themselves.

"Notoriously poor sources of historical information, those history books," Mae giggled as she quoted one of my fondest sayings.

"Yes, well," I continued, "they were taken from Greece to adorn the triumphal arch of the Emperor Trajan in Rome. When Constantine moved himself, the seat of the empire, and the
Christian religion from Rome to Constantinople, he took the horses with him to decorate his Hippodrome. During the Fourth Crusade, the Venetians took a bit of a detour on their way to the Holy Land and attacked, then sacked, Constantinople, and brought the horses back here."

"Why did they do that?" Mae asked, sliding off the statue's back and dusting snow from her hands.
"Christians sacking the Christian center of Eastern Europe? You see, I do know a bit of history, Michel."

"The pope wanted to know the same thing. The Doge then, I forget his name, said something like `Well, you see, we are Venetians first and Christians second and looting Constantinople was a good deal for Venice.'"

Mae laughed. It tinkled out over the square and echoed down the canals until I thought the icicles above us would fall to shatter on the pavement below, waking the city.

"How wonderful," she cried. "What happened then?"

"Nothing happened then," I answered. "Let's go

202

back inside. It's cold out here. I'm cold." And God knows, undead flesh is cold enough without added environmental factors like snow, ice, and wind chill factors.

"There must be more," Mae insisted, tucking her arm into mine.

We reentered the church and began to stroll through its darkened nave, seeing it in the darkness far more clearly than humans could in the light. "The legend is that every time the horses are removed from the facade above us, an empire falls," I said. "Look at this marble, Mae."

I stopped her before the altar and pointed to the green veined floor beneath our feet. "It's called La Mar, not only because of its color being so like that of the sea, but also because the uneven settling of the building has given it a wavy look, like waves."

"It's lovely. Now don't tease me, Michel. Tell me about the empires that have fallen."

"I'm not teasing you," I said. I was. "I thought you didn't want a history lesson."

"I don't. And I don't want a guidebook tour of this church either. Tell me about the legend. I love legends."

She moved away from me and seated herself on the marble slab, where rumor has it, Frederick Barbarossa knelt to Pope Alexander III on July 23, 1177. Before my time and I wondered if should want to hear that legend. Probably not. No ghostly doings there.

I sighed, but from the happiness, the joy of having her near with her attention on me and not shared out with others, even others as dear to me as Tony had always been, and as Ronald was becoming.

"The first time they were removed from the facade was in 1814," I said, seating myself across from her. Her eyes sparkled at me, like frozen topaz in the darkness. "Napoleon had them taken down and transported back to France."

"Well, even I know what became of Napoleon. Any others?" She wrapped her arms about her knees and rested her chin on her elbows, staring past me to the altar.

Her posture was a sudden false note, a warning of something wrong. Her eyes became pensive and darkened. I had not seen her look like this, or sit in that position, knees to chin, since she had been human.

"The next time was in 1918 when the Venetians removed them because of the allied bombing," I said, watching her carefully. "They didn't want the horses damaged. They are supposed to be the only real example of Roman bronze chariot horses in existence, even if they were cast in Greece. The Austro-Hungarian Empire fell that time. The last time was in 1940 when they were again removed so they wouldn't be damaged by allied bombing raids and the Italo-Ethiopian Empire fell."

"I didn't know Ethiopia had an empire," Mae said idly. "Let's hope they never take the horses down again. Who knows what might happen? Nuclear war, I suppose, and then what happens to us?"

I shrugged. Was this what was bothering her?

Thermonuclear war is a persistent worry to us, for even a vampire is not immune to sudden immolation in the heart of a nuclear fireball, but as a grounds for whatever was causing Mae to withdraw into herself, it didn't feel right. Like a superstitious child, I began to wish I had never told her the falling empires legend. Perhaps she would not now be watching me with those hidden eyes if I had made up some little fable of treasures secreted in the horse's inaccessible tails or something equally silly.

"What was Rome like?" Mae asked then, hugging her knees tighter.

"I wouldn't know," I said, moving closer to her. I pointed to the altar. "That slab of granite the altar rests on is said to be the same one John The Baptist was beheaded on. I imagine Rome was as violent, as deadly a place to live in as Judea in the first century A.D., or as living now is wherever we are in the world." I reached out to touch her hair. It was still wet with snow. "What is the matter, Mae?" I asked softly.

"Are there any of us who would know?" she answered. Not an answer at all.

"Would know what?" I stalled, but I knew.

I thought I knew, too, why she was always pursuing those poor creatures who share our unlife, but who are as unlike us as humans are: the ragged army of blood drinkers called vampires

that live in sewers and condemned slums and the rusted out hulks of cars in junk yards, in New York, London, all large cities, even Venice.

It was like a mental disease common in some of these young ones, a desire for a past, or for ancestors, somehow, a lineage, or maybe just jealousy at all they thought they had lost by being newly made in their own century instead of one perceived to be more exciting and in the far past.

"Are there any of us who were alive back then? When John The Baptist was beheaded, when those horses were cast, when Jesus walked, when Ankhenaton built that city of his Tony loves so much? Do you know?"

"I don't know," I said after a moment. "The Others, it is said, are truly immortal. And it is said that

205

they are unborn, too, therefore it is possible that they have been always been alive on this earth and seen all things since the beginning of time."

Mae looked at me sadly. "And they will not speak with us, will they? They hate us, and we do not even know why, is that right?"

"Yes," I sighed. "Mae, the true and only curse of immortality is the endlessness of our existence. We must find things to keep us interested in continuing, but this curiosity about the origins of our kind will never lead you anywhere except to frustration. It is a question none of us will ever be able to answer, unless we chance to meet with some first-born being. Even if such a first-born exists, he or she is likely to be a solitary, like all the others of our kind you've tried to contact." I leaned forward and clasped her hands in mine.

"We are not a social demon, Mae. We may have a circle of companions, those we have created ourselves, usually, but even that is rare. When you have been among us a while longer, you will realize how rare Tony and Ana and I are, to have retained our love for one another through these many centuries."

"Even if I never find the answer," Mae said reflectively, "at least I will have used my eternity in the search, and will never desire to end myself from boredom or despair."

"Maybe so," I replied wearily. I could conceive of nothing that would ever cause Mae to tire of her existence.

With a little shock I realized that she was enough for herself; she would never wander the cities of the world searching for love, as I had, never give her blood kiss out of love, to create a thing of love, never contemplate death as an end to loneliness. When she transformed others, it would be to demonstrate her power over them, the power to give immortality to those who are dying, perfection to those who decay. Someday she would transform Fred, as she had tried to do Waldo, not from affection or love but to have a slave, an eternal admirer and the beauty of it was, the children she created would not have to remain with her to fulfill their function. Once a century, meeting in a city as near strangers, she would be able to weave her enchantment over them repeatedly.

She was not like me, I realized with a sharp, quick pain in
my heart.

Perhaps she was stronger in her destitution of soul, I weaker in my need to love and be loved in eternity. It was a depressing recognition.

"Come," I said. "Let's return to the hotel. Tomorrow we'll go to the island of the truly dead." I held out my hand to help her up. "It's called St. Michele and you have to be very, very wealthy to have your bones laid there."

"Why would I want to go there?" Mae asked, but she did so playfully, not indifferently or spitefully, as she would have done a month before; playfully, yes, but with eyes still folded in upon her thoughts.

"Because I have a story to tell you," I said. "About a woman I once loved and changed, as I have changed you. A story of the dangers of recklessness and being too sure of yourself. A warning, if you like, about the vagaries of human beings."

The dawn was beginning was to come up, washing in through the gothic arches, the high mullioned windows. It was going to be a bright, sunny day. One to sleep through, certainly, arms about each other beneath heavy blankets, behind blackout curtains.

"If you transformed her, why is she dead, lying in a

207

human grave?   What kind of immortality is this, Michel, when we may yet die a second time?"

"We'd better hurry back to the hotel, Mae," I said, watching the pearl and rose light creep through the cathedral nave, thinking of her delicate skin and how it smoked in direct sunlight.

She turned her eyes, too, toward the light and nodded.   "How many meters of mosaics do you think there are on these walls?   Isn't that an excellent tourist question, Michel?   Isn't it just the sort of question, my poor Higgy will clutter up his eternity with?" she laughed. I began to giggle, then to laugh loudly with her.

We staggered out into the dawn with arms about each other's necks, just as the mimes had walked together earlier in the night.

And that night, at its close, was somehow redeemed for me, by that laughter, our closeness, her sweet kisses in that glowing dawn.

CHAPTER 12

She rests, she sleeps, her stone head and stone shoulders nestled high upon the stone pillow.

Her face is turned toward us, the brilliant moonlight tracing her stone lashes, shadowing stone breasts that peer modestly from beneath a stone chemise.

There is a date and a name engraved in the lentil above her resting place, but the date is a false one, carved there over a hundred years ago by myself.

The truth is that I buried Sonia here in 1716. It is the statue that was laid in the shallow grotto in the 1880's and at the same time, I carved the date above her head.

I asked the stone mason to sculpt her lying thus, with head fallen to the side, arms limp beside her, so that she would resemble in this stone death, how I found her all those years ago, lying at the bottom of the staircase in our home beside the Rio S. Vidal canal, her neck broken.

Between her slender stone waist and her arm, I have set flowers in a riot of blue and yellow and red and gold and white, a blanket from elbow to shoulder. The flowers are all silver in the moonlight. Mae's eyes are silver in the moonlight. Only the blood tears that fall upon the stone fingers of my Sonia have color in this night, and they are black, like age and death and night.

I, too, am rigid as the stone. Mae has reached out to cradle my hand in hers, and I say, "I wanted to bring you here, to share with you this place and my memories, but not like this. I did not believe, with you beside me, there could still be so much pain."

She squeezes my hand comfortingly and I begin to tell her.

****

In 1714 Venice was beginning to wind down her life's clock as an empire.

Well, that is not quite true; Venice had wound down her clock already, she just could not accept it yet. It would be another year before the last possession she held in Crete would fall to the martial hands of the Turks, another 60 years before the Carne-Vale, the `flesh-farewell', now called Carnival, would expand to encompass over half the year as the Venetians strove to forget their economic and political defeats in the pursuit of endless, and delicious, pleasures.

In 1638, the nobleman, Marco Dandolo, had been granted a gambling concession by the Doge. He opened the doors of his personal palace, which stood next to the church of S. Moise and which stands there still, to those who wished to gamble, converting his family's winter quarters to a card room.

Gold was the primary impression one had upon entering these rooms, for they were done all in that lustrous color, from the geometric designs on the parquet floor, to

the heavily decorated
walls and ceilings with their renaissance moldings, paintings
and mosaics. One could only feel rich in those rooms,
even when he had lost everything gaming throughout the
night.

With so much gilt and gold leaf about, how could a
man, or his city, ever fall into true poverty? Thus it was a
popular place and most of Venice frequented it in those
years between 1638 and 1714. By 1714 it seemed as if all
Venice came to the card rooms to breathe in the gold and
the glamorous illusion of wealth and empire, and to gamble.

On July the second, 1714, I saw Sonia Szforcini
there.

I believed at first she must be a courtesan, for no
noblewoman would have appeared in the gambling rooms,
not even on the arm of her husband, in the Venice of that
time, and although the courtesans had been outlawed a few
years before, men still kept them privately, as wealthy men
keep mistresses in the twentieth century.

I searched the crowd that night to see who she
might be with, for she was too lovely for me to resist.
Thick, russet hair, wide chocolate eyes, skin like the milky
cast of cream on peaches in a white china bowl, an
improbably slender waist, and a full, rich laugh such as
Anne had had before Henry and his divorce darkened her
laughter and took her life.

Anne Boleyn was not so far in my past then, and I
still looked for her in every woman I met. In this
unknown beauty, I thought I could see what had been best
in Anne and my desire to possess her flared hot and new in
the cool night. I was instantly in love, and determined to
feed on her male keeper as soon as I was able to identify
him and then to replace him in her affections without delay.

When I could see no man familiar with her, and the

211

night was wearing thin down to the dawn, I finally asked the gentleman who sat beside me at the table, bereft of his last florin and quite cross about it, who she was.

"That is Szforcini's daughter. I can't imagine what he is thinking of, bringing her to a place like this. He must be hoping some man will pick her for his jilly. They do say he is completely without money now, but if you, Sir, are thinking of being her banker, let me warn you. The girl is said to be quite a minx and utterly uncontrollable." He laughed harshly and threw his cards down upon the table in an untidy, multicolored pile. "I, myself, seem to be without a single coin, as well. I bid you good night, Sir, and better luck than I have had with these games."

But I was already forgetting him, staring through the crowd at the glimpse of Sonia's dress moving down the hallway, and did not answer.

Over the next few nights I asked for, and was given, more information about the lady by those with whom I gambled at Dandolo's palace, still called so, though that worthy and visionary gentleman had long since been in his tomb.

I learned her name was Sonia, and I learned her father did have little control over her, though none could point with assurance to any man she given herself to intimately. She did as she pleased, when she pleased, defying custom, rules, and fashion, engendering gossip and envy, but no scandal.

She was, indeed, a rarity. A swan among banty hens.

I set out to make certain that she would be pleased with me.

When one is in love, one wishes to be loved in return. I began the tortuous process of courting the lady's favor by purchasing tickets for the box next to hers at La

Fenice, Venice's most famous theater of the time, and bowing to her when she entered in a rustle of satin and gold velvet.

I began to attend Mass at St. Mark's, and always sat within a few feet of her, smiling whenever she chanced to glance in my direction, which was often enough to convince me of her lack of devotion to the Blessed Mass.

I was completely visible whenever she came to the gambling rooms with her father and eventually, I met her brother over a friendly game of dice, lent him a small amount of money, and joined his Compagnie de Calza after a suitable period of acquaintance, and a few more small loans for which I never pressed repayment.

These Compagnie de Calza were clubs for the wealthy young men of Venice and because each club wore a different colored silken hose, they became know as the Stocking Companions. Rodolfo's club wore scarlet, a color that has always enhanced my cold, blond looks, and, as his companion, I was now able finally to inveigle an invitation to his home for dinner.

The Lady Sonia was everything I had been told she was. Strong hearted and highly intelligent, she ran her father a merry race to keep her barely on the correct side of respectability. Fully educated and even more well read than I, it was she who taught me all the ancient history I would pass on to Mae in the Basilica.

On a night full of stars and the soft lapping of canal water against the sides of her personal gondola, she began a conversation about immortality with me, quoting Plato, rather than Holy Writ, and when she paused to ask for my opinions on the matter, I offered her my gift.

She did not hesitate for a moment.

She ripped the high neck of her gown and flung herself at me, nearly knocking me over the side of the

213

gondola and into the canal in her eagerness.

We told her family we had gone to the mainland and there married. As sometimes happens, not often because of the difficulty of keeping even a thin veneer of normality, Sonia wished to remain living in her father's home. She wanted to be near her father and brother, to finish out with them their normal lifetimes, and at first, there were no suspicions or questions about the odd hours we kept, or the less explicable changes, particularly Sonia's now amber eyes.

If neither she nor I went out in the hot afternoons when the sun flounced off the canals like a sheet of white wax, well, it was because she developed headaches so easily now that she was (probably) pregnant and I was too devoted to leave her side.

If we only attended evening Mass with her father now, it was because he had grown so old, and needed our companionship, more than her brother, who always attended morning services.

If we stayed out most of the night and slept well into the afternoon, why that was because the Lord de Brissault was wealthy enough to do as he pleased, and wasn't Venice, after all, a gay city, a city that awoke at dusk to pleasure itself till dawn? My wealth, besides being an object of gossip, became an excuse to cover all our oddities.

Except for the change in the color of Sonia's eyes.

And no one ever spoke of that.

My Lord de Brissault and his lovely wife were too wealthy,
in a city full of noble families rich only in name and pedigree, and I was more than generous with my money. No one wished to offend by questioning the strange manner of our marriage, our odd hours, or the change in Sonia's eyes from deep chocolate to amber. Better to

214

whisper that she had undergone some new treatment in Italy then to risk cutting off the flow of largess from my hands.

I financed Sonia's family whenever they chanced to think they might want to try a new business venture or fix up the villa a bit. I lent money to Rodolfo's friends and forgot to pursue repayment. I gave vast sums to the Church, the City, and to any of the family's friends who were in need. People began to whisper that I was a bastard Medici, one of the family who ruled Florence as virtual tyrants, and it was thought impolitic to offend me on those grounds alone.

I could not really understand Sonia's desire to remain with her father and brother. It had been enough for me to keep a long distance eye on my own family until the last of them died in 1437, but if she wished this, I would not stop her.

They would, after all, die after some years, while we would go on forever. Soon enough, I told myself, I would have her company to myself and meanwhile, everyone was much too pleased with the advantageous marriage she had made to rock the gondola, so to speak, with rude questions and suspicions that all was not quite right in the Szforcini palace.

When Rodolfo married, I funded his honeymoon to Egypt and the Orient. When he died a year later of fever contracted in the Delta, I buried him in such style even the Doge was envious. I set money aside for his unborn child's education and supported his widow.

Old Enrico, Sonia's father, had new stables with Arabians brought in specially built conveyances from the Egyptian desert. He gambled each night at Dandolo's and consistently lost.

We gave lavish parties. We were the happiest

couple in Europe, everyone agreed. We lived like royalty without the pressures of royalty, people said, and we were so good to others in our own good fortune.

I was in love. I was completely content. My wife was beautiful, intelligent, and she loved me. We had unlimited monies. We were immortal. We had everything.

But Sonia began to mope, then to sit sighing in the windowseat staring out over the canal, then to raging about the city streets crushing skulls with her bare hands even as she wept.

I remonstrated with her repeatedly for her recklessness. I feared she would be seen, carelessly rampaging about as she was, committing murder after midnight.

The city began to grumble about the number of bodies appearing in the canals and alleys and there was talk of a citizen's watch to patrol the warrens at night. I had been asked to volunteer for the group, to keep a watchful eye on that section of the Rio S. Vidal beside which we lived.

Finally she stopped feeding.

After four days and four nights of abstinence, for I would not leave her to go and feed myself, I grabbed her forcibly from the windowseat where she sat and flung her against the wall, pinning her there.

"What is that ails you?" I howled. "Why are you acting like a mortal woman who pines for some silly bauble? Is it a child you feel your arms so empty of that you will not even feed? Is that it? I will steal a child for you, buy one, for God's sake!"

She began to weep. Women and tears. How they weaken a man. A vampire's tears, shadowed by the blood we drink, are the most heartrending of all, and I gathered her to me and smoothed her hair and kissed her eyelids and murmured my apologies. "Tell me, my sweet," I crooned. "Tell me why you are so unhappy, that I may attempt to right whatever is wrong for you."

"Are there no others like us?" she asked, still sobbing against my chest. My velvet shirt was beginning to feel a bit sticky against my skin from all her tears. It was doubtless ruined and I had been fond of it, the color being so flattering to me, but one's wife is more important than a shirt, I supposed with a sigh, so I lifted the bottom of it and wiped away her tears with it.

"Certainly there are," I cooed in my most soothing tone of voice. I stroked her hair gently and her sobs gave way to little hiccups and gasps. "I have two very dear friends in Europe I would gladly take you to meet. Is that all that is bothering you, my lovely Sonia?"

"I feared we were alone, yet I knew we could not be. Someone had to create you as you created me. I have been wandering the streets, looking into faces, thinking, you, or you, are you as I am? But they never are, and then I must smash their poor mortal skulls between my palms or die of my despair, and all you have been able to do is shout at me for my carelessness. Oh, Eric (for my name was Eric then), when can we meet these friends of yours?"

I smiled indulgently. This was a problem much easier to solve than I had feared and I, too, would be happy to see Tony and Ana again.

Preparations for our departure began immediately and Sonia, happy to be going to meet others of our kind, laughed and sang as she packed our baggage, just as she used to do before the depression came upon her.

We went to Egypt first. There we tramped along the tourist trails, Tony, Sonia and I. She was enthralled with the pyramids, the sphinx buried to its chin in sand, the

217

ruins, the mummies that were sold in the marketplace. Before long she began to ask Tony if he knew any vampires older than himself and me.

In Egypt, she said, where such antiquity layered the earth and the river and the streets where we hunted in the darkness, vampires more ancient than ourselves must also exist.

Tony answered that he had never met any of our kind in Egypt at all. He had never even felt the presence of others, he said, but later, when he and I went out for the kill alone, leaving Sonia curled up with a book on Egypt's history, he confided to me that he had often sensed another being somewhere in the black, Egyptian night.

"Not one of us," Tony said, a small frown marring his upper lip. "It's something not alive and yet it walks. Or perhaps it is something living, but not in the mortal sense, for it has never died as we have."

When I asked him his impression of the being, he could say only that he did not feel it was a threat to him personally, as long as he stayed far from it. And, thus it was that I first heard of the Other Immortals.

Sonia and I passed on to Holland and I introduced her to the Countess, of whom my wife again asked if there were others older than Ana or myself.

Ana rearranged her skirts, reached out to grasp the thigh of her human boy lover, and said blandly, "I do not know any such myself, but it would seem logical that should be others older, wouldn't it? Seeing as how we are immortal."

The boy's eyes turned lazily to me. They were hungry eyes, chips of sapphire in a fair, milk-fed face. Ana must have promised him transformation in return for his services. It was a lie, of course; she had never again given immortality after learning of the Fear Year, but her cruel

218

promise kept her paramours faithful and silent.

"Aren't you curious to meet them?" Sonia insisted.

"No, child, why ever should I wish to? The man who made me was a thoroughly evil creature and I am quite as happy not to have seen him again. He was older than I. Obviously."

"But perhaps not older than Eric," Sonia mused, tapping one fang with her fingernail. "Eric, what about the man who changed you?"

"It was a child," I said. "A female child. A member of my parish who I saw birthed, christened, and finally buried. I, too, have never seen her since the night she made me. It was a sloppy business, Sonia, this making of new ones back then. It was done from lust and hunger and not from love, as you were made. There was no desire, on either side, for Ana or I and our creators to bind together afterward."

"It just seems to strange to me," Sonia complained, sinking her chin into her palm. "I don't understand why you have so little curiosity about our history, our origins."

"De Brissault has always been a singularly incurious man," Ana said smoothly. "It truly is an unimportant thing to idle after, this history. As like as not, my dear, we have no history. Only centuries of bloodlines passing down, each to each. Savor your time with Eric. Create a history for yourselves."

Ana was always so intrinsically wise. The wisest of us all. I wonder why I still have not learned to listen to her when she speaks.

"If I may," the boy said. Ana looked at him in amusement and nodded.

"Man always searches for cause and a reason for being. Meaning. We believe God created us. Perhaps Satan created you, to despoil mankind."

219

Ana laughed, rocking back and forth among her cushions. "And who created Satan, my precious love?"

"Why, God," the boy said.

"Then God created us," Ana said. "That is our origin, Sonia. God has made us, as He made all else."

"But why?" Sonia persisted.

"I do not know, any more than I know why He created the Other Immortals."

In spite of my well known lack of curiosity, my ears stood up at Ana's casual words.

"Other Immortals?" Sonia exclaimed.

"Yes, the Others," Ana said. She brushed her lover's face with her lips in a languid, indifferent way. "There are Others, although I have never seen them. I have only sensed their presence near me occasionally. They are not blood drinkers and they are certainly not friendly to us. I have felt only hostility from them myself and I take pains never to cross their paths. I do not think they were ever mortal at all, as we once were. Perhaps they are the gods of the pagans, still walking, though their worshipers have all gone to their graves.

"But I recently heard that they have begun to kill ones newly made when the vampire who has made them leaves them unprotected."

"You have heard that?" I asked, aghast at the implication for us who must survive that first year of a new one's life by assuring that they somehow survive.

"Yes, but I do not know if it is true," Ana said gently. "It just seems best to be careful when giving the Blood Kiss and to avoid meeting one of these Others under any circumstances."

Sonia did not care about other immortals, about gods. And once she had seen Ana and Tony, she lost interest in other vampires as well.

Now she knew we were not alone and not freaks, though we might be monsters, her interest turned to bloodlines. In the twentieth century she would have made an excellent geneticist, but in 1715, no one had yet envisioned such a science though the breeding of hounds and horses and roses for the best traits of their predecessors had been carried on for centuries.

Ana's eyes were a glacial blue, more white than blue, and quite striking. Tony's, Sonia's and mine were amber. I am unobservant, as well as being criminally incurious, and I swear I had never noticed until Sonia pointed out to me that Ana's eyes were not golden like mine because she had been made by someone other than myself.

"It's the bloodline," Sonia said, over and over again. I couldn't see what was so fascinating about all this, especially since it didn't explain why she and I cast no reflection in mirrors while Tony did (an oddity that did interest me), but she was happy again and therefore I was happy again.

She ceased idling after some history of vampires she felt must exist. Now she asked insistently why a blond mother and father would produce a blackhaired child, or how blue eyes on her father's side and green ones on her mother's side had produced her own lovely chocolate eyes, questions that seemed so foolish to me that I hardly knew how to answer her. And she asked me why neither Tony nor Ana had created another as mate for themselves as I had done.

"Ana has never believed in love," I explained. "She believes only in infatuation and the satisfaction of the flesh and its desires."

"And Tony?"

"He has tried to capture love as I have done with you, my sweet." I pulled her down on the fireside bench,

221

enveloping her in a tight hug, and she settled into the crook of my arm. "He changed a woman back in 1430, but she left him after the first year. He changed another in 1560, but she also left him. He also transformed his sister, but she disappeared some 150 years ago while in Africa and we feel that she is dead."

They always leave. Or we always lose them, I thought and shuddered in a sudden chill of fear for Sonia. The fear thundered out of nowhere, sweeping into my heart like ice on the walls of my vessels.

But I would not lose her, I assured myself, looking down into her calm face, leaning forward to kiss the sweet, bowed red of her lips. The fear receded, then vanished. Just vapors, like breath in the coldest part of the night, I sighed.

"Then there are many of us."

"I am sure that there are. But we are a solitary race of beings," I said. "Love does not last with us." And felt the fear beginning to prickle along my arms and back again.

"I will never leave you," Sonia whispered urgently, wrapping her arms tightly about my neck. "I will never cease to love you."

"Nor I you," I answered.

And that is the truth. I have never stopped loving my lost Sonia.

We returned to Venice.

Months passed and things seemed as they had been before the melancholy had gripped her. If she had changed in any way it was only to become more gay, more involved in our life together. We hunted together, attended the theater together, had dinner parties, and on the anniversary date of her transformation that marked the end of the Fear Year, we gave a masque for the entire City that lasted two weeks.

But then she began to evidence restlessness again and with it came the carelessness, the reckless kills. I tried to speak with her about it, but she brushed me aside as if she hated me. One night I came home from a business meeting (for unlimited monies do not grow on almond trees) to find her in our bedroom, slowly feeding on a girl of about ten years of age, while the child's identical twin stood frozen in horror against the far wall. They were the daughters of a high city official who had attended our masque not many weeks before, and the only twins in Venice.

"What are you doing?" I hissed, grasping her throat and throwing Sonia back upon the marchpane of the bed. The twins looked me with the eyes of drowned animals and I swiftly snapped both their necks.

"Why have you done this?" I raged at her. "What were you thinking of? We shall be very lucky if we do not have to flee the city, you foolish, wretched bitch. You know who they were. Do you think their deaths will go uninvestigated? Unavenged? Ah, God, Sonia!" I screamed in the excess of my frustration and pain.

I threw the bed pillows against the windows. I was afraid I might kill her, so I smashed our furniture instead.

"They were twins," she said, appealing to me for understanding. "Identical bloodlines."

"You are insane," I roared into her tear stained face. I gathered the children up, wrapped them in the velvet hangings from the bed and bore them from the house, too angry to care if I were seen lugging this unlikely burden through the crowded streets.

It was the season of the Carne-Vale and all about me wore strange masks with feathered eyeholes or the horns of beasts sprouting from their temples, or bloody mouths grimacing black in the torchlight. The sounds they

223

made, both with their voices and with musical instruments, were distorted, colorful screechings and sighings, as if after donning the masks and costumes they had found themselves doomed forever to live as these animals they had only meant to pretend to be for a little time.

Trapped. We were all trapped in some manner, by our very natures, vampiric and human, and the sad mixture of the two.

I consigned the children in their rich velvet shroud to a deserted gondola on the far side of the city. I could not resist a small prayer for their peace as I turned away, though I no longer believed in a benevolent Father In Heaven.

Someone would find their bodies, return them to their father, and Sonia and I, with much pomp, must make a show of traveling to London for holiday within the week. It would be a century or more before we could return to this, my favorite city, and anger against her flared in my bones again.

I returned home through the great festival of the Venician streets. Sonia was as I had left her, lying on the marchpane, sobbing weakly.

"Clean yourself up," I commanded. "Wash the blood from your face and change your dress. You have dribbled onto it."

She did as I ordered. As she dressed, my rage began to fall away from me, like clots of blood from an old wound.

She was mad. There could be no other explanation, I decided, although I had never known a vampire to become so before, yet it must be true and I must care for her. I had created her, I loved her. I was responsible for her, and aside from this madness with bloodlines, she was reasonable enough yet, could be reasoned with, I thought frantically, must be reasoned with somehow.

When she had finished dressing, she came and stood before me, her posture both defiant and subservient.

"You must never do such things again," I said quietly, taking her hands in mine. "You must never endanger us like that again."

"What danger?" she pouted. "We are immortal."

"Not always," I whispered. "We can be destroyed. We can cease. If humans begin to suspect our presence they pull out their wooden stakes and heavy chains and garlic corsets and sometimes, the Goddess Fortuna aids their endeavors, and we are killed."

"Impossible," she laughed contemptuously. "We are immortal."

I shook my head, grinding the small bones of her hands against themselves and she cried out at the pain.

"We are immortal compared to them," I said, "but we still feel pain, my Sonia. We still need the life of the blood to exist. I have heard the Inquisition in Spain kept a vampire chained in a darkened cell for many years, until he had starved to nothing but a mummy's bundle. Do you want that to happen to you? To me? We can still be killed, Sonia. That is what the Inquisitors did best, snapping our necks as I did those of the children tonight. Do you want to die like that? You will be killed, Sonia, if you do not restrain your madness. They are weak and we are the stronger, but you can still be killed by them. How can I convince you of this?" I crushed her hands yet tighter in my agony to make her understand. It caused me pain to hurt her, and it made me angry once again.

"I only wish to discover how physical traits are passed among the generations," she said in a small voice, her head bowed over our clasped hands. "It is in the blood, I know it is. If you would only help me in my investigations, Eric. Please," she begged, lifting her eyes to mine.

"Investigate all you wish," I said in disgust. "But do so without this foolish recklessness. Be cautious and wary. Alert no human to our presence or, I assure you, much blood will be spilled and not all of it will be human blood."

"Where are you going?" she cried as I crossed the room and flung open the bedroom door. "To celebrate the Flesh Farewell," I answered. "Don't worry, my darling Sonia. I could never leave you." It was a simple truth and it angered me the more that I should have to reassure her of it again.

I moved among the crowds that night, allowing my anger and pain to goad me into acts every bit as reckless as Sonia's had been as pain, guilt and rage won over my better sense.

Near dawn I returned to the villa, exhausted, bloody sweat streaking down my forehead and into my eyes, gorged with too much blood taken too quickly. I vomited a great, clotted puddle of it on the step and leaned for a moment against the stout wooden doors of the Szforcini villa, weeping helplessly. Finally I reached out and pushed open that front door ... and saw Sonia lying at the bottom of the staircase, her neck askew only slightly, her eyes closed, the fingers of one hand trailing on the terracotta tiles.

He stood silently in the shadow of the library door. Old Enrico. Her father.

We stared at one another and I heard his thoughts, like heavy heartbeats, pounding in my head.

He knew.

226

He knew his daughter was a slaughterer of children, his son-in-law a demon who had made her so in blood and madness.

Her careless hunting, her hubris, Tony would have said, had aroused his final suspicions, but it had been the change in her eye color that had first caused him to wonder, to follow, to watch.

He wanted to me to know all this. I did not have to suck it from his mind. I was not eavesdropping on the confession of his heart, as he had eavesdropped earlier outside our bedroom door. He wanted me to know it all, because he wanted me to live with the memory of what I had done to his family, with the agony of my loss of Sonia, the pain of separation and loneliness. And he wanted me to know that if not for my words to her tonight, he would never have known how to destroy his daughter.

He believed he could kill me as easily as he had her. Looking into his eyes I saw him come up behind her, push her. I saw her tumble down the staircase, heard her scream, in his memory, saw her lying stunned at the foot of the stairs, and her father coming slowly after, taking her head in his hands, those large hands that once had been so strong, but which now shook with an old man's weaknesses, strong for just the moment more he needed them to be, twisting her head until her neck snapped as dry and clean as the twins' had in my hands hours earlier.

He believed I could be as easily destroyed, but he did not want to kill me. He wanted me to remember. He thought that a more fitting punishment and he was right. I lowered my head and heard him take a step toward me.

"Never a viler thing happened in this house, than the night you fell in love with my daughter, Monster," he said quietly. Then he turned away, shuffling into his library, closing the door silently.

I slumped to the floor beside Sonia. I took her head in my lap. I kissed her lips, now blue with death.

What happens to us when we die? I wondered dizzily, patting her cheek, my tears rinsing her open eyes. Did we pass on to whatever awaits mortals in the normal course of death, heaven or hell somewhere, or nothingness, perhaps?

Or was there a special place for the physical souls of the un-dead? Some transcendental net where we were caught and struggled, unable to leave our useless bodies, and unable to repair the gross damage of a torn spinal cord, ripped nerves?

Were there endless ages of awareness without movement, without the feeding, growing weaker and finally `dying' only when our bodies passed into dust? Where was Sonia now, and if still in her body, for were we not nothing more than body? where would she be when that body had rotted away or was burned in the crematorium? Would her soul be freed? Was there even such a thing as a soul for us? For anyone?

I had never thought of these things before and I have not thought often of them since then. They are questions I cannot answer and I have no time in my eternity to waste on unanswerable mysteries.

****

"I am sorry," Mae sobs, standing to embrace me.

"It was long ago," I say. "I did not know it would be this painful to recall."

"You loved her," she whispers, raising her eyes to mine, those amber eyes that are my only mirror for myself. "Do you love me as much?"

I do. I love Mae more, and with greater passion,

than I have ever loved anyone, and suddenly what I have told her seems no longer a private burden for me alone to bear.

Love does that. Halves the sorrows. Increases the joys.

That is why it is such a necessary thing, for mortals and vampires alike. That is why, needing love so greatly, I could look into her eyes, the bloody tears streaking down her cheeks, and believe, because I must, that it was an answering love for me that I saw there, even as she said, "Poor, poor Michel. How unlucky you have been in the choice of your lovers."

CHAPTER 13

"Today I want a history lesson, Michel," Mae cried, stretching as a kitten does, with complete abandon and an almost disgusting display of exuberance for just past sunset of an evening. Her body, so like that of a young boy, lithe and androgynous, swirled among the rich furnishings of the Danieli's most expensive suite, fingertips raised to graze upward to the farthest height those small toes could take them.

Truly disgusting exuberance considering how late we had been up the previous afternoon. Still, all that upward movement of her body was causing a rising in a part of mine, and I threw a pillow at her.

"Confounded wench," I muttered, "get thee back into this bed at once."

She came, of course, and afterward sighed against my belly some trite words of love and fulfillment that made my heart beat too fast and my eyes tear with gratitude.

Mae had changed since our coming to Venice, just as I had hoped she would, changed again into the woman I had loved enough to risk even the Fear Year and its possible final death.

She was attentive to me, she was loving toward me. She was tender. She was acquiescent.

And I, as Tony would have said, had he been there to see all this, was being a sap.

In my gratitude for her devotion, I was failing to ask myself why she should have changed so quickly and so completely: why, to state it plainly, did she desire to please me now, when she had not since her awakening?

"Come on, Michel," she said at last, taking a fold of skin on my lower belly between her teeth and nipping it. "I want one of your history lessons."

"Before dinner or after?" I teased, sitting up and punching the one remaining pillow into a comfortable lump behind my back. She snuggled into the curve of my arm. Her hair smelled like sunlight on clean snow.

"After."

Of course.

I had never met a vampire as avid for the hunt as Mae. But then, I reminded myself, I hardly knew any other vampires, as talking of Sonia a few days before had so distressingly demonstrated.

Mae, who seemed to be developing a rather disturbing ability to read my mind, said, "Are Tony and Ana and Dickie the only other ones you've known?"

"Is that the history you want to hear?" I moaned. What was it about my women and this question? I had never wondered about vampires and where they came from, and how they could exist, and why they existed, not even when I had been first made. "I knew both of Tony's women, and his sister, of course. I knew an old man in Belgravia once who used to complain that the vampire who created him deserved to be staked for making a 73 year old

232

man into a vampire. Being undead was for the young, he said, for those with beauty and virility. I once met an entire family, in 1866, in New Orleans. Mother, father, grandfather, two sons, three ravishing daughters."

"More ravishing than me?" She giggled and nibbled at my earlobe.

"There has never been any woman to match you, Mae," I said seriously and then threw her share of the covers off her. "Go open the blackout curtains and tell me what kind of night it is out there."

She leaped from the bed, stretching again, and pushed the heavy velvet hangings away from the windows. "A million stars, my Michel," she sang. "A beautiful night." Then she abruptly fell silent.

"Think, Michel," she said finally, when I was about to go to her in anxiety at her silence. "Think. You and I will see this same sky a millennium from now. We will see the future. To never see the sun blazing upon a beach or feel its rays upon my skin again is no sacrifice. I would exchange all the daylight, if I had to, for this immortality. This not-life." She spun on her toes to face me. "And you, you never wonder about anything, do you? What life will be like in a hundred years, whether there are other groups of companions like ours, about those Other Immortals wandering the darkness somewhere."

Ah, so. That was her new obsession. The Others. The immortals who were not blood drinkers. The eternals who lived, without ever having died, that Tony and Ana had sensed occasionally as the centuries passed; who I had sensed myself once or twice in the past couple of hundred years. I had not mentioned my personal impressions of them to Mae, not even when telling her of Sonia. I wanted her to remain with me, not dashing off to chase after some other, different, brand of immortal.

"Certainly, I wonder," I said lightly, "but there's no sense in dwelling on things that we will either come to discover in time or not, as fate decrees."

"I don't dwell on them, Michel," she said casually, going to the closet. She thumbed through her things and finally chose a pair of black satin leggings, a see-through black silk blouse with a sunburst of rhinestones at the shoulder, and a pair of black spike heels. "But it's only human to wonder about the others out there. How they live, what they've seen."

She brushed her hair into a shining, metallic helmet around her face and applied a rich, red lipstick to her rich, full mouth.

Sometimes love feels just like a heart attack. A numb kind of pain, a presentence of love's death.

"Well, you're not human, so you might as well quit thinking like one," I said crossly. "Damn it all, where are my jeans?"

"You've never quit thinking like one."

Why did the casual tone of her voice set off my interior alarm? Why did I turn to her then and finally ask myself, after those two perfect weeks in Venice during which I had never questioned any of it ... why she was here with me, why she was so loving and careful of me ... why, in short, she was acting like the human Mae, and not the undead version of that Mae whose love I had tried to bring into immortality with me? For she was acting.

I knew it suddenly and completely.

My heart tightened again, but not from love this time. From something that might have been terror.

I remembered her on the steps of the brownstone saying, "What do you imagine you are? Do you think you are still human despite your death?" What did she want? To be a glittering monster without my restraining hand to

234

hold her to some semblance of humanity? To find some other who would allow her to indulge her cruelty, her hunger for fear-tainted kills?

She stood straight before the mirror, like a bronze statue done in golds and blacks and a smear of red. Because of the mirrored walls of the suite, I was confronted with a dozen statues of Mae, ordered and frozen in files, marching forever through the glass.

She was alone in that room.

I was a impotent ghost, haunting her.

It could not have been more clear to me in that horrific moment of stillness between us, but then, suddenly, the feeling, the insight, whatever it had been, was gone. I felt weak and sick. I wondered if she meant to murder me. I wondered if I should let her by killing her myself.

"Hurry and dress," she laughed. "I hunger, and after our feeding, you shall take me on a tour of the Doge's Palace in St. Mark's Square. Perhaps tomorrow we can visit the Devil's Bridge on Torcello? Oh, and I am thinking of writing a book. `A Vampire in Venice'. What do you think?"

"Why would you want to write a book?" I asked, shaking off the last of the feeling that the vision in the mirrors had laid over me. Suddenly finding my jeans seemed as earthshaking as discovering a cure for cancer. As a final resort in the search for my clothing, I pulled open a dresser drawer and found my jeans, just where they were supposed to be, neatly folded.

"I want to be famous," she sighed. What a dolt I was. Of course.

"Vampires don't get famous, Mae. Come on, I'm ready, let's go."

"Why not?" she asked as we stepped out into the night. It was wet still from earlier rain, and the drops fell from the roof tiles onto our heads like the afterthought of tears. "All the vampires in the books I've read lately are famous. They write, or are rock stars, movie idols ... "

I had lost my appetite and I wished she would stop chattering so I could think about what I had seen for that one terrible moment, rushing out of the mirrors at me, but she would not stop babbling on about Lestat and his crew and finally I said crossly, "That's fiction. You are not. One day, though it seems a long way off to you now, you will have to stage a death for yourself, so that those who knew you as Mae Remotti in this life, will allow you to disappear from memory with their passing. It's difficult enough to do when only a few dozen people are involved. Think what it would be like if hundreds of thousands knew your name, your face, followed your every step in movie magazines or rock-u-mentaries. Can you imagine Stephen King trying to disappear?"

I thought of Ronald Higgenbothum discovering what I was.

She knew the story, just as she now knew about Sonia's father. She knew how dangerous human belief in our kind could be; at the very least, how troubling the decisions to be made were when a human did uncover our reality. To live intimately with a mortal is foolish, but necessary sometimes, when the loneliness begins to eat away the caution, and the hunger to create another like yourself to love you and stay with you forever begins to gnaw at your good sense.

To become famous, to be intimate with thousands, to have all those people interested in your slightest cough, your past, your future, to have fans following you, photographers dogging you in hopes of a candid shot, was to invite discovery, was to invite the danger home into your lair with you. She knew it and yet she craved it.

Sometimes I thought she was modeling herself on Anne Rice's `Brat Prince' consciously.

I thought of reminding her of Ronald and the decision I had had to make about him, or about the night she had killed Rachel, but before I could articulate the words, she reached up and bit my cheek playfully, pointing down to the end of the alley, toward the canal.

"You're very grumpy tonight, Michel. Look, there's a couple of strong, young gondoliers. Shall we dine, my love? I'm sure you'll feel better after some fine, fresh blood." And then she was gone, the rhinestones at her breast flashing hot fire in the night and those poor gondoliers did not even have time to scream before she was upon them.

But she was right. I did feel better after we had fed.

In a city like Venice, where history is lying about everywhere to be picked up as shells are upon a beach, it was not abnormal for her to wish to make a history for herself, I told myself. On these streets, where the famous and the nearly so, had walked through long centuries, it was not unnatural for her to think of her own longings for an ersatz immortality made up of the worship of mortals.

When she had been dead awhile longer, she would lose interest in this newest desire for human fame, recognizing it for the meaningless moment it was, I assured myself, and so, replete with blood and the warmth of her fed body pressing against mine as we walked to St. Mark's Square, I felt much better indeed.

"It's an interesting question, though," Mae said, tilting her head on my shoulder, burrowing closer.

Mae had this disconcerting habit of picking up a conversation, sometimes days after it had begun, in midstride.

237

Usually I hadn't any idea which conversation she was attempting to finish and I always felt just a bit slow next to her, always a half-step behind her. She was streaking through unlife with the same velocity she had as a mortal.

I decided she must be referring to her earlier remark about what the world would be like a hundred years from now. "Absolutely," I agreed.

"These Others, who are immortal but have never died, must have some answer to our existence."

I groaned. "Not likely. Why should they?"

"Because they have been here since the beginning. They must have watched man himself come into being."

I grunted.

"But to live as an immortal in a mortal body can hardly be possible," she continued, as if she were still mortal and arguing again with me about whether vampires could actually exist. "I can't imagine it."

"Our bodies have changed," I said sharply. "We are no longer subject to disease. Only a broken neck or destruction by fire can now kill us."

"If we can still die, then even our changed bodies have not ceased to be mortal, Michel."

"All right, then, we are not immortal. Are you happy now? Look, there is the Doge's Palace, as ordered, and the Bridge of Sighs. Plenty of history there." I pointed to the bridge she had so wanted to walk across.

"Michel, be serious. We are immortal to all intents and purposes. You have lived for 700 years, so long that I cannot grasp it. So long that I cannot believe that I shall live that long. But, how do we exist in mortal bodies?"

"I don't know," I sighed. "But I do know why the Bridge of Sighs is named that. The prisoners used to be led across that bridge from the prison on this side of the canal

238

to the chamber of the inquisitors, there on the other side, for questioning and sentencing ...", but she was not listening.

She was staring up into my eyes, her face tight in that total concentration humans are never capable of, even in times of their greatest need or desire.

She was looking at my skin, my hair, trying to see how this miracle could be: an immortal life, in what had once been a mortal shell.

"It is the blood. Sonia was right, for it is our life. Without it, we cannot continue, at least not as animated beings," she whispered. "Yes, it is the blood, but we also must have a soul, Michel!" Suddenly she was leaping in the night, her hair aflame with moonlight and rain, twirling a dozen inches above the street in her ecstacy.

"The soul has somehow fused with the flesh, for only a soul can animate a body made for death, giving it life for eternity beyond imagining. Forever unchanged, forever unchanging, yet possessed of great strength and the ability to shapeshift, to fly. When we were alive, do you remember," she cried, her voice filled with eldrich power, "how in dreams our souls could fly, take on the bodies of others in visions? Only a soul can dream of life forever. Melded to the flesh, a soul could produce what we are, Michel." She paused. She drew a deep breath. She settled back down on the cobbled pavement, sparks seeming to fly from hair and eyes and that sunburst of rhinestones at her breast.

"What are we, then, Mae?" I asked, filled with awe at her.

"Earth bound gods," she said softly. "The soul made flesh."

I stopped walking and pulled her close to me. Moonlight ran into her eyes and shattered there. I have lost you, I thought, and did not know where the thought came from or why it pierced me so surely and with such keen torment.

"Michel, you're trembling," she whispered against my chest and I held her closer, while in my memory her form marched away from me in the mirrors of the Danieli Hotel.

CHAPTER 14

Things were different after that night by the Bridge of Sighs, different in a subtle way I could not specify, even to myself.

Mae continued as bright and glittering as ever she had been and I continued as muddled and confused as always, but something had come into our existence, or gone from it, something that rustled like a ghost in a child's closet after the parents are safely sleeping, and within the month we decided to cut short our visit to Venice and return to England.

Spring would be just brightening the English moors and I dreamed of sleeping in the scent of heather as it returned to the breezes that danced about my father's manor house.

On the evening we decided to leave Venice there was only one train out of the city, an old and ornate ten-car, of a type I had not seen since the 20's. Renovated for modern use, it nevertheless retained glamorous sleeping cars with glass vases filled with roses and tulips on the space of wall between the windows and an elegant, formal dining car.

Mae was enchanted, by the train itself and by the fact that we boarded in what she considered good company: there was a European prince, an American movie star, and an exiled shah's son waiting to entrain at the station with us.

"Don't worry, Michel," she said, patting my cheeks lightly with her gloved hands as we settled into the gold leather seats of our private car. "This thing moves so slowly we will easily be able to fly out as hawks, feed and return, without anyone missing us. I shan't nibble a soul on board, my sweet."

And she didn't, for the train was slow. It rocked along its tracks as trains used to do, and I relaxed on my bed, my hands behind my head remembering other train journeys with other lovers: Helena, Caroline, a delicious beauty in 1888 named Greta. It would take six days to reach Calais, from which we would catch a flight back to London, and although I hoped to spend these last lazy days alone with her, from our first night on board, Mae and I passed less time together than we had ever done, even while on the Queen Diana.

She easily charmed the prince, the shah's son, and, surprisingly, the female movie star. She spent much of her time in the lounge car with these three and the other four passengers ... I spent most of mine in the dining car, reading and sipping an excellent Chablis during the long nights as the train rocked and thundered across Europe.

On the fifth night, I raised my eyes from a page of Dylan Thomas' poetry to see a man, on the far side of the car, watching me.

I had seen him often enough before, but we had not spoken. He came to the dining car, as I did, after dinner was cleared, sat on one of the couches that lined the sides of the room, and read (always a paperback mystery) while smoking thin, black cigarettes and drinking thick, sweet wine. We had not so much as nodded to one another, but that night I felt his interest in me and, more, his familiarity, somehow, to me.

"Do we know one another?" I asked politely, laying aside my book.

"Not formally," he answered, his expression remaining serious. I wondered if he had ever smiled, and suddenly my guts knew what he was. His essence rolled over me in a stunning wave of color and polish and I started up from my seat, terrified.

"You have nothing to fear from me, Michel," he said, lighting one of his black cigarettes. "Come sit by me and try some of this wine. It is rather fruity, but still quite good."

"Why now?" I asked, seating myself carefully on the couch beside him and accepting a glass of wine from his exquisitely graceful hand.

"Why ever not now?" he shrugged and smiled.

It was the most beautiful smile I had ever seen. It moved over his face like awakening light, beginning in the deeply amber eyes, traveling down to the wide, mobile mouth, over the skin, dark as an Egyptian's, resting at the strong chin and high cheekbones. I ceased to be frightened of him.

"What are you?" I asked, awestruck and more than a little in love with him already.

"I am, as you say, an Other. An Immortal. One of a very few and perhaps, as your friend, Ana described us, a pre-Christian god." He laughed at the surprise on my face. "Don't worry. We do not listen to your conversations, nor follow you about, as spies do. I see her in your mind. I

243

see your entire life in your eyes, Michel. Or your soul, shall we postulate?"

"Why are you here now?" I asked again. "And why didn't I feel your presence as I have before when one of your kind was approaching?"

"You could not feel me, because I did not want you to do so. Truly it was me and none other you have felt near you many times in the past two centuries, but only when I have wished you to know that I was so close."

"But why?" I pressed, bewildered and beginning to be
frightened again.

"Because you are our children, Michel. Unwanted, unasked for, but ours, nevertheless, and for all eternity."

"But it is said that you hate us. Destroy us at every chance. My blood-child, Ronald Higgenbothum, had an encounter with one of you."

"Yes, unfortunate. She has been punished for her effrontery in approaching one of my offspring without my permission," he said, nodding into the smoke of his cigarette. "Oh, in the beginning, we did follow you, track your kind, destroy it wherever we found it. But we do so no longer."

I sipped on my wine, which was very fruity, and not at all to my palate. "I don't understand," I said diffidently.

"You are an abomination, Michel," he answered, somehow, surprisingly, with kindness. "You are creatures never meant toexist. Neither man nor god, despite the ideas of your pretty, treacherous, little Mae." He drank, too, from his wine, and toasted me with the nearly empty glass.

"And now?" I asked.

"Now we merely co-exist. My brothers and I avoid your kind, we send signals to let you know when we are nearby so that you will flee in the opposite direction, but we do not kill you any longer."

"Then why come to me?" I pressed. "For centuries I have felt your presence and fled, as you wished, in the opposite direction. Why appear now to converse with me of this?"

"I have lived since the beginning of this world. I awoke one evening in the sands of what you now call Egypt. I was as you see me now. I have watched you since your transformation. You were a good man in life, Michel. You remain, somehow, good in death. You do not deserve what has happened to you."

"What has happened to me?" I asked, truly baffled now and beginning to feel not a little irritated with his oblique riddles and evasions.

"Mae," he answered shortly.

Shocked, I said nothing.

He gazed at me sadly, poured us both another glass of wine and sat back, his arms extended along the length of the couch back, his hand lightly pressing my shoulder.

"Do you know the true definition of `vampire', Michel?" he asked. He did not wait for me to answer. "A vampire, in early times, was an evil spirit that took over the body of a dead human being, usually for sexual purposes, and reanimated it for a short time. It, like you, devoured the blood of living humans, but more it ate their bodies. The American Indians called this spirit a Wendingo, a cannibal demon. The Rumanians called it vampire. You are no more a real vampire than I am an actual god, Michel."

"What am I then?" I asked slowly. I thought of Tony, how he would love to be here now, speaking with this being, learning what I, who had never wished to know, was being taught. Tony would know the right questions to ask.

"You are an accident," he answered gently. "The creature born of a mating between myself and a body inhabited by one of those spirits. Our offspring was a creature such as yourself, a creature able to procreate others of its kind, as I cannot do. As true vampires cannot do, being only evil spirits that may temporarily reanimate a dead or dying body, and as you cannot do without great risk to yourself."

"The golden eyes," I said stunned.

"Yes, my eyes. Passed through centuries of generations from undead to undead."

"But Ana ... her eyes are blue. There were others than, besides yourself who did this thing?"

"Yes. I was the first, but the demons, once they learned of my offspring and their capabilities, began to seduce others of my kind."

"And what are our capabilities besides the obvious ones of shapechanging and living almost forever? Are we so special then?" I glupped the rest of the wine in my glass and he obligingly poured me more.

"Oh, certainly, you are very special. At first we saw you as a threat to ourselves. You drank blood to exist and were ten times stronger than we, physically. What if you should capture one of us, keep us captive, suck our blood into eternity? Would it make you as invincible and completely immortal as we? We did not know and so we began to kill your kind as often as we found them and could catch them by surprise. Won't you try one of these cigarettes, Michel?" He proffered a finely carved wooden box filled with black Egyptian cigarettes and I took one numbly.

"But then we realized that you were not the demon in another form, but that you were a creature, completely

246

new, retaining its human personality, its human hungers, its human slyness. In those times you bred new ones as quickly as rabbits still breed, and we came to know that we would never destroy all of you, so eventually most of us ceased to even try and none of us ever interfere with the children of another Immortal, unless asked to do so. Now we have no contact, your kind with ours, except occasionally. Like now."

"I am still confused," I confessed. "Why now?"

"Mae," he said again.

"Mae?" I repeated stupidly.

"She is not one of you," he said, and now he took my hand and held it comfortingly. "She laid in death too long to be one of you, Michel, and you have always known it, in your deepest heart."

I shook my head in denial.

"How long before she awoke, Michel. Think. How many days ... four, five? Had you ever known anyone to lie so long without waking before? Mae died, truly, when you sought to transform her. Her spirit was pushed aside by what now inhabits her body. It is clever. It imitates her well, for a small part of her remains in the memory of her body's cells. That memory teaches it, but it chooses only to learn the negative lessons her life taught her. It knows her fears, her hatreds, her desires, but it has none of her loves, her goodness; that innate goodness you fell in love with and wished to preserve with your Kiss. It is not Mae you have brought into your eternity. It is only the beast wearing her lovely face. And, be warned, it will not die when her body does so."

I looked at him, into those compassionate eyes, felt his hand tighten on mine. I realized suddenly that I was weeping.

She <u>had</u> loved me.

Ana had been wrong, despite her wisdom and her caring. Mae could have loved me, even now, had she been the one to awaken in that underground room of the Coral Castle.

"You asked me why I come to you now. I came because you are my child. Because, sometimes, we find one of you to love, one we wish had been created as one of us. So do I love you, Michel. And I have come to warn you. I have watched Mae closely and I fear the spirit now feels itself strong enough to cast you aside. Do not try to stop it from going. It is not Mae. Let it go its way whenever it wishes to leave you. Then search for another to love you, for there are many women alive who will gladly follow you into eternity and you may rest easy that no one of my kind shall ever attempt to harm the one who you may choose to be your mate in immortality, nor through her, you."

"No," I said, wiping my face on a fancy cloth napkin. It was streaked red with blood tears when I set it down on the table and the attendant would think one of us had cut himself on the
sharp, thin glasses when he came later to clean the car. All around us we leave clues to our being, and humans rarely perceive them. "No, I will not. It might happen again," I said wearily.

"That is unlikely," he said kindly. "There are not many of these spirits, though they have always and everywhere appeared. Not one of them had manifested itself in over a thousand years before this one came into your Mae's body. And I give you a further piece of advice, if you will be kind and wise enough to accept it. Do not change the next one so slowly, as you did Mae. Take her swiftly, as you did Sonia and Caroline and Tony and Ronald and Dickie. Give the beast no chance to rob you of what

248

you love by alerting it to a possible home."

He rose from the couch and smiled down at me, his sad and beautiful smile. Was he what the ancients had seen and named `angel'?

"Be wary of it, Michel," he said quietly. "Enough of the spirit of your Mae, as distinct from her soul, remains in the cells of her body so that the spirit is confused as to its own identity. I think it is unsure yet just what it is. If it should find out that it is not Mae, I do not know what it would do. Certainly it would be free of the limitations it places upon itself as Mae."

"Thank you," I whispered.

"Treat her no differently than you have done. Simply let her leave when she desires to go, then begin your life anew. Do not thwart it, for as I have warned you, it will not die, and may perhaps one day return to seek revenge against you personally." He leaned down then and kissed my cheek. "I will see you again, Michel," he said. "In years to come, I will visit again. Often."

"One last question," I said suddenly, urgently, as he turned to go. "What would happen if she were to die, to be killed? What would happen, I mean, to me in that moment? There are several months left before the end of the Fear Year."

"I do not know," he answered. "The body is Mae's, but it is not animated by your essence, your blood. On the other hand, your blood was used to create its perfection initially. I do not know if you are in danger of the final death should she be killed. It is perhaps best if you allow nothing to happen to her as long as she remains with you which I do not think will be long now. When she leaves, I will assign someone to protect her until your year is up."

"Thank you," I said again.

249

He walked from the car, pulling the heavy connecting doors shut behind him almost before I finished speaking the words, but his smile seemed to linger in the air for minutes after he was gone.

I did not see him again during the remainder of the trip, and did not expect to, and when we pulled into Calais, he did not disembark with the rest of us. I think he must have disappeared from the train the moment he walked out of the dining car, just as Mae had disappeared from not my heart, but from my life, instantly, with his words.

Though what walked beside me out of that train and into the rain of France wore her body, Mae had died for me at last, and only her memory still lived like a glassy wound cleaving my heart into gore streaked halves.

CHAPTER 15

Ronald had prepared a welcome home for Mae worthy of the Lady Anne herself.

A Lalique crystal bowl sat in the entrance foyer of my London flat, filled with amber liquid and awash in floating orchids in Mae's favorite colors of faint pink and peach. In the dining room he had set huge sprays of white lilac, her favorite flower, on every surface, bludgeoning out of blindingly red vases of too thin china.

"I missed you," he said simply to her, and she gently wrapped her arms about his neck and kissed him.

My heart broke for him, for he had never known of her cruelties, and still saw her as the beautiful woman I had pursued and won. I could not disillusion him, even now that I knew what she genuinely was. I would let her go from me when the time came and he need not ever discover that the Mae he loved had ceased to exist in the hour that I took her blood and stopped her heart on a terrace overlooking an ocean afire with torches in the night.

It was enough that I should know it and bear the

agony for both of us.

"We missed you, too, my friend," I said and bent to place our bags on the floor.

At that moment, Father Ray stuck his startling white hair around the hallway's bend. "Well, look who's home!" he shouted, as if it were completely normal for him to be in my London house without my knowledge.

"Ron," I said quietly, though I could feel my face heating up to a fine shade of plum with the newly ingested blood of recent feeding, "where is Tony? What is Ray doing here?"

"Tony had to return to Egypt," Ronald said stiffly. "He had some kind of emergency with his Afghans. At least that is what Ana said when she came to collect him, so I called Father Ray and asked him to come and stay with me. I knew you would feel easier if I had someone here to look after me."

An emergency with his Afghans? Was this a joke? Tony had left because of dogs, no matter how beloved? No. Absolutely not. Ana, alone had the power to persuaded him to leave Ron in a lurch, but not for the mere sake of vampiric dogs.

"We are grateful for your care of Ronnie," Mae said with cool politeness and the priest nodded happily. "Come, Michel. You have been so gloomy since we left Venice. It is no problem that Tony has left."

It might not have bothered Mae, but it troubled me as an ant bite had once itched and irritated when I had been as human and vulnerable as Father Ray. I had lost Dickie over this silk clad demon who smiled and laughed softly now with Ronald and his friend. I feared this abrupt leaving on such a flimsy excuse must mean I had lost Tony, as well.

Suddenly I remembered, and it was like a brilliant

252

stream of sunlight in my darkened heart, that I need never again be afraid of the Others killing my children, and myself through their

deaths. Ronald would have been completely safe, even if he had been left all alone in this house. The Immortal, whose name I only now realized I did not know, had so assured me, and I knew it was true.

We did not need Father Ray here to protect Ron and I did not want a human in my home for any reason. Not now. Not until this hell with Mae was over.

"We do thank you for your trouble, Ray," I said. "But I must ask you to return to America now that I am are back."

"Michel," Ron protested.

"I am sorry, Ron. I have some family matters to attend to and this is nothing an outsider can be involved in," I said firmly. I wanted to tell him of the Immortal. I had been bursting with the joy of telling Tony once back in London, but that would now have to wait.

"Can he at least stay the night?" Ron pleaded.

"Oh, yes, do be genteel, Michel, and let the Good Father stay the night," Mae said with such complete disinterest that I felt ashamed of her and of myself.

"Fine," I said. "Ray, would you mind if I used you as a servant and asked you to take this luggage upstairs for me?"

"Not at all, Mr. de Brissault," he smiled. "I believe Ronald has something he wishes to speak to you about in private this evening. Mae, would you care to join me in the study?"

"Thank you, no," Mae yawned. "I prefer some early hunting." She pecked me somewhere in the region of the chin and faded through the tiny space between door and jamb. As she never did things like this, I knew it was solely for Ray's benefit. She was showing off and perhaps hoping to frighten him, too. I frowned at the place where she had stood.

Ray winked at me, as if he could read my thoughts, hefted the luggage and disappeared into the depths of the house.

Alone with me in the hall, Ron took a newspaper from the entrance table and thrust it into my hands, then stood humbly against the fireplace, head bowed and hands deep in his pockets, as if I might suddenly howl and throw the cherrywood armoire at him.

The paper was open to the Arts section and showed a picture of several long-haired musicians grouped in a standard publicity still, surrounded by a black background and shining white guitars. The caption read, `Freddy Z and the TarotBoys play Wednesday through Friday at London's premier Acid House'.

"What the hell's an acid house?" I said. I felt an unfocused gratitude reading that article; it meant the time had come, so soon and so easily.

I would not much longer have to bear her close to me, contaminating my friends, disrupting our lives, and tears of relief filled my eyes. Ronald shifted uncomfortably from one foot to the other, misinterpreting my emotions.

"Who knows?" he said miserably. "I think it's a place where children take LSD and listen to kinky bands, but the important thing is that he's here and she'll want to see him."

"Then she will, of course," I said, tossing the paper back onto the hall table. It landed with the picture face-up. "She will go with him, too, you know."

"I can stop that, if you want," Ron said earnestly. "I can destroy him for you."

I shook my head. I remembered the mirrors and

the terror
that had marched out of them. I remembered the face of
the immortal, swaying in the train's easy roll. I was glad
my time as her ghost was nearing its end.

When she was gone, I could begin mourning my
real and lost Mae. The Mae who had died in my arms
before the French doors and the sea covered in fire.

****

But of course it is never as easy as that.

Mae did not mention that Freddy was in London
and I did not draw her attention to it; that would have been
out of character, and the Immortal had warned me not to
let her suspect that I knew of her true nature. Instead I
tried to keep our lives as they had always been and I
allowed Father Ray to stay in the house as well, because I
was beginning, against my will, to enjoy his conversation
and company.

He had a mind that fancied philosophical dialectics
and we passed many evenings discussing Christianity (as
any two priests might), Neo Platonic thinkers and, because
of Ron's newest craze, UFO's. It was restful to spend time
with them in the darkened study, sipping wine and lazily
drifting from subject to subject, while Mae hunted with
nightmare ferocity throughout London, coming home at
dawn covered in blood, sometimes with brain matter or
flesh matted in her hair.

I continued to take her about on sightseeing
excursions, too, as this was something we had done before
the train ride back from Venice and the Immortal's
revelations.

We took a boat from Westminster to Greenwich on
a stormy day and I walked with her through the park there.

255

Once I had meandered these same paths with Anne Boleyn and felt the same melancholy of impossible love.

At the gift shop, I bought Father Ray a silver headed cane, a replica of one of Henry VIII's favorites, because he had admired the original when we visited the Royal Portrait Gallery together.

Friday came and went. Mae and I hunted together on the banks of the Thames that night of Freddy's opening, and attended the Theater in the Strand.

Saturday. Sunday. Like blood dripping from slashed veins, time fell drop by drop, sounding as it fell, heavier and heavier upon my heart, like the slow ticking of a tired clock. I wanted her gone, yet did not know how I would live without even this false Mae by my side through the years to come.

On Monday night, he came.

No mistaking the fine, translucent white skin, the lustrous black light of his hair and eyes, the enhanced sexuality, the preternatural grace. Mae had changed him. She had been lost to me before the Immortal had come to me, no longer present, even as I had held her; waiting, simply for a time when she felt herself strong enough to leave me for him. And then I noticed his eyes. They were not amber.

They were glacial blue. Ana's eyes.

"Hello, Michel," he said, putting out his hand for me to take, his look a curious mixture of sheepishness and defiance.

"Hello, Fred." I managed to shake his hand. "How long have you been one of us?"

"Ana came to me the night Mae returned to you in New York. She saved my life, to understate the matter. Mae was trying to change me, and it just wasn't working. I was dying when Ana flew in out of nowhere and snatched me away. I tell you, as near dead as I was, I wasn't far enough gone. I've never been so terrified in my life as when that wonderful old woman swept me into the sky underneath her arm and I could see all Miami spread out below me like a magic carpet of jewels and mist." He shook his head in wonder at the memory.

"I'm glad she was there for you," I said woodenly, still astounded that Ana had broken her centuries long rule not to transform anyone, much less a stranger. Perhaps her hatred of Mae had been so great she was willing to save Freddy Z from her even at the cost of making him undead. I meant to ask her why she had done it, if I ever again had the pleasure of her company.

"Well, you know, I suppose, that I have come for Mae. She asked me to take her on tour with the band," he said and shifted about nervously, his eyes not meeting mine any longer. It came to me that his discomfort stemmed from guilt.

He thought he was stealing her from me, and if not for the revelation of the Immortal, he would have been. I thought then that I could have liked him under other circumstances and I felt a sudden pity for him.

He did not know what he would be leaving my home with upon his arm. I debated telling him about Mae, and knew he would never believe me. He would think me only a creature trying desperately to hang onto his lover, when in truth, I could hardly wait for her to be gone. It was him I was frightened for, and by extension, Ana, though he might never know it.

"Well, I hope there won't be too many hard feelings between us over this," he said awkwardly when I only continued to stare, without speaking, at him. He stuck his hand out again as if we had not yet shaken hands. "If not for you, I would never have had this gift," he continued, his fine vampire skin amazingly coloring with a deep, true blush.

I cannot bear this, I thought. But I will bear it. I will say nothing.

Mae slipped into the room and stood beside him. Her chin was up and set, her eyes blazing with something like triumph and something not a little like fear.

I remembered the Immortal's warning that all appear as normal and said, "Would you like me to fight for you?"

"It wouldn't make any difference," she said curtly. "I will leave you, even if you kill him. I am joining his group for the rest of their European tour. It was the deal we made. Immortality for Freddy. Stardom for me. I'm to be his new lead female vocalist, and I will be, even if you crush his head and snap his neck. I have a contract with the band. All I want from you, Michel, is a simple answer."

I saw a look of uneasiness pass over his face, the way his eyes cut to her at her apparent unconcern over his physical safety. "Answer?" I asked, astounded.

"Yes. Why could I not change Freddy? I tried to transform him as you did me, but I was only killing him until Ana came and took him away. I want to know why."

Fred, still a bit alarmed at her words, said nothing. Mae merely looked at me, her eyes closed and cold, waiting for my answer. Time ticked down to a final, stuttering halt and I turned away from them both.

I thought of my love for the living Mae, the Mae I had wanted to save from death and had hurried to it. I thought of Fred's love for her, of my love for the Mae we had both known and who no longer existed except as tiny

258

grains of cellular consciousness within the body that had once been hers, and I came to a decision.

"I will answer you in a moment. I will let you go and I will do nothing to hinder your going," I said, with my back still to them. "You know all I ever wanted was your happiness, Mae. But I am going to ask you first to do one last thing for me. I want you to go and say goodbye to Ronald properly and kindly. He loves you." I turned to her and saw surprise in her eyes, though her face did not change at all. She nodded and left the room.

"Fred," I said softly, moving close to him, "I must tell you something now. You may choose not to believe me, but perhaps having heard her just admit she cares nothing for you, you may at least think, in the future of what I say now, and save yourself and Ana, later."

He listened puzzled, while I fumbled for the words, and then, shocked, as I told him what the Immortal had told me. When I finished, he shook his head like a diver breaking water after a long swim, breathing in deep gasps.

"It can't be true," he said finally. But not with finality.

"It is," I said, quietly, firmly. "Your love, like mine, lies on her like a dusting of starlight upon her skin. She will quickly rub you off with the palms of her tiny, white hands, and you will be forgotten as quickly as I am forgotten now. The form is Mae's. The spirit within her is not. It is not even nosferatu, which is why she could not change you."

Behind us there was a sudden and appalling scream. We pivoted to see Mae standing at the drawing room doors, her arms outstretched, fingers clawed, fangs extended, her voice a medley of sounds and sights and colors felt only on the surface of the mind, contempt and hatred washing from her over the two of us like the rolling and lapping of the sea at Waldo's body.

She was on me before I had time to raise my arms in defense, her fangs tearing at my throat, blood splashing up into her eyes. Fred tried to grab her from behind as I had once done when she fed upon Waldo, but she was stronger in her knowledge of herself, in this new knowledge of what she truly was, and he was flung back across the room to smash, forehead first, into a heavy brass cabinet, jarring the portrait of my father hanging on the wall above it, swaying and tilting it until it fell, striking him across the bridge of the nose, stunning him into semi-consciousness.

I saw this happen through a mist of blood ... my blood pumping out from the torn carotid and jugular even as I fought with her, trying to catch hold of her throat, her head, her hair, anything to pull the tearing fangs away from my face, but she was slippery as the satin and silk she habitually wore and I could find no purchase for my fingers.

She moved in quick, deadly strikes, her head descending like that of cobra again and again to rip at my cheeks, my throat, my hands. I hit her with all my remaining strength finally, in desperation, and connected. She tumbled back for just a moment, and then we were rolling about the floor together, locked to each other, snatching at each other, rending flesh, vampiric and demonic, screeching, but she had torn my throat out with her first attack and I had lost too much blood, was far too weak, to do her much damage.

My blood soaked her, pumping in gouts from my throat. Her blond hair lay red and streaming on her cheeks. In less than two minutes she had nearly destroyed me, and now, seeing my weakness upon me like death, panting, she straddled me, raising her hands to take my

260

head between those soft, bloodsoaked hands, readying herself to snap my neck and then, strangely, her head caved in, and she wailed, a final, despairing, defeated wail as the silver headed cane fell again and her face dissolved in the impact of silver and wood.

Her body fell full length upon me.

I screamed, a feeble sound, pushing her corpse from me.

Ronald stood above me, a kitchen cleaver grasped in his hands, his face whiter than even a vampire's face could possibly be except in dreams.

He struck down and separated Mae's head from her body, his face screwed into a tight mask of disgust. The head rolled a few feet with the violence of his thrust and came to rest, staring from what was left of its eyes directly at Father Ray, who stood behind Ron, the cane I had given him, still half-upraised.

"Is she dead?" he asked, dropping the cane to the floor.

"I think so, yes." I managed to cough out. "But I find it hard to believe that I am not."

The Fear Year was not yet ended, but she was dead and I was not. The demon had truly been the only animating force then. Nothing of myself had been within Mae's body.

I tried to sit up and found I couldn't.

Fred, stunned, blood pouring into the collar of his fashionable punk rocker's outfit from a slash on the back of his head moaned, "Oh, Jesus ... ", pointing at the door and we turned to see her head rocking back and forth on the stump of its neck.

Ronald, still, calm, and white, walked over to the head and cleaved it in two, then stepped onto the back of her corpse, chopping through it repeatedly, severing the

261

spinal cord again and again until bits of flesh and bone were raining down throughout the room in a grisly white drizzle.

I watched him in dull, gray wonder, my life draining from my throat, pooling beneath my head, staining the valuable, ancient carpets. I could no longer speak, but he lifted his eyes to mine, recognized my condition and came to kneel beside me, closing the largest tear with his hands. Father Ray got down beside him and nodded at me encouragingly, while ineffectually, but with great love, chaffing my wrist.

"You will be fine," Ron said gently, and Ray bobbed his head up and down in agreement. "I will not let you bleed dry."

I smiled as best I could and went softly to sleep, my head cradled in Freddy Z's ample lap.

Ronald held the flesh closed long enough for my body to remember its true shape and close the wound. He sat by me until I awakened some hours later and when I opened my eyes it was to see him there beside me, with an unconscious young male, a commodities trader perhaps, by the look of his suit, lying at his feet, ready for me to feed upon.

An hour later, nearly fully recovered, although my voice would be rusty sounding for many days to come, I joined him in the drawing room where Fred sat waiting, twisting one waist length lock of black hair in his fingers.

They had cleaned up the blood and dispensed with her body. Not even her perfume lingered in the room.

I thought of the wheels of time, turning forever, grinding love to scattered shards between them, and the smell of old blood in this room for years to come.

I would sell the flat, I decided with vehemence, sell it and go to Egypt where Mae and I had never been. I turned then and saw, on the silver salver used to present visitor's cards, the diamond and emerald bracelet. Without her wrist to wrap itself around, it was only a tawdry and dull ornament.

I picked it up, looking at its inner fire dancing over my flesh, holding it in my palm as if it were a small, very venomous snake, while Ronald, Father Ray and Fred watched me with careful eyes.

"I can't imagine what I am supposed to do with this now," I said at last.

"Keep it, to remember her by," Ray said.

Ron rose from his chair and crossed over to me, putting his arm around my neck. He reached out to touch one exquisite platinum link. "She said to me, when she came to say goodbye and I asked her why she had to leave us, she said, `You cannot keep me, anymore than you can keep a flame within your hand or a memory fresh with a mere photograph, or your humanity by imitating the life of a man. Better to grasp at the wind or clench mercury in your fist. Better to let me go now before I destroy your love completely, for you have never known me.' I was going to go out after that, going to walk awhile with Father Ray so I would not have to see her leave, but I heard her scream."

He began to cry, the pink tears falling down the front of his white, ruffled shirt in perfect, round dots. "We rushed in and saw her throw off Fred as if he were no more than a blanket stifling her on a hot night, so I went for the cleaver. I was thinking I had never known her, just as she said. If I had been thinking clearer, I wouldn't have left the room. It was Father Ray who had to save you because of my muddledness and I thank God he was here."

"It's all right," I said, ineffectually, using his words of comfort to me in hopes of comforting him, putting my

263

arms around him, as he had put his around me. "It was not Mae that you killed, and you <u>both</u> saved me, Ronnie, in killing her. An evil took her body between the time I drank her blood and her awakening and that evil is what you killed. An Immortal told me this and I will tell you all else he said when we are far away from here."

"But you must keep the bracelet, don't you see?" Ron said urgently. "To remember the real Mae, the one you loved and the one who loved you, for I know she did love you. You must keep it to remember that Mae."

"It was the human Mae who loved you," Fred said, speaking for the first time. "The fragile, dying thing you tried to save from death. She told me she loved you, worshipped you, back when you and she first began going round together. You were everything to her, everything she had ever wanted and she loved you the more because you were the first and only being she had loved. She used to say, `I will marry him, if he will have me.' Ronald and the Father are right. Keep the bracelet in remembrance of her."

And I thought of Mae, standing there with my arms around Ronald, his tears staining both of our clothes, the bracelet draped on my hand, with Fred, shyly and solemnly watching us and Father Ray, embarrassed and lowering his eyes.

I thought of Mae with her dark, childhood horrors, her empty heart, her desperate gaiety.

I thought of her as she had been, childlike and charming on the beach, white muslin dancing about her thighs, the black sea kissing her calves, laughing.

I thought of Ana warning me that Mae's love for me would not last the transformation, as if she had known even then that the being that would awaken would not be her, and wished with all my soul that my poor, doomed and

264

cherished Mae had had the chance to love me or not, as she choose, as an immortal. I could have borne losing her after a few years to another much more easily that I could bear this.

For I had murdered her. I had killed her body so that she might awaken immortal with me and instead some dark being from a lost, unholy time had taken that body and Mae was truly dead. Because of me.

I thought of what her life might have been had I not answered her call. Perhaps she might have married Fred in a year or two, or Waldo, or some imperfect stranger she met in a club or at work, had children, lived to wrinkle up, get arthritis, die in a nursing home. Perhaps she would never have married, gone to a university and become a career woman of some kind.

Whatever she might have been, I had stolen it from her and now I, too, began to weep with the heaviness of my guilt.

"Don't," Fred said softly. "Don't. I can guess what you're thinking and it isn't true, any of it. Mae was desperately unhappy. She had tried to kill herself before you came to her and, if you have never appeared in her life, she would have tried until she succeeded. She had happiness with you. She loved you. That is what you must remember."

I snuffled a bit and wiped my nose on my sleeve. Ronald released me finally and I looked at all three of them, finding a smile somewhere inside me to give them.

"Thank you," I said. "You are all very dear to me."

"Does this mean I can stay with you awhile?" Fred asked. He grinned, trying to lighten his words, but I could see how much he wanted to remain with us. It is hard to be newly made with no friend beside you.

"Stay forever," I said, and to Father Ray, "Stay as

265

long as you like."

Ronald smiled hugely, happily. "Stay!" he cried. "Yes, stay!"

Fred stepped forward into our circle of arms and we embraced one another like the lonely children we were while Ray smiled on us all, like the Father he was.

EPILOG

Sometime during the long night, Celine and I had ceased to sit separated by careful, forlorn inches on the wooden bench in Mattheson Hammock Park and now, with dawn beginning to lighten the sky and my recital done, I found I was lying with my head in her lap. She brushed my hair from my forehead gently, as if she had been doing so for a long while, but had not yet tired of doing it.

"There is one thing I cannot understand," she said when she discerned by my silence that the story was finished.

"What?" I asked softly.

She lifted several locks of my hair in her fingers and kissed them gently. "Why did you never realize that your Mae had not awakened? I have not been a vampire very long, yet even I know we do not change from what we were when living."

She hesitated when naming herself a vampire, and I was obscurely comforted that Celine should have difficulty with the word. Only Mae, of all the undead I have known, had ever been able to call herself `vampire' with no qualm, and, of course, she was not undead, at all.

"There was nothing in Mae's behavior before you changed her to indicate she would be so evil as she was when transformed."

"I don't know," I admitted. "Perhaps it was easier

to believe Ana's interpretation. Mae, as hidden monster until I came to her, giving her the power to indulge herself. And, too, how could I have guessed what had really happened? I knew nothing of the demon the Immortal described to me. I could not have known anything about it, for it had not made an appearance, as he said, in over a thousand years." I sighed and grasped her hand to hold it tightly on my breast. "The one warning sign I had was the length of time she spent in death. I have never known nor heard to this day of anyone to lie so long without waking, but I did not know what it meant then. I shudder when I sometimes think that all those days she lay dead on the coral, her soul and the demon might have been fighting for control of the body, that she knew what was happening and that she would never have the immortality she so desparately wanted from me."

I fell silent, brooding as ever Heathcliff on his moors did, and in the quiet we could hear the birds waking up, singing, and the ocean rising with its tide beyond the park.

"Where are they now?" she asked into the silence, brushing my blond hair back behind my ears. "Your friends."

"Ronald and Fred?"

"And Tony and Ana. And, of course, the Good Father." Celine smiled, a wisp of a smile that said I was so blessed with good friends and yet there I had been last night, alone on the beach, as if I were as lonely as she.

"Tony's in Abu Simbal, Ankhenaton's old city; it's autumn again, and he is always there in autumn. Ana loves Monte Carlo this time of year."

"Is the hunting good?" she asked, laughing like wind causing daisies to dance on a mountain field. "For young men to love?"

I laughed, too, and raised her hand, kissing it. "You have been good for me," I said.

"And I have learned so much from you, aside from the pleasure your company has given me," she answered shyly. "I don't know why we newly made are so frightened of you older ones."

"I don't know either," I said. "Perhaps it is another myth, like that which says the Others will kill us if we should fall into their hands. Once it may have been so, the older ones killing the newly made. I don't believe it is so now."

Her eyes were really so incredibly violet. With the new sun lighting the world more and more brightly, they deepened in color until they resembled hot house lilacs. She seemed to blush as I continued to hold her eyes with mine, but it may have been only the rising dawn that colored her cheeks. It is hard for vampires to blush when they have not fed in hours.

"But where are Fred and Ronald now?" she asked again, recovering herself, but still not trying to reclaim the hand I was holding so tightly. "And Father Ray?"

"They are `on-tour', as Fred says. In Russia. I saw a video not too many nights ago. Fred was talented as a human, but as one of the undead his performance is devastating to see. The Russians were holding banners over their heads that read things like `Freddy, you're our God!'. Ron is managing his group, booking their dates and checking out the groupies, I imagine." I laughed. "He has some theory that any latent psychic power one has while alive is augmented by the transformation to nosferatu. He wants me to fund a study and he says the best place in the world to find psychics is in Russia. He has Father Ray completely sold on the idea and they both lose no opportunity to expound on how the

Russians consider such people human weapons and treat them like royalty. I think the next step is that they'll persuade me to build some kind of experimental clinic or something, to house the psychics they gather, then to find the most powerful one and transform him or her to see what happens to the psi gift."

"Why didn't you go with them?" Celine asked, smiling broadly. "You would have enjoyed checking out Fred's groupies, too, wouldn't you?"

"And have been on hand to keep Ron and his theories from costing me too much money," I agreed cheerfully, "but after what happened to me in Moscow in 1440 when I was collecting manuscripts from abbeys for Cosimo de Medici and his friend, Niccilo Niccili, I have had no desire to see Russia agian. People think the Communists are bad, and they are, but they learned all they know from the Tzars."

I sat up. The rim of the sun was showing at the horizon. We must go," I said. "Is there somewhere I can drop you?"

"Yes, of course," she said. "I sleep in the husk of the Jefferson Hotel on Miami Beach. The one that burned down a few months ago."

We walked to the car, neither of us speaking.

If I could feel her longing so strongly, then surely she could feel mine, I thought, even though there is no telepathic communciation between vampires as there is between humans and our kind.

We drove to the Jefferson Hotel, still not speaking, and as I opened the door for her, I decided, `What the hell?'. She must have been thinking the same, for both of us spoke at once.

"You never had a chance to tell your story ... " I said, and, "I would love to hear about the time in Russia ...

269

" she said, and we both began to giggle like children.

"Stay with me awhile," I said hesitantly, soberly.

"I should like to stay," she answered. "Until you tire of my company. We can be the best of friends, like you and Tony and Ron and Ana and Father Ray and Fred, for however long you choose."

"We will be a family," I answered, and closed her door again, sealing her fate to mine, whatever it might be in the centuries to come. "Forever, perhaps."

It was full daylight now and the heavy ocean breeze smelled damp and salty and good.

I reached for her hand as we drove and the sunlight turned her eyes to the color of lush plums growing beside glacial streams, their colors reflecting in the pure sun-washed waters, and unlike Mae, her skin did not smoke where the sunlight brushed it.

I laughed aloud.

"Good times," I laughed. "We will have such good times. We have all eternity before us, after all."

She smiled and kissed my fingertips, echoing my voice in her joy, "Yes, loving times, my sweet prince."

I could hardly wait to get her to Russia so Tony and Ron and Father Ray and Fred could meet her and share my newly found treasure with me.

And the Other. I would see him again, as he had promised, and he would see my Celine and my family, and be proud of me, as I was, proud that I had not again made some fatal mistake in the choosing of my lover.